T0304918

MINOR DISTURBANCES AT GRAND LIFE APARTMENTS

MINOR DISTURBANCES AT GRAND LIFE APARTMENTS

Hema Sukumar

CORONET

First published in Great Britain in 2023 by Coronet
An imprint of Hodder & Stoughton
An Hachette UK company

3

Copyright © Hema Sukumar 2023

A CIP catalogue record for this title is available from the British Library

Hardback ISBN 9781399708463
Trade Paperback ISBN 9781399708470
eBook ISBN 9781399708487

Typeset in Swift LT STD by Manipal Technologies Limited

Printed and bound in Great Britain by Clays Ltd, Elcograf S.p.A.

Hodder & Stoughton policy is to use papers that are natural, renewable
and recyclable products and made from wood grown in sustainable forests.
The logging and manufacturing processes are expected to conform
to the environmental regulations of the country of origin.

Hodder & Stoughton Ltd
Carmelite House
50 Victoria Embankment
London EC4Y 0DZ

www.hodder.co.uk

For Amma and Appa

1

Kamala

Every evening, Kamala stood purposefully in front of her gods, armed with a carefully planned and numbered agenda. First and foremost, she prayed for her daughter Lakshmi's health and happiness. Second, she prayed for her daughter to do well in her studies – a subject she considered important enough to be discussed as a separate line item. She had prayed for this every day, and hadn't that worked? Didn't Lakshmi top her class and win a scholarship to study abroad? Her third prayer was somewhat half-hearted, and she only included it because she considered herself a good person. She prayed for the well-being of all mankind, but even as she mumbled words in Sanskrit, she knew that however almighty her gods, and however numerous their numbers, they were simply not equipped to deliver adequate results on this front.

On that particular Saturday, with her daughter's annual visit less than ten days away, the sense of anxiety that usually underlined her prayers was replaced by a sense of eager anticipation. However, she didn't let that tempt her into taking any short-cuts, and she opened her eyes only when she was finished. She struck a match and carefully lit the lotus-shaped silver lamps in front of her gods as they continued watching her actions impassively through a smoky haze of jasmine incense.

The sun went low in the windows, casting a pool of amber light in the corner of the kitchen partitioned into a prayer room. Kamala could hear the shrieks of children playing in the distance, muffled by the sounds of a cement mixer at a construction site nearby. She did the time-zone conversion that she was now very familiar with and knew that it was noon where her daughter lived, where a more mild-mannered sun ruled the British summer sky. Wiping her hands on the edge of her cotton saree, she decided to check if her daughter had replied to her question about what she wanted for her first meal back at home.

She stared intently at the screen of her laptop as her emails loaded, as if it would not do its job properly if left unsupervised. Whenever Lakshmi visited, she would tease that this was the only laptop in the world that was never moved from its place nor was ever kept on a lap. Kamala would smile indulgently in response but make no attempt to move the laptop from its designated spot on the coffee table, where it sat importantly on its own tassel-edged embroidered mat.

Kamala felt a small flicker of disappointment when she saw that there were no new emails from Lakshmi. Peering at the keyboard with her spectacles perched at the edge of her nose, she typed with the tips of her index fingers, reminding her daughter to let her know whether she wanted potato roast or ladies finger fry for lunch the day she arrived. Sweet potatoes would also be in season, she added, making a mental note to buy some from the shop across the road, just in case.

She switched the television on and walked back into the kitchen to cook rice for dinner, humming the familiar theme song of her evening soap mindlessly. Her saree was hitched up to her waist and her long hair, which had suddenly turned very grey at fifty-five, was tied into a neat bun at the nape of her neck. Her heart-shaped face had aged gracefully, and girlish dimples still puddled her cheeks when she smiled, but she didn't believe in smiling unless it was absolutely necessary.

In the time that it took for the pressure cooker to puff up and whistle, she came back to her laptop and clicked the button that fetched new messages from the internet. When she saw a new, unopened envelope appear next to her daughter's name, her heart leapt with familiar pleasure. However, she soon felt a frown arrive on her lips as she started reading the message. Lakshmi sent her regular emails, but they were usually short messages giving cursory updates about her life. She would say things like, *The weather is so cold. I need the wool monkey cap you use in Chennai – lol*, or *Made Maggi with vegetables for lunch.*

Her message that day was unusually cryptic – *Amma, there's something I need to tell you when I'm there. Hope it doesn't make you too upset. See you soon.*

She read the email carefully again, adjusting her spectacles to be closer to her eyes. Her brain cycled through various worrying possibilities. Was something wrong with her daughter's health? Was she planning to change her major from computer science to something that made no practical sense, such as history, like her colleague Dr Raman's son? Or worse, did she want to marry a British boy whose accents she had previously described as – using one of those peculiar modern words – 'cute'?

She was just about to reply to her daughter's email, when Sundu rang the doorbell, arriving early for dinner.

'Unbelievable,' Sundu declared as soon as she walked in through the doors, shaking her boyishly short hair for additional emphasis.

Kamala simply nodded in response and motioned her inside. Sundu, shortened from Soundaravalli, was Kamala's closest friend and had the habit of using the word 'unbelievable' to describe a wide variety of topics, which, on closer inspection, turned out to be entirely believable.

'This General Motors diet. I told you about it, didn't I?' Sundu asked, still sounding belligerent.

'What about it?' Kamala enquired, although she was unable to recall any conversation about a diet that seemed to have an unlikely association with a company that sold motors.

'I gave up that diet yesterday. I was supposed to eat nothing but bananas and milk on the fourth day. Can you believe this nonsense?'

'No, I cannot,' Kamala replied with appropriate indignation, although she could. Sundu constantly worried about her weight and approached diets in the same way that cats approach a ball of yarn – with a sudden burst of frenzied attention before assuming their natural state of doing nothing. Kamala, on the other hand, had always been on the thinner side, and was often reminded by Sundu about how lucky she was that she didn't have to worry about losing weight. Like most people born with some sort of good fortune, Kamala didn't understand why others valued it so much – so what if you had a few extra kilos here and there? she would ask Sundu, who would look back at her with unconcealed exasperation.

Sundu stood leaning against the kitchen sink eating peanuts and Kamala was about to ask her to save her appetite for dinner, when she smelled the rain – the sweet smell of salt, mud and summer reprieve – before she noticed the darkening clouds outside the kitchen window.

'I've left clothes out to dry on the terrace,' she exclaimed, and they picked up a plastic bucket each and went briskly up the stairs.

The terrace was shared by all the residents of Grand Life Apartments and was sliced by a zigzagging clothesline from which sarees and towels hung crisped from the day's heat. The tops of mango and coconut trees encircling the terrace rustled softly, and dark rain clouds hung low and ripe from the sky. The rain still seemed undecided whether to start pouring or not and was leaving large, thoughtful circles on the concrete floor.

'Not too long to go now, for Lakshmi's visit, is it?' asked Sundu as she removed a saree with one hand and folded it deftly into the bucket.

'Yes, only eight more days. By God's grace.'

Sundu had a newly-married son, who lived within easy reach in Bangalore. Although Kamala couldn't be more proud of Lakshmi, she wished she could see her whenever she wanted as well, without having to wait fervently for her annual two-week appearance. The days before her visit would pass by slowly, with her stripping off each day eagerly in her calendar, and the two weeks Lakshmi was at home would pass by quicker than the time it took to fry mustard seeds in a pan. After that, she would have to start the excruciating countdown for the next year before she could see her again.

'Both of you come home for lunch when she is here.' Sundu's assertive tone tapered away distractedly as her eyes fell on Jason, who had also come up to the terrace. Tilting her head towards him, she asked, 'That new tenant in the apartment – he is a foreigner, isn't he?'

Kamala replied that blonde-haired, blue-eyed people in Chennai usually tended to be.

'Why would a young foreigner choose to stay in Chennai of all places? Instead of lying around half-naked on the beaches of Goa? Or getting up to no good on houseboats in Kerala?'

'Well, there is the Marina beach here, I suppose,' Kamala said, feeling the need to defend her city.

Sundu continued in a louder voice than Kamala would have preferred. 'He looks like a young James Bond, doesn't he?'

Kamala, who didn't watch English movies, but had a functioning knowledge of who James Bond was, thought that Jason looked nothing like an action-movie hero. If anything, his lanky frame and shy demeanour made her think that he must be pursuing a good, sensible profession, like accountancy. Nevertheless, she nodded in agreement.

Jason, who was removing clothes from the other end of the terrace, seemed to sense their interest and waved at them with a hesitant, friendly smile. Sundu smiled and waved back over-eagerly as if it were actually James Bond who had made an appearance on their terrace to rescue some towels in distress. Kamala waved diffidently back.

The rain suddenly seemed to make up its mind and started sending sharp slivers of water down their way. Kamala and Sundu ran down to the sheltered safety of the apartment, grinning widely, the act of running with swinging buckets in their hand making them feel younger than their years. The rain soon gained momentum, and they listened to the cracks of thunder and the sound of water pouring down in torrents while seated at Kamala's dining table. Rice, tomato rasam and potato kari were laid out in stainless steel vessels, and a few fried appalams were heaped in a blue Tupperware bowl.

Kamala doused a heap of rice in the fragrant, soupy rasam and mixed it with her hand. With her other, she served Sundu the potatoes that were cut into exactingly thin pieces and fried a deep golden brown, just the way she knew her friend liked them.

Sundu protested that she was serving her too much but ate all of it appreciatively, exclaiming, 'Your potatoes are excellent, as always.'

'I made more than enough. Let me pack some for you to take back.' Kamala had already kept some aside in a stainless steel box in anticipation of Sundu's compliment.

As they were eating, the nasal sound of a cell phone ringing called for their immediate attention. Kamala got up to check her phone to see if it was Lakshmi calling her, flakes of rice still stuck to her hand. The call turned out to be for Sundu, who mouthed to Kamala that it was her assistant. She continued to give elaborate instructions on the phone while still seated at the dining table. Sundu had only started studying law in her late thirties but had managed to build a successful career, and now had a retinue of assistants who fell over each other to do her bidding. Kamala worked flexible hours as a dentist at a hospital nearby and often found herself summoning up the courage to remind her part-time nurse that she was expected to work for part of the time.

After dinner, Sundu switched on the TV and changed to the sports channel where a cricket match was in progress. 'At least it isn't raining in Australia. The Indian team was giving those Sri Lankans a run for their money when I had checked the score.'

Kamala would have preferred to continue watching her evening soap that involved a standoff between an evil heiress and a righteous cop on Sun TV, but on listening to her friend's exuberant cheers, she resigned herself to the corner of the sofa in front of her laptop. This was one of the reasons why their friendship worked – Kamala felt more comfortable giving up control instead of putting Sundu through the perceived discomfort of what she would have liked to do instead. However, on the rare occasions that she did have a strong opinion, she could be very stubborn and Sundu usually knew when to back off by just looking at the set of her jaw.

Kamala leaned forward towards her laptop and typed an email to her daughter, asking her what this important thing she needed to tell her was. Sundu was also typing emails on her phone while the cricket match on TV was interrupted by an advertisement for mineral water claiming to be freshly bottled at the foot of Himalayan glaciers. Without looking up from her phone, Sundu asked, 'So, what is our girl saying?'

'Well . . .' Kamala started, trying to translate her concern into words. 'Nothing. Just the usual one-line telegrams,' she finished. Sundu's attention turned towards the television again and the noisiness of a sports stadium filled the living room.

*

The next day, Kamala tried calling Lakshmi, but Lakshmi declined her call swiftly. She texted back, saying that she was in classes all morning. Kamala closed her laptop after checking for new emails one last time and sighed, feeling vaguely distressed. Kamala and Lakshmi used to lead lives that revolved around each other, as it had been only the two of them for such a very long time. At the end of a long day, they would sit on the terrace folding away clothes that had been left out to dry, enjoying the late evening breeze from the coconut trees nearby. Even as a teenager, Lakshmi used to accompany her to the vegetable market, although she would stand a little distance away from her mother in embarrassment while Kamala haggled over the price for a kilo of carrots. However, ever since Lakshmi left for Oxford, Kamala had felt herself become slowly obsolete from her daughter's life. Perhaps, this was inevitable, she surmised. Parents spend their entire lives trying to make their children more equipped for the world, and maybe this was the end goal – the bittersweet liberation of not being needed.

She went to Lakshmi's room to check that the air conditioner hadn't died from lack of use. Summer had truly arrived, accompanied by a humid, all-pervasive heat, and she couldn't have her daughter sweltering during the short time that she was here.

Kamala sat apprehensively on Lakshmi's bed as the air conditioner made a strange wheezing noise at the effort it took to cool the room.

This room had been Lakshmi's since she was a toddler, when Kamala had moved into Grand Life Apartments so that they could be within walking distance of a good school that produced students delectable enough to be immediately consumed by the best engineering and medical colleges in the country.

Now that Lakshmi had followed the path paved for her by Kamala, her room was preserved in the same condition that it had been on the day she left for her studies abroad. A framed photo of the two of them, taken on the terrace of the apartment to mark one of the rare occasions in which Lakshmi had worn a saree, was displayed on a shelf, protected by two layers of crinkled plastic wrapper. Bottles of nail polish, moisturisers and perfumes stood unused on the dressing table, although they were dusted periodically. She made a mental note to finally confer with Lakshmi this time on which ones to keep and which ones to give away.

She opened the grey cupboard in Lakshmi's room and decided to pick some kurtas that she could send for washing and ironing, so they would be ready for Lakshmi to wear when she got here. The cupboard was packed with clothes from Lakshmi's teenage years that had not made the cut for a spot in her going-abroad suitcase – salwar kameez sets, hand-painted T-shirts from her fabric painting phase and some unused exercise clothes. There was also her photo album in the middle of these clothes, and as Kamala reached for it, she found a faded blue dupatta wedged underneath.

The long piece of cloth unfurled a memory from over fifteen years ago when Kamala had returned from work to find an eight-year-old Lakshmi pacing the floor of the house with a very adult-like, worried expression on her face. Lakshmi was part of a school play the next day and was urgently in need of a blue dupatta. Kamala had brought out her own blue dupattas for her to inspect, but with each one, Lakshmi had started looking more teary-eyed because it wasn't the correct kind of blue. Perplexed, Kamala had asked, 'Well, what is the correct kind of blue supposed to be?'

'It needs to be the colour of copper sulphate because I am going to be playing that compound in the science play tomorrow!' Lakshmi had wailed, sobbing into a clearly not-copper-sulphate coloured dupatta. Kamala was familiar with these educational plays – children would hold a placard indicating which chemical they were and wheel around on stage, forming chemical reactions in accompaniment to some exuberant commentary from their science teacher. 'Why can't you play something simpler, like sugar or salt?' she had asked playfully, which had made Lakshmi's saucer-like eyes well up with tears.

They had then walked to Ranganathan Street and climbed up and down the stairs of multiple shops without luck. Finally, they landed in a musty tailoring shack with walls filled with sketches of necklines for blouses. The owner took them up a flight of cramped stairs and brought out a blue muslin cloth from a spool and rolled it over the splintered wooden table. Lakshmi jumped up and down with excitement as if she were seeing the Indian ocean glinting under the morning sun for the first time.

Kamala vividly remembered the image as if she had taken a picture of it – Lakshmi's dimpled grin over her braces, her eyes sparkling with happiness while her head was draped in that blue piece of cloth. She wished that she could take the same little girl out of this mental picture and ask her to confide all her worries to her.

As she folded the dupatta pensively, she was interrupted by the loud trilling of the phone. It was Sundu, continuing a previous conversation without any preamble. 'So, what did we decide – are we going to Aruna's daughter's wedding? I need to confirm my schedule with my assistant.'

'It is the second Saturday of the month, isn't it? I won't be at the clinic, so we can go together,' she said resignedly. She usually didn't look forward to social events that involved more than a certain critical mass of people. Kamala and Sundu were now more than used to being viewed differently for going about their lives without husbands by their sides, but now their children's lives had started to come under scrutiny as well. ('Sundu, two years since your son got married – any good news?', 'Kamala, I know this boy in the US, good family, doesn't drink or smoke – would be perfect for our Lakshmi! You just say the word.') However, Aruna was a good friend who had also been Lakshmi's teacher at school, so she decided that she was worth running the social gauntlet for.

'By the way, I had meant to ask, do you want me to send my car to pick up Lakshmi from the airport?' Sundu asked.

'No, I have booked a taxi already,' Kamala replied and, after a moment's hesitation, added a little sheepishly, 'Lakshmi sent a strange email the other day, actually.'

'Strange?'

'She said she had something important to tell me when she got here. Not sure what it is.'

'Young people these days,' Sundu started, in the exasperated tone adopted by middle-aged parents all over the world, 'have no clue what is important. My son said he had something important to tell me the other day. Turned out he was getting a tattoo. Of his wife's name of all things. Can you believe that?'

Sundu continued without waiting for Kamala's response, 'I told him that his forehead would be an appropriate place for the tattoo if he still needed my opinion on anything, that is.' She then paused for appreciation from Kamala for her sassy retorting skills.

However, Kamala's eyebrows were getting increasingly knitted with worry. As if Sundu could see that down the phone, she added, 'I wouldn't worry about Lakshmi, though. She is such a sensible and clever girl.'

When Kamala got off the phone, her eyes roamed over the various proofs of this cleverness, framed and displayed as certificates and golden goblets in the living room. They were arranged behind a glass-walled shelf, interspersed with multiple photos of Lakshmi. Amid all these pictures of her daughter, however, there was only one picture taken with her father. It was a picture of Kamala's husband holding a two-year-old Lakshmi in his arms, both of them pursing their lips seriously at the camera. Her husband, a surgeon whom she had immediately liked from the kind and respectful way he had addressed her parents on the day they met, had died in a bike accident shortly after that picture was taken. Life had been hard afterwards when she had to continue living with her in-laws, but she was grateful to them for allowing her to continue working. Although this was all long ago, the memories of her husband evaporated like pickling mangoes under the summer sun, she still missed having someone who would marvel along with her at her daughter's achievements or share seemingly frivolous concerns such as the one she was having right now.

Kamala redialled Lakshmi's number, and when she heard her daughter's voice after a few rings, she was momentarily suffused with happiness.

'Hello? Ma?' Lakshmi's words came out in a straightened accent that usually indicated that she was surrounded by friends.

'How are you doing? All well, I hope?'

There was some murmuring on the other end before Lakshmi's voice came on the phone again, louder and without the accent. Kamala could now hear the sound of traffic in the background, which probably meant that her daughter had stepped outside from wherever she had been.

'Hi, Ma. Sorry, I was eating lunch at that Mexican place I have told you about. Is everything OK? Is it about the email? I probably shouldn't have sent it.'

'Oh, did I disturb your lunch? Go back and eat properly. I will call again later.'

'Is it anything urgent, or is it just about my email?'

'Nothing urgent. I was only wondering what the important thing you wanted to tell me was. I am just worried, you know. But you go back and eat. We can talk later when you have finished.'

There was a pause before Lakshmi replied, 'I wrote that email very late at night – I know that I should have just spoken to you when I got home. Listen, Ma, don't worry about it.'

Kamala detected a catch in her daughter's voice that made her more persistent. 'If it's nothing to worry, you should be able to tell me what it *is* about? Is anything wrong with your health?'

'No, Ma, my health is fine.' Lakshmi was now using the mildly annoyed voice that she usually adopted just before she was about to dismiss Kamala.

'That's good to hear. Then what else is wrong?' Kamala pressed.

'Listen, Ma. I know you think that I don't drink.'

Kamala was silent. She could hear a bus honking thousands of miles away. Had her daughter, the one who didn't even drink coffee until she was fifteen, now succumbed to the allure of alcohol in this new country? Maybe it was just a passing phase. This wasn't as bad a revelation as she had feared, though.

'Not the kind of heavy drinking in your television serials, but a glass of wine now and then.' Kamala could hear Lakshmi half-smile at the other end at her own description. 'Anyway, I wrote that message after a couple of drinks. I didn't intend to make you worry unnecessarily. We need to talk in person and not over the phone like this, Ma.'

'Oh,' said Kamala in surprise. She had thought that Lakshmi's confession was over. Lakshmi used this pause to explain that she needed to get back and quickly ended the call.

Kamala had meant to ask Lakshmi a couple of things – whether she wanted cashew nut or plain Good Day butter biscuits to be bought before her visit and whether she had remembered to pre-order the Asian vegetarian meal for her flight home. Instead, she just looked at the phone accusingly as if it were the one that had ended the conversation. The phone hummed back unsympathetically in response.

2

Revathi

The last time Revathi had met Shreya was over a year ago. These yearly meetings were a recurring theme with Reva's friends – they had all left Chennai for foreign shores and she met them during their annual visits home, accompanied by a fog of new accents, hand sanitisers and baby powder. Shreya was one of her closest friends in college, so she was glad that this would not be another superficial conversation where she would need to pretend that her life was extra-awesome just to keep up with the more awesome lives that allegedly happened abroad.

Reva waited by the entrance to Hotel Saravana Bhavan, standing next to a man setting up a cotton candy machine, who smiled leeringly at her. She hastily broke eye contact and looked at her phone, trying to adjust her usually friendly demeanour to appear less approachable. Reva believed that she wasn't exactly good-looking by Chennai standards – she had a small frame that elicited questions about whether she still bought clothes from the children's section, and was self-conscious enough about her skin colour to have used fairness creams in her teenage years. If she were forced to pick one thing she liked about herself, it would be her fish-shaped eyes set under thick lashes that she unfailingly outlined with kajal every time she stepped out. Today, she was dressed in a sleeveless top and fitted jeans, which she diagnosed as a potential reason for such untoward glances being directed her way. Out of the corner of her eye, and not without a touch of satisfaction, she watched the restaurant's security guard stride purposefully towards the cotton candy man and ask him to set up shop elsewhere.

Shreya was late but made up for it with the exuberance of her arrival. She jumped out of her father's black BMW and enveloped Reva in a tight hug, her skin feeling pleasantly cold to the touch from the air conditioning in her car. Their conversation was a continuous squeal, both of them talking in excited, overlapping sentences. They exclaimed about the slow-moving traffic on the main roads ('A bullock cart would have been faster!') and mutual compliments on their appearances ('You look great – have you done something new with your hair?').

The man packing up the cotton candy machine stopped whatever he was doing to stare openly at both of them. With the affected air of nonchalance that came with years of practise, they pretended they didn't notice him and walked inside.

The restaurant was brightly lit and noisy. They could hear the clanging of stainless steel utensils in the kitchen, and the smell of frying oil and chilli hung in the air. They seated themselves at a table as a tired-looking waitress gave them their menus. Shreya thanked the waitress effusively for the bottle of mineral water, but the waitress barely nodded back at her in acknowledgement. Shreya recovered quickly from her newly acquired American ways, saying politely, 'One plain dosa and a filter coffee,' without adding a 'please' at the end.

'So, how long are you here for?' Reva asked, retying her shoulder-length wavy hair that she had straightened unevenly in her hurry.

'Well, a month, or however long it takes to renew my H1B visa, if I am lucky enough to get it renewed, that is.'

'Time to make a trip to visit the Visa Ganapathi then,' teased Reva, a suggestion of a smile in her voice. She was quite familiar with these acronyms – H1, B2, H1B. Named like flu strains, these visa types seemed to elicit symptoms of constant anxiety in all her friends who made contact with the US immigration system. One of the more popular locally sourced cures was to visit the Ganapathi temple where the resident deity specialised in visa-expediting services.

'Perhaps I should.' Shreya nodded with exaggerated seriousness. She looked around the restaurant, taking in the old couple eating their meal wordlessly next to them and the loudspeaker blaring devotional songs outside. 'I do miss all this, you know.'

'There are probably more Saravana Bhavan branches in the US than here,' Reva replied, rolling her eyes goodnaturedly. Reva had been to the US once, for a conference somewhere on the outskirts of San Francisco. Her colleagues who had travelled with her had started craving food from home after consecutive meals of bland pasta and sandwiches, and they had decided to go to the nearest South Indian restaurant for dinner. Reva had been surprised at the authenticity of the restaurant that they had ended up going to, which was playing Tamil movie songs from the eighties, making her wonder whether she had travelled back in time and not across oceans.

Both of them paused the conversation in hushed respect as their dosas arrived, looking golden and lit from within. Tearing a corner of the dosa and dipping it into coconut chutney, Shreya continued, 'There is one thing I would probably not miss that much, though. The constant pressure to get married here, you know? The way my parents sometimes look at me with those eyes – half-sad, half-fearful – as if I am a walking time bomb that needs to be defused by a husband.'

Reva laughed loudly in agreement. 'So, you haven't told them about Anwar then?'

Anwar was the Iranian American whom Shreya had started see-ing during her MBA in Chicago. Reva had looked him up on social media and found that he was one of those relentlessly cheerful over-sharers – she not only knew where he lived and worked, but also knew that he ran 4.25 miles on alternate days, liked drawing smileys with blueberries on his Sunday pancakes and that if he ever had a dog, he would name it Captain Bark Sparrow.

'Hell, no. Anwar's parents are Muslim, and he is also ten years older than me. I am not going to risk giving them a heart attack unless we know for sure that we want to get married.'

'Totally agree, especially given my own experience.' Reva nodded, making a wry face before looking down to carefully unstick the tumbler of filter coffee from its saucer. Shreya took the cue to not mention what happened with Sebastian and changed the topic.

'How is your mum doing these days? Remember the time that she tried to set you up with that fellow whose family was in the firecracker business?' Shreya chuckled.

Around six years ago, Reva had received a box of firecrackers with a card that read, 'U the lite of my life'. It would have been an incredibly romantic gesture (admittedly, for the grammatically challenged), if not for the fact that they had never even spoken to each other at that point. This was one of the anecdotes that Shreya and Reva recalled every time they met, and with each retelling, the note sounding more hapless.

'She's good, still looking after my grandmother in the village. It goes without saying that she is obsessed with my unmarried situ-ation. Now that I have turned thirty-two, she claims I am way past my expiry date in the arranged marriage market.'

Shreya smiled commiseratingly at her and took a sip of her frothy coffee.

'So, have you heard from anyone else from our college?' Reva asked, her voice turning lighter as she changed subject.

'Remember Kavita? The one that went to the Hanuman temple every day and pinned her dupatta to her salwar? I almost didn't recognise her in her tiny shorts and tank top when I bumped into her at a shopping mall in Chicago.' Reva had seen Kavita's transformation unfold on social media and nodded in the gleeful, guiltless manner that came with gossiping about someone you didn't know very well.

'Oh, remember that guy Natarajan who always came first in maths?' Reva countered, mischievously wriggling her eyebrows.

'Yeah?'

'He has now found God and joined an ashram in the Himalayas.'

'No! You're joking!' Shreya shrieked.

'You're right. I just made that one up. He still lives a few roads away from me and is working on his PhD,' said Reva as they both hooted with laughter.

Reva had missed having Shreya around – it had been nice to have a friend who was always available to hang out during those irregular pockets of time on Sunday afternoons and empathise with her when she complained about her mother's obsession with marriage. Reva had other friends in Chennai, but almost all of them were married, with young families. She hardly saw them, and even when she did, she felt guilty for trying to prise hours out of their already time-impoverished lives.

'How are things at work? Your company recently changed its name to Zip Technologies, right?' Shreya asked.

'Yes, I think I need a change, though.' Reva shrugged casually, in the manner of someone who has said this several times before and done nothing about it.

'Listen, why don't you apply for an MBA as well? Come to the US? It will make for a good change of scene.'

'Maybe,' she said, without mentioning that she just didn't have the confidence to sign up for that kind of loan in exchange for an education that seemed somewhat superfluous to her.

'You can repay the loan within a couple of years, what with US salaries and signing bonuses and everything, you know,' Shreya said, as if reading her mind.

The loudspeaker outside cranked up its volume, ensuring that everyone within a ten-mile radius could not have much of a conversation. They both grinned at each other and signalled for the bill.

Reva was pensive on her way back to her apartment, as meeting her friend had inadvertently made her examine her own life. As she waited in the evening traffic on her two-wheeler, shielding her mouth from the grey exhaust fumes of a water lorry ahead, she couldn't help thinking about how little had changed for her in the last few years. She had worked in the same software company as a project manager for several years now, and although the level of responsibility had increased, the context of her work had not changed by much. She had, however, taken one step towards becoming a grown-up by moving out of a cramped flat shared with distant family to living by herself in Grand Life Apartments.

She opened the black iron gates and pushed her scooter inside, enjoying the sense of calm she felt whenever she left the dust and grime of the city roads and entered the green interior of the apartment block. It had originally been a bungalow, which was then renovated and renamed, rather optimistically, as Grand Life Apartments. The building was butter-coloured and had a large verandah with a sloping red roof at its mouth, which always looked like it was in need of another coat of paint. Jasmine-studded vines tumbled down its sides and reached out to the garden in front of the house that was carpeted with lush green grass and perfumed by rose and jasmine bushes. Reva's favorite part of the garden, however, was the extremely purple bougainvillea bush that leisurely spilled outside the walls of the house like an all-year wedding festoon.

She noticed that Mani was seated on his verandah, listening patiently to one of his friends who often dropped by at this time of day. Mani was the owner of the apartments and Reva often thought that the building felt like an extension of Mani's personality – it stood with the reserved air of an ageing writer who observed the world quietly, but not entirely without the capacity for wonder.

'Revathi! There you are. I have some mail for you. Wait right here – I will bring it from inside.' Mani got up slowly from his candy-striped chair. As if he remembered something he had forgotten, he paused and asked her and his friend, 'Lemon juice?' and without waiting for her answer, he nodded to himself, saying, 'Let me get the two of you something to drink.'

Reva sat on the low wall of the porch, next to an emergency lamp and a pile of mosquito repellent coils. She picked up a folded newspaper that lay next to her.

'Nothing good in the news these days – all murder and theft everywhere,' Mani's friend announced cheerfully, resting his arms over a belt that looked like it was bursting at the seams. He was wearing formal trousers and a neatly pressed shirt that showed the outline of his undershirt, although Reva was fairly certain that his only plans for the evening involved a stroll, followed by a discussion about the fluctuating costs of petrol with Mani.

'So, tell me, Revathi, do you like living here in Grand Life Apartments?' He took out a small comb from his front pocket and began combing back his sparse, well-oiled hair.

'Yes, I do like it, especially the garden here.' Even though the sky had darkened, she could make out a small round shape amid the leaves of the guava tree next to the porch. 'Look, the guava tree has started bearing fruit!' Commenting upon any new change in the garden – a bush starting to flower, a new fruit – was the kind of small talk that she usually engaged with Mani. He would then adjust his spectacles and peer closely with interest at the plant she had pointed to before surveying the rest of the garden with a look of satisfaction.

However, his friend seemed to take on an aggrieved air at the mention of the garden. 'This garden is such a luxury in the centre of the city. I keep telling Mani that he could make a lot of money by converting this area into apartments, too. Don't you agree?'

Reva wanted to come up with a sarcastic yet inoffensive response that showed her disagreement with that statement. Unable to come up with one quickly, she simply shrugged.

Mani came out with glasses of lemon juice that were sweating from the journey made from the cool confines of the refrigerator to the humid porch. Mani's friend took one and finished his juice in a single gulp before speaking again, 'So, Mani, didn't that big construction company offer you a handsome sum of money for this land?'

From Mani's tired nod, Reva guessed that this topic had been discussed recently and was now being re-remembered for Reva's benefit. She knew about this – Olympic Constructions, the company that had bought the house next to them – was now keen to buy Grand Life Apartments as well so that they could raze it and build one big luxury, high-rise apartment block of the type that now hovered all over the city.

'I have no desire to live anywhere else,' Mani murmured softly, surveying the lengthening shadows of the house cast by the soft glow of the streetlamps outside.

Mani's friend shook his head in a manner that indicated that Mani was being unnecessarily sentimental. He looked at his watch, then announced, 'Dinner would be ready at home. I need to get going.' He turned to Reva and asked in a rather commiserating tone, 'Do you now need to go and start cooking dinner for your husband?'

Reva spluttered, swallowing a lemon seed along with her juice. Thankfully, Mani intervened and changed the topic of conversation. 'How is work going, Revathi? You have been working long hours these days?'

'All good, Mani Uncle. Same old, same old.' She made a point to only smile at Mani before making her excuses to leave.

As Reva walked up the steps to her apartment, thinking about Mani's friend's enquiry about her husband, she was relieved to realise that she actually liked the fact that the evening ahead was entirely her own to squander as she wished. She did not always feel this way and had moments of severe self-doubt when she worried that she was never going to find someone to be less lonely with. There were also other changes she would ideally like to make in her life. She had been meaning to find a job where she felt more valued and to use some of her savings to travel and see more of the world. As she fumbled to find the right key to fit the door of her apartment, she resolved to actively try and make these changes happen.

However, once she reached the other side of the door, she noticed her phone glowing at her reproachfully with four missed calls from her mother. She also remembered that she needed to make some changes to the client presentation that was due the next morning. Before long, her resolve slowly drifted away, and the tiredness of the day settled in instead. After finishing her presentation, all she had the mental bandwidth for was to pour herself a glass of wine and sit in front of her laptop to rewatch a familiar episode of a sitcom that had stopped airing over a decade ago. She sank into the corner of her sofa as the familiar jingle filled the room, her mind comfortably numbed by the fact that she didn't have to concentrate to follow the conversations and didn't even have to bother with making the decision on when to laugh. She could wait one more day to start making changes to her life, she decided. Just like she had decided every day before.

3

Jason

It had all been too much of a change for Jason.

He was waiting to cross the road, standing under the glare of the unforgiving afternoon sun. He looked towards his cool apartment waiting across the street and at the unmoving traffic in his way and decided to take the plunge. Weaving through bicycles, buses, cars and mopeds, he was almost near the other side of the road when the traffic suddenly started to move. A young boy on a bicycle lunged towards him, causing his heart rate to double as he tried to quicken his pace.

'Please stop!' he cried, raising his palm towards the speeding bicycle as the boy braked two inches away from him, grinning like the devil. 'Cheeky bastard,' Jason muttered, mopping his brow with the handkerchief that he had begun to carry in his pocket as a new habit. Close to a month in this city, and crossing the street still made his heart thump like the stuttering engines of the canary yellow auto-rickshaws that flitted across the busy roads.

He climbed up to his flat on the third floor of Grand Life Apartments and sat on his sofa, heaving a sigh of temporary relief. The house was cool and quiet, except for the whirring sound of the dust-sprayed fan that circled overhead at a dizzying speed. It was a simple apartment that came with no furniture apart from a black imitation leather sofa and an iron bed. It had patterned mosaic tiles on the floor that felt cool to his bare feet and freshly painted cream walls that made the apartment smell pleasantly of turpentine. The living room had rectangular glass windows against which the leaves of an overgrown mango tree pressed hard, like the cheeks of a curious child.

There were two bags of unpacked luggage lying in the corner of a large living room, which he ruffled through whenever he needed clothes instead of unpacking them into the cupboard in the bedroom. He couldn't tell if he did not unpack because he didn't have the time or because it would signify that he was finally going to accept that he was going to stay here for however long it took.

He walked towards the kitchen to make some tea. The kitchen was its own room and had a large amount of sunshine coming in through the windows that faced the road, making the few stainless steel vessels on his shelves dazzle with brightness. In other circumstances, this bright and spacious kitchen would have made him happy – it was the exact opposite of the kitchen that he had left behind in London, which was cramped and mouldy, with a window that overlooked a discoloured wall. Jason lit the stove with a matchstick and watched the pot of water blister as it got heated. He could hear the faint sound of a mewling cat coming from outside the kitchen window.

'Now, who do we have here?' he murmured softly as he watched the grey eyes of a cat peer through the metal bars of the window, its ears perked up warily, in the manner of felines everywhere. It was white, with smudges of orange, as if it had tumbled around in a mostly empty jar of apricot jam. The cat entered through the window and lapped up the milk even as he poured it into a bowl from a plastic sachet. Jason's doorbell rang loudly, and the cat glared accusingly at him before gliding out through the bars of the kitchen window in one swift motion.

Jason walked towards the door, wincing at the loud, unfamiliar tune that the doorbell seemed to play every time it was pressed. On the other side of the door, he could hear an unabashedly confident voice singing tunelessly along. It turned out to be a boy of around ten carrying a large keg of water on his shoulders with surprising ease. He paused mid-song to stare at Jason for a moment and then announced rather formally, 'Mineral water, sir. From Diamond General Stores.'

Jason beckoned him inside, and the boy removed his sandals before following Jason into the kitchen. He was wearing worn-out shorts and a blue T-shirt with a faded Superman symbol that hung loosely around his shoulders.

After placing the water on the floor, the boy turned to him with a bright smile. 'My name is Salim, sir. Nice to meet you.' He said this in unbroken English, with his hands on his hips and his chest chuffed up in pride, as if he were auditioning for the role of Superman himself.

'Hello, Salim, thank you.' Jason fumbled in the pocket of his shorts and thrust a twenty rupee note into Salim's hand. The boy looked at the note with barely concealed glee. However, his expression soon changed to one of stoic sacrifice. 'But, sir, you have paid the entire amount for water already.'

'This is extra for you. A tip,' Jason replied, smiling at him. It was the equivalent of twenty pence, an amount that would not even buy a bar of chocolate in London. However, from the wide smile on Salim's face that he was trying unsuccessfully to hide, Jason gathered that this was perhaps a generous tip for carrying water across the road in Chennai.

Salim thanked him profusely and tucked the note deep into his pocket before Jason could change his mind. He then skipped down the stairs, whistling the tune of the song that he had been singing before.

'Salim!' Jason called out from the top of the stairs, remembering something. 'Where's the nearest barber? Haircut place?' He mimed the action of chopping his hair with a pair of scissors.

'Oh, haircut?' Salim blinked. 'Be back in ten minutes, sir,' he said, holding up all his ten fingers and mimicking honking a horn.

True to his word, Salim was back, carrying a large pair of scissors and a metal box of unidentifiable colour and contents. Jason looked at the boy warily as he pulled a chair to the middle of Jason's living room and beckoned him to sit, brandishing a red towel to wrap around him.

'You will look even more handsome after my haircut, sir,' Salim smiled, opening his box and giving Jason a pockmarked mirror to hold up in his hand.

Jason couldn't recall the last time someone had actually used the word handsome to describe him. Perhaps it had been his grandmother as she looked over one of his old school photos with him wearing a blazer and a shirt buttoned up till his neck. Although he hadn't gone to visit her in her care home before leaving for India, the memory of her trying to keep her pen steady while writing in her bingo numbers suddenly made him more homesick than anything else had in the last month.

Salim was showing him photographs of men sporting exuberant hairstyles and striking contemplative poses. 'Which one do you want, sir?'

Jason looked at the stack of photos one by one with increasing trepidation. He thought that these could only be considered acceptable hairstyles if he happened to be a poodle.

He cleared his throat. 'You know what, Salim, we can maybe arrange the haircut for another day,' he said finally, in as firm a voice as he could muster.

Undeterred, Salim tried to mimic the men in the pictures by styling his hair with his comb and standing in different poses. Jason chuckled aloud for the first time in weeks.

As Jason watched the boy cheerfully pack up the red towel, he admired the fact that Salim was so relentlessly upbeat. He wondered if Salim's situation in life might warrant him to be otherwise, but then reproached himself for making assumptions about someone else's life that he perhaps had no idea about.

'So, are you here for holiday, sir?' Salim eyed the unpacked luggage on the floor.

'Kind of,' Jason replied, although it wasn't true.

Salim continued with the upbeat voice of a television commercial, 'Tamil Nadu – very beautiful. I have a friend who can give you a car with a driver and take you to see temples for a good price. Want to go to Mahabalipuram?'

Jason hesitated, which made Salim press on. 'Or Pondicherry? He can show you a good time.' Salim stretched out the word 'good' and winked exaggeratedly for additional measure.

Jason shook his head and replied in a mock formal tone that was meant to match Salim's, 'No, I will request your services the next time I need them. Thanks again for bringing the water.'

*

For the first time since Jason had moved in, he found himself climbing up the staircase of Grand Life Apartments at the same time as Kamala. It was only early evening, but the cement staircases looked bleached under the bright glare of tube lights. Kamala was a few steps ahead of Jason, carrying a cloth bag distended with vegetables. He debated whether to speak to her or walk slower so that it wouldn't seem rude if he didn't make any conversation with her.

As they reached the landing of the first floor, he caught up with a quick jump, cleared his throat, and said, 'Excuse me.'

Kamala appeared surprised to be spoken to but looked back at him kindly.

'I wanted to ask about your vegetables? They look so fresh? Where do you get them?' He uncharacteristically added an inflection at the end of each sentence, turning them into questions.

Kamala brightened. 'From the vegetable market on North Street. It's opposite Srinivasa Theatre, next to the auto stand.' She shifted the bag from one hand to the other and used her right hand to point towards the corner of their street. She then turned to look back at him, appraised his evident foreignness, and added, 'There is a supermarket around the corner of this road, if you want something quicker.'

'Thank you.' He was already fumbling for the next topic of conversation. 'So, you're a dentist?' He gestured to the wooden sign with its hand-painted lettering.

'Yes, I am.' She looked up at the sign, too, almost as if she needed reaffirmation that she was indeed Dr T.S. Kamala Sundaram, B.D.S, M.D.S.

'I am a chef,' he offered in return. 'I work in a restaurant here.'

'Oh really,' observed Kamala with surprise, but didn't continue the conversation. She was still looking at her sign, seemingly lost in a distant memory. Jason realised that Kamala's attention was wavering, like the swivelling pedestal fans he had seen in Chennai.

'Also, to travel and experience a new culture. And to have a bit of an adventure on the side, you know,' he added hastily, now regretting having started this conversation.

'Why don't you come inside?' she asked, surprising him. A cool blast of air.

As they entered the apartment, although Kamala didn't question him further, Jason found himself explaining, 'I work at one of the restaurants in the Radisson hotel – The Tamarind Room?'

'I usually don't go to those types of places,' Kamala said decisively. By 'those types of places', Jason guessed she meant fancy restaurants that served food that didn't bear much resemblance to what she cooked at home.

'Jason, isn't it? Let me make you some coffee. I still have plenty of decoction left over from the morning's drink,' she said, tucking the end of her lilac saree to her waist in a practised motion.

He nodded vaguely, not sure whether it would be rude to refuse. Kamala didn't give him much of a choice and walked straight into her kitchen without waiting for a response. He sat on one of the wooden chairs by the dining table and looked around. It was definitely more lived-in than his apartment above, and everything in the living room, from the sofa to the television, seemed to have its modesty protected with plastic or crochet when not in use. There were jewellery-laden, round-cheeked gods everywhere – enclosed in mahogany frames, flapping on monthly calendars, and painted on prayer books. Right next to him, there was a Ganesha idol stuffed with what looked like puffed rice, and a passport-sized photo of a young girl was placed at the idol's feet. She looked like a younger version of Kamala and was staring sullenly at the camera through thick spectacles, her hair tied in two plaits that were so tight that they defied gravity. He suspected that this girl would be embarrassed if she found out that this photo, perhaps from high school, was being displayed to all visitors to this house.

Kamala came back with coffee, hers in a stainless steel tumbler, and his in a red porcelain mug that had Oxford University printed on it. 'That's my daughter, Lakshmi,' Kamala pointed at the photo Jason was looking at. 'She studies at Oxford now.' She gestured towards his cup.

'Oxford? Quite impressive,' he replied. Oxford University had been completely out of the question for him with his grades – he barely scraped through a psychology course at a little-known college, and looking back, he wished he had skipped that to start cooking earlier.

Jason took a sip of his drink and murmured his appreciation – it was frothy with milk but still had the delicious bitterness of coffee steeped in it. They sat silently for a few moments, sipping their drinks. Jason looked around the room, trying to find something to talk about, and his eyes fell on a purple badminton racquet hanging from a nail above the sofa.

'Oh, do you play?' he asked.

'Play what?' Kamala turned around to see what he was looking at. Noticing the racquet, she tilted her head and gave a loud chuckle, in the manner of someone not used to laughing loudly.

'That's not really a badminton racquet.' She brandished it in the air in demonstration. There was a zap as it swished, stunning a mosquito mid-flight.

'Ah,' said Jason, almost as stunned as the mosquito.

She seemed to loosen up a little after that and spoke about her daughter with visible pride. She quizzed him about various aspects of the UK, reaffirming facts that her daughter must have already told her. How cold did it get in the winter? Was there enough vegetarian food in restaurants? Were the roads safe to walk alone at night? She listened carefully to Jason's answers while intermittently asking him if the coffee was all right and whether he was really sure that he didn't want some bondas that would be no bother at all and would take only two minutes to make.

When Jason went back to his apartment, he was greeted by a voicemail from an unknown number. He put his phone on speaker and went to the kitchen to refrigerate the curry leaves that Kamala had asked him to try cooking with. When he heard the voice on his phone, he rushed back to the living room and stared at it, his heart beating a little faster than necessary.

'Hi, Jason. This is Emma . . . I'm just calling to see how you're doing. I got this number from your mum. How is India treating you? Ring me back when you hear this? Bye for now.' Emma's tone had the sing-song lilt that she normally adopted when trying to be breezy, but he could sense that her voice was strained. Or at least, he hoped it was.

Jason listened to the voicemail again and was taken back to that evening, two months ago, when his world had been turned upside down. It had been an ordinary Friday, and he had opened the door to their apartment with a minor sense of elation on remembering that it was his turn to pick that night's movie to watch. When Emma, who had been waiting for him on the sofa, mentioned that she had something to say, he had followed her line of sight to the dishwasher and momentarily wondered if it had stopped working again.

'I think our relationship has run its course.' She had eyed him sadly as if he were the one saying these words. 'Surely, you've noticed that it hasn't been working for a while?' she had asked. How could he have noticed when he had stopped to buy her favourite candies shaped like tiny teddy bears on his way home, while she had been busy packing her belongings into a suitcase? How could he have noticed when he had foolishly assumed that their relationship of three years was meant to last forever.

For weeks after, he tried to entreat Emma – reasonably at first, then pleadingly after she refused to budge, and finally fervently, as she remained stuck in her resolve that she wanted their relationship to end. The problem was that he couldn't stop loving her just like that – even though she left half-drunk teacups underneath the sofa, even though her long blonde hair stuck annoyingly to his sweaters, even though he had given her everything that he could and it hadn't been quite enough. It was this thought that still gave Jason a mild pain in his chest, even though he was thousands of miles away from her now, sitting in the uncomfortable embrace of a sofa in Chennai.

His decision to come to India was down to sheer happenstance, like most things in life. He had been spiralling in self-pity and wanted to escape from the city where everything reminded him of Emma. One of his friends had suggested a much smaller shift in location to somewhere like Edinburgh, perhaps. However, on a rainy evening in the neighbourhood pub, he had heard about a friend's friend moving to a restaurant in India. Jason had asked for more details, thinking that somewhere very far away sounded like where he needed to be, and now, here he was. Although, if he were honest, if he had heard about a friend moving to Mexico, he would probably be folding tacos and downing tequila right now.

Dusk was settling in, and honeyed fingers of light reached through the windows of his living room. He looked outside the window and saw a playground in the distance where a few boys were playing cricket, refusing to stop until there was absolutely no sunlight left. He got up and pressed delete on the voicemail and went to bed wishing, like many have wished at one point or the other, that his mind had a delete button, too.

4

Kamala

Kamala tried to jostle her way to the front of the railing so that she could have an unobstructed view of the passengers coming out of the airport. It was only four in the morning, but the place was teeming with activity and lit up by lights so bright that they hurt her eyes. The area outside the airport was filled with families huddled in hour-long farewells, taxi drivers trying to hustle everyone walking out of the gates and security men milling about with the slow, casual air of overfed guests at a wedding. Kamala could feel a headache setting in from this excessive early morning noise and wondered if she should get some of the overpriced coffee that came in flimsy plastic cups from the airport kiosk. She decided against it, as she didn't want to lose the good spot she currently had – with a vantage view of the exit door through which her daughter would emerge in another half an hour.

Standing next to her was a middle-aged couple sending off their daughter to far foreign shores, judging from the tear-filled eyes and trembling voice of the mother. Kamala didn't intend to eavesdrop, but they were standing so close that she could not help it. The mother was giving her daughter rolled-up aluminium foil that contained home-made rotis, along with instructions to eat them during her layover in Dubai before her second flight.

The girl was flying first to Houston in Texas, where her third cousin lived, and then driving to Austin, where her university was. With the casual American accent with which the girl was naming these cities, Kamala would have never guessed that this was her first time on an aeroplane until her father brought it up.

'Here, have some cotton,' her father was saying, pushing wads of fluffy cotton into her hands. 'I've heard that the flight take-off and landing can harm your ears.' Even if her father couldn't take care of all the problems that his daughter was going to face when she was thousands of miles away from him, Kamala empathised with his attempt at protecting her from what little he could.

Their conversation reminded her of the day Lakshmi had left for the UK. Lakshmi had been more excited than sad to leave, and Kamala had listened with a heavy heart as she said her goodbyes on the phone to her friends, punctuated by conspiratorial whispers and nervous laughter. They had fought when Lakshmi had refused to take the boxes of home-made snacks and pickles that Kamala had spent all day packing and sealing with wax from a candle to keep them safe. Lakshmi had complained that there was no space in her bag and, eventually, Kamala had relented. Her daughter's bags were indeed overflowing with newly purchased winter clothes and shoes that she would need for the colder climate of her new home. However, she had been surprised at the airport when Lakshmi, who was seldom sentimental, hugged her tightly and nestled her face in Kamala's neck, just as she used to when she was a child.

'Take care of yourself, Ma. I will miss you,' her daughter had said, and Kamala had tried to temper her tears. 'Don't do anything that I wouldn't do!' Lakshmi had added, smiling, in an attempt to lighten the situation. Kamala still didn't understand what that last phrase meant. What would she ever do that Lakshmi would not? She should perhaps ask her.

As a new group of passengers started trickling out by the exit sign, Kamala perked up and carefully squinted at each person walking through the gates. After twenty minutes, she finally saw Lakshmi walk out in the hesitant, shy manner of hers that still tugged at her heart. It had taken her an embarrassingly long moment to recognise her own daughter – Lakshmi looked even frailer than she remembered, and her curly hair, which had been cut short the last time she had seen her, was now long enough to be tied up in a knot.

Kamala waved at Lakshmi vigorously, the golden bangles on her wrist jangling with the movement. Their eyes met, and they rushed to meet each other, wading through the crowd near the exit that was over ten people deep. When they finally met, Kamala gave her daughter a brief embrace and patted her on the back, exclaiming, 'You have become so thin, Lakshmi *kanna*. You must be starving yourself. You will soon disappear if you keep up like this.'

Lakshmi also appraised her mother's appearance but didn't comment on it. She smiled and said, 'That's why I am here now, Ma. So that you can feed me properly, isn't it?'

Lakshmi refused to give Kamala her bag despite a short tussle, and they walked towards a pre-booked taxi, waking the driver, who was fast asleep with a towel covering his face. He looked displeased to be woken up, but once Lakshmi and Kamala got in, he obligingly adjusted his seat to accommodate Lakshmi's long legs. It was still early in the morning, and the amber-lit roads were just coming to life with hawkers setting up stalls selling coconut water, grey-haired men going for their morning walk in veshtis and sports shoes, and stray dogs lounging near tea shops waiting for the morning's first act of kindness.

Kamala kept talking like a wound-up clock that simply had to keep going until its lever finished unwinding.

'Did you sleep well on the flight?'

'What did they give you to eat?'

'I've made your favourite onion sambar with sweet potatoes. You can eat that right away or after sleeping a bit, whichever way you prefer.'

But the real question she wanted to ask hung between those sentences like an apostrophe that she didn't know quite where to place.

During the brief silence that descended just before they reached home, Kamala looked at Lakshmi – at the profile of her curly-haired face and slender neck as she looked silently out of the taxi window – and felt a surge of happiness that this was her daughter, here, in flesh and blood, and hers to keep for two whole weeks. She reached for Lakshmi's shoulder and squeezed it in affection. Lakshmi squeezed her hand back and smiled at her, somewhat distractedly, before returning to her vigil to check if they had arrived home.

*

The next morning, Kamala bustled around in the kitchen planning Lakshmi's meals for the day. She decided to make uthappams for breakfast, recalling Lakshmi mentioning that these savoury pancakes were not easily found in the menus of Indian restaurants abroad. For lunch, she had already confirmed with Lakshmi that she would be making pineapple rasam, a dish that she made only when Lakshmi was around as Kamala herself didn't particularly like its sweet and sour taste. She reminded herself to check on what Lakshmi wanted for dinner as soon as she woke up, just in case she needed to make a quick trip down to Diamond General Stores in the afternoon for any ingredients.

Kamala had just brought the lentil and rice batter for the uthappams out of the fridge when the doorbell rang. It was Reva from upstairs; she had come to return one of Kamala's pink Tupperware boxes.

'Thanks for the mor kozhambu, Aunty. It was too good. I ate it over several days,' she enthused, as she always did, but it didn't stop Kamala from feeling flattered.

'No mention, please.' Kamala peered through the transparent box. Reva had placed something inside – a glossy black and gold chocolate bar.

'You shouldn't be buying me these expensive chocolates, Revathi,' she chided. This was a familiar routine – whenever Kamala cooked something that involved a bit of additional effort, she set some aside for Reva because she knew that it would be eaten appreciatively and, when Reva returned the empty container, she would slip a bar of chocolate inside. Later, Kamala would cluck about the strange flavours of these chocolates to Sundu ('*Goodness, isn't lavender supposed to be used in talcum powder?*') as they passed the chocolate between them, finishing it in one sitting.

'Come in, come in. Don't simply stand at the doorstep.' Kamala gestured the young woman inside. 'Lakshmi is still sleeping. *Jet lag*,' she added knowingly, mentioning the term recently added to her vocabulary.

'Ah yes. She must be quite tired after her flight. How long is she staying for again?' Reva asked, taking a seat on the sofa, which was now propped with extra, perfectly plumped-up cushions for Lakshmi's visit.

'Only two weeks.' Kamala sighed in the practised manner of someone who had been complaining about this for a while.

'I am sure she is looking forward to being pampered at home for that time, though,' Reva responded warmly, and Kamala found herself smiling back.

She was quite fond of Reva, whom she considered to have been brought up well by her mother, with a sensible head on her shoulders. She thought that Reva was quite pretty, too, and often wondered why her mother was finding it so difficult to find a suitable boy for her. However, she had been at the receiving end of enough disapproving glares from Lakshmi on such topics to know that she shouldn't be asking this question directly to her young neighbour. 'Is your mother doing well?' Kamala asked instead.

'All good. And she was very happy to hear that I am eating well, thanks to you.'

'If you stop by later, you can take back some pineapple rasam that I was planning to make for Lakshmi.' Looking at Reva's uncertain expression, she wondered if the humble lentil rasam needed better marketing these days, and added, 'You can just drink the rasam from a tumbler like soup.'

They paused their conversation as Lakshmi walked into the living room in her pyjamas, her hair knotted at the top of her head. Kamala noticed that Lakshmi's hair looked as dry as a tamarind husk and made a mental note to give it a good soaking in coconut oil later.

'Good morning, *kanna*. Do you want to have breakfast now or in a little while?' Lakshmi smiled sleepily at Kamala but didn't answer her question.

'Long time no see, Reva,' Lakshmi nodded at Reva and proceeded to sit cross-legged on the sofa.

Reva and Lakshmi soon started talking in the fast, casual English that Kamala had trouble keeping up with, and she settled for merely watching their young, bright faces in animated conversation.

'Revathi, you can stay for two more minutes? I will quickly make some uthappams for both of you,' Kamala interrupted them, getting up from her chair. Before Reva could protest, Kamala continued, 'I've already kept the batter out of the fridge to rest. It will take me no time to make it.' She tucked the end of her saree to her waist purposefully and headed to the kitchen.

As she sliced onions, tomatoes and capsicum into small pieces and scattered them over the batter, spread into a perfectly shaped circle, a burst of laughter reached her from the living room. She hadn't heard Lakshmi laugh this loudly in a long time, and listening to her throaty laugh that tapered into a high-pitched giggle, she smiled to herself, although she had no idea what had been so funny.

She came out of the kitchen holding two steaming plates of uthappams, accompanied by cups of drumstick sambar, and successfully stopped herself from asking what they had been talking about.

'I can't recall when I last had an uthappam! Must be the last time I was in Chennai, almost a year ago,' Lakshmi exclaimed.

'I don't eat them often either,' admitted Reva. 'The last time I had it must have been at Murugan Idli Kadai a couple of months ago, and it was nowhere as good as Kamala Aunty's.'

'The sambar we make at home is different from the hotel ones,' Kamala deflected the compliment. 'Those hotel fellows add jaggery,' she added, her voice suggesting that it was an addition that she didn't quite approve of.

'You are not eating any, Aunty?' Reva asked with the politeness of a guest, while Lakshmi asked no such question, on account of Kamala being her mother.

Kamala waved her hand in a manner that indicated that she would eat later. 'How is work going, Revathi?'

'Same as usual, Aunty. I have a difficult manager right now, so it's been a little challenging, I must admit.'

'Managers come in all varieties. The important thing to remember when you are young,' Kamala paused to look directly at Reva and Lakshmi for emphasis, 'is to learn a skill. You shouldn't worry about what A or B thinks about you or your work.'

Reva nodded earnestly, murmuring, 'Very true, Aunty,' while Lakshmi seemed to be eyeing her mother extra attentively. The evening before, Lakshmi had brushed off her questions about the important thing she had mentioned in her email, but the seriousness with which her daughter was observing her now made Kamala very anxious about what it might be.

*

Both Lakshmi and Kamala were seated at their usual spots in the living room – Lakshmi in the far corner of the sofa, and Kamala on the divan, a small pillow propped up against her back. The first rays of translucent sun after the morning's rain streamed through the half-open window. A squirrel that had jumped off the mango tree scurried around on their windowsill, chirping intermittently. It turned to look at them with wide, startled eyes before hopping back onto the tree.

'Do you remember the story from the *Ramayana* about why squirrels have three stripes on their backs?' Kamala asked agreeably in an attempt to draw Lakshmi into a conversation.

'Maybe, why?' Lakshmi shrugged, looking up from her phone to give Kamala a vague look before going back to typing something.

Kamala thought back to the ten-year-old who used to quiz her so intently about the stories in Indian mythology as she stood frying onion vadais on Sunday afternoons. Surely, that young girl must be in there somewhere, wandering inside the unfathomable maze that Lakshmi's brain now seemed to have become?

Lakshmi had been back for two days, and she had spent most of that time either sleeping or chatting with the friends who seemed to be perennially available on her laptop and phone. Kamala had insisted that they go to the neighbourhood temple, and although Lakshmi didn't refuse, she didn't really submit to praying and had acted as if she would have preferred to be someplace else. Kamala had asked her repeatedly if there was something bothering her, but her daughter brushed those questions aside with a quick hand motion, as if Kamala's words were mosquitoes buzzing too close to her ear.

'Does the phone have something really interesting to say?' asked Kamala. Lakshmi's eyebrows rose in surprise at Kamala's displeased tone.

Kamala tuned her voice to a more placatory setting and asked, 'Do you want something to drink? I can make some fresh juice.'

'Yes, I would really like that.' Lakshmi curled her legs up on the sofa and reached for the magazine section of the newspaper that was neatly folded on the coffee table.

Kamala had already peeled some mangoes early in the morning, thinking that she would make some juice for Lakshmi later in the day when it got hotter. She quickly blended the mango pulp with ice and sugar and brought it out. She sat back on the divan with a sigh directed towards her knees and took a small sip of the filter coffee that she had made for herself.

'So,' Lakshmi said, looking contemplatively at the mango juice that glowed a bright crayon yellow in the light streaming through the window, 'as you have rightly guessed, I have been meaning to say something to you.'

She looked up, her eyes meeting Kamala's resolutely. She took a deep breath, then continued as if she had rehearsed this moment many times before. 'Ma, I am a lesbian.'

Kamala furrowed her eyebrows. 'I don't understand, Lakshmi. What are you saying?'

'I am a lesbian. It means that I like girls. Not boys,' said Lakshmi, eyeing her mother's face carefully. 'I know that this will be a really difficult thing for you to digest, Ma, so maybe just take some time to think about it, OK? I am sorry to trouble you with this, but I really hope you understand,' Lakshmi continued, averting her eyes guiltily from Kamala's.

Lakshmi's words ran circles around Kamala's brain, making her feel dizzy. She clutched her tumbler of coffee tightly in her hands for support.

'Do you want to talk more about it, Ma?' asked Lakshmi tentatively. She looked scared of the shocked expression on Kamala's face.

The silence in the room ticked away, heavy with parental disappointment. Finally, perhaps unable to bear the weight of it on her shoulders, Lakshmi picked up the glass of mango juice and left the room.

*

Lesbian. A sharp migraine had burrowed into Kamala's head ever since Lakshmi had uttered that word. Her mind was full of questions. Did Lakshmi feel this way because she grew up without a father? Was this just some experimental phase that young people living abroad went through? Most importantly, what would happen to her grand plans for Lakshmi's wedding and her lifelong yearning to play with her grandchildren?

After the revelation, Kamala had been so shocked that she had spent the next few days acting as if the conversation had never happened. Lakshmi seemed relieved and hence eager to please – she kept offering to help around the house, accompanied Kamala to the vegetable market and enthusiastically engaged in detailed discussions about what she wanted for lunch.

However, one evening, when Lakshmi had returned home from meeting a friend, Kamala had been sitting on her bed, looking through the jewellery that she had collected over the years for Lakshmi's wedding. Every year, for Lakshmi's birthday, Kamala would take her to T-Nagar and buy her a piece of jewellery, the cost of which was paid in monthly instalments into a gold-deposit scheme. Kamala would proudly declare that Lakshmi would look like a divine goddess on her wedding day when she wore these jewels, to which Lakshmi would exclaim in a mildly horrified voice, 'I will only look like a temple cow if I wear all of this, Ma!'

Lakshmi stood by the door, watching Kamala wistfully stroke the ruby necklace with the mango motif they had bought for her eighteenth birthday, and burst into tears. 'I am sorry, Ma. Sorry to be such a disappointment to you,' she sobbed, before running into her room and locking herself in.

Kamala did not ask her daughter to open the door. She was not sure if she wanted to hear more of what Lakshmi was going to say, the distance between them feeling much bigger than the few metres that separated them inside the house.

Knowing that the only thing that would help ease her mind was praying to her gods at the temple, Kamala set out of the apartment, unfurling her umbrella absently for shade. She walked slowly and purposefully, armed with additional offerings of coconuts, bananas and silk dhoti for the deity. She decided to stop at Karuthamma's stall and buy some flowers as well. Just in case.

'I will get the jasmines today,' Kamala said, and then after a pause, 'might as well get some of the kadhambams.' She pointed to the coral and violet flowers strung together and looped like a skipping rope tidied away.

Kamala watched Karuthamma swiftly measure the strand of flowers using the distance between her hands and elbows. 'Hope the children are all doing well?' she enquired, as she had done every time she had bought flowers from Karuthamma for the last fifteen years.

When Kamala had first met Karuthamma, she had been running a provision store with her husband at the very same spot, and sold flowers by measuring strands with hands that jangled with golden bangles. However, her husband had died suddenly, leaving her with debt and children to feed, and one by one, those golden bangles had given way to glass ones. Finally, the shop had also been sold and replaced by a service centre for electronics. At least the new owners had been kind enough to let her set up her rusty iron chair on the pavement and continue selling her flowers.

'What to say, Kamala-ma.' Karuthamma flashed her a wry smile, showing teeth stained crimson from chewing betel nut leaves. 'The oldest, even at the age of two donkeys, doesn't show any signs of becoming useful. He drinks away everything he earns and, even yesterday, needed his mother to get him out of jail after a good-for-nothing fight.'

'Hopefully, he sees sense soon, by God's grace. Children these days don't want to listen to any good advice from their mothers,' Kamala replied. She thought more about this statement as she reached for the flowers and felt more exhausted than she remembered being in a long time.

'You don't look too good, Kamala-ma. Are you not well?' Karuthamma asked, shading her eyes from the sun so that she could take a better look at Kamala's face.

'Just a small headache, nothing to worry.' Kamala rested the handle of her umbrella on the crook of her neck so that she could dig out the money from her handbag with both hands.

'Here, Kamala-ma, take this. Some more for your prayers.' Karuthamma handed her a cluster of bright yellow samanthi flowers, waving her hands in dismissal when Kamala insisted on paying for them as well.

The temple had various gods stationed in different rooms, and you could choose the one you wanted to pray to depending on what ailed you, not quite unlike picking a pill from Kamala's medicine cabinet at home. There was the idol of Hanuman, in the far corner, who gave you strength, and Pillayar in another corner, who removed obstacles from your life. On this day, Kamala chose to pray at the central multi-purpose altar of Vishnu, as she felt that she needed to be fortified with everything that the temple had to offer in order to ease her worries.

'So, an *archanai* in your daughter's name, as usual?' The priest nodded at her familiarly as he took the basket of flowers and fruits from Kamala's hand.

As he started reciting his hymns in Sanskrit, Kamala closed her eyes and folded her hands in prayer. She prayed for Lakshmi to see some good sense and realise that this was all just a passing affliction, negotiating that she would conduct a more elaborate prayer, involving a saffron-scented bath for the idol, in exchange for giving Lakshmi's mind a little nudge in the right direction.

Once she had finished drawing up these mental agreements, she opened her eyes to find the priest reaching out to her with a plate of tulsi leaves, on which she placed some money. She was very generous that day, placing several notes on the plate, and it did not go unnoticed by the priest.

'We also have another *archanai* later today, where we can include your daughter's name for a special blessing. Ticket is five hundred rupees,' he added, with the practised ease of a salesman at the belief shop.

'I will get two tickets. Both in my daughter's name,' said Kamala, taking up the opportunity to double the chances of getting her prayers heard.

By the time she returned home, the streetlamps had started glowing yellow, but Lakshmi had still not returned from visiting her friend. Sundu, however, arrived on time for dinner and walked into the house surrounded by a cloud of jaggery and ghee. 'I bought Lakshmi's favourite – polis from the stall opposite my house,' she said, handing over the bag of coconut-stuffed pancakes to Kamala.

'She should be back anytime now, that busy girl.' Kamala took the polis into the kitchen and placed them in an airtight container. Sundu followed her inside and picked up a laddoo from the plate of sweets that Kamala had placed on the praying altar so that the gods at home didn't feel unattended to.

'Sundu, that was kept as an offering!' Kamala exclaimed in disapproval even as Sundu finished the laddoo in two quick bites. She then shrugged, letting the matter slide in the manner of someone who has had the same argument with the same person many times before.

'Did I tell you what unbelievable thing my son is up to now?' Given the cheerful tone of Sundu's voice, Kamala surmised that it was nothing like Lakshmi's shocking news.

'—He is doing something called "stand-up comedy",' Sundu announced and, although Kamala hadn't looked particularly concerned at this announcement, Sundu waved her hands as if to dismiss any potential concerns. 'Nothing to worry, his wife didn't let him quit his normal job.'

Kamala feigned interest. 'What is standing up comedy? Is it like Crazy Mohan's comedy shows?'

'Nothing funny like that. He just stands on a stage and tells jokes,' her friend explained, giving a young people-these-days shake of her head. 'I didn't tell him this, but between you and me, it sounds like a very difficult way to not make any money.'

Kamala couldn't help giving Sundu a small smile. Sundu's presence was a good distraction from her immediate worries, and she felt her headache lighten just a little.

She wiped the kitchen countertop while waiting for the pressure cooker to finish whistling and blowing off its steam as Sundu foraged through the large stainless steel box where Kamala kept her fried snacks. Sundu was going on about one of her friends who was on a package tour around Europe, tailored exclusively for middle-aged South Indians. She had heard Sundu mention these tours several times recently. It seemed like Sundu was trying to drop a strong hint or she really had a suspiciously large number of friends going on these trips.

'—Did you know that they actually take a cook along with them so that they can eat curd rice in Paris?'

Kamala didn't understand what was wrong with that. She herself was not too big on travelling for pleasure. She imagined that if she did end up going abroad, she, too, would like to have the comfort of having some familiar curd rice to accompany her wherever she went. Normally, she would have said this, which would have then led Sundu to retort that they should at least go to that Italian place on Mount Road, if not travel all the way to Europe, but today, Kamala just kept quiet.

She opened the pressure cooker on the dining table wrapped with clear plastic, and the steam misted over both their spectacles. The old friends looked at each other, half-blinded through their moon-coloured spectacles, and wordlessly distributed the steaming trays between themselves.

As Kamala scooped out the round idlis onto a plate, she asked Sundu, making her tone as casual as possible, 'What do you think of all these people who say that they are gay or lesbian these days?'

'What do I think? I think that they are the same as anyone else. And it's not like it's something new.' Sundu continued prising the idlis from their steaming trays with a spoon without looking up. 'Remember Sarala from high school? She had that thick, long hair, plaited till her hips?'

Kamala nodded. They had been in high school three decades ago, but Sarala still lived two streets away. 'She and that college librarian, that strict-looking woman who would never crack a smile – they used to exchange secret love notes inside books all the time.'

'Ah, yes. And you used to help them ferry these books back and forth. I remember that, too,' Kamala recollected. 'She ended up marrying that fellow who owns that big cement factory and has two sons who are around Lakshmi's age now,' she added, as if making a point.

'That is because she didn't have a choice,' Sundu said emphatically, ladling generous spoonfuls of sambar on top of her idlis so that they now flailed in a spicy lentil pool.

Kamala had to admit that she wasn't very surprised by Sundu's opinion on this topic. Sundu herself was a divorcée, a fact so remarkable for someone her age that she had grown not to care much for the reckless gossip that preceded her wherever she went. Still, Kamala thought that it was always easier to be charitable in one's opinion as long as it concerned other people and other people's children.

'I hear that there is this new shop near the LIC building that sells sweets for diabetic people,' Kamala changed the subject.

Sundu looked at her closely, not registering what she just said. 'You look a little off-colour. Are you sure you are feeling all right? When was the last time you had a full health check-up?'

Kamala looked at Sundu's concerned face and found herself wavering on whether she should speak to her friend about Lakshmi. It was too much of a stretch even for Sundu's imagination to guess that her questions had something to do with her own daughter. She wanted to talk about it, but somehow talking meant that she needed to voice her fears aloud, which made them more real. If she just kept it to herself, she could at least pretend for a while that everything was just as it used to be.

'Just a mild migraine, Sundu. I will take paracetamol later,' she replied absently, keeping an eye on the window facing the entrance, watching for Lakshmi's return.

*

The sight of her daughter's suitcase in the middle of the living room was making Kamala's migraine thrum even more ferociously than before. It was time for Lakshmi to return to London and they had managed to avoid each other for the last few days, except for some perfunctory terse exchanges about food in the refrigerator and spare keys. Kamala eyed Lakshmi as she walked back and forth from her room, adding more clothes that she rolled up like newspaper before placing them in her bag. Usually, Kamala would have asked her why she was rolling her clothes instead of folding them neatly, but today, she didn't.

Lakshmi pretended that her mother didn't exist by carefully avoiding eye contact with the corner of the sofa where Kamala was seated. Lakshmi finally zipped up her hard-shell suitcase and made it stand upright. It rattled emptily, as it didn't have the cardboard boxes containing the jars of pickles and sweets that Kamala usually insisted on adding to her bag every time she visited.

'I forgot to give this to you. Here,' Lakshmi said finally, her face carefully cleared of any expression. She was holding something shiny in her hand, causing Kamala to get up faster than her arthritic knees would normally allow. It was a metallic keychain that also doubled as a bottle opener. Kamala clasped it tightly and ran her hand over the university logo embossed on it.

'The flight is at four in the morning, isn't it? Have you checked in online?' she asked, although she knew every detail about the flight from previous conversations with Lakshmi when they had been on normal speaking terms with each other. She knew that the flight was actually at quarter past four, with a vegetarian meal booked, and there was an afternoon class Lakshmi needed to attend the next day despite the effects of jet lag.

'Yes,' said Lakshmi, walking back to her room. Kamala could hear the sound of drawers being opened and shut and tinny laughter coming from her laptop. Lakshmi returned and unplugged the phone charger that was still in the socket in the living room, carefully avoiding eye contact with Kamala again.

As she watched her daughter's frame – thin and wiry, drowned in oversized spotted pyjamas – walking away from her, she knew that she couldn't see her daughter leave like this – couldn't allow her to leave while being so furious with her. She fought all her innate instincts to avoid confrontation and blurted out, 'Are you *sure*?'

Lakshmi walked back out of her room, looking defensive and uncertain at the same time, 'Sure? About what? The keychain?'

She then looked closely at her mother's face, eyebrows arched in worry. 'Oh, about being a lesbian?'

Kamala flinched at the word.

'Unfortunately, I am sure.' Lakshmi turned away as she said this.

'Lakshmi, you will get over this. You have always liked to make things unnecessarily complicated,' Kamala replied, almost as if she was reassuring herself rather than speaking to her daughter.

'You think I wanted to be complicated? I can't believe that you think that this is a choice.' Lakshmi sounded very tired. 'You know what?' She was standing in the middle of the living room, holding on to the suitcase very tightly. 'I should have never brought this up. I was really stupid for thinking that you would understand. That you were different. That *we* were different.'

Before Kamala could respond, Lakshmi quickly carried the suitcase in jerky, righteously angry movements to her room and slammed the door shut.

5

Revathi

It was the small slice of time in the Chennai evening, when it was late enough for the day to have cooled down and yet early enough for the mosquitoes to still be asleep in their watery beds. Reva and Mani were seated on Mani's porch, playing carrom under the yellow light of a naked bulb that hung from the ceiling. Reva flicked the striker and a coin fell inside the slot, making a sharp sound like a gunshot. Mani surveyed the remaining coins on the board with grim concentration, his hands placed on his knees. They played in companionable silence, occasionally interrupted by the clanking of metal from the construction site nearby.

Reva noticed a man with a briefcase hovering near their iron gate, half-heartedly looking for the doorbell as if he really didn't want to find it. 'Looks like we have a salesman at our door.' She tilted her head questioningly towards Mani who recognised the man and beckoned him in.

Reva couldn't hide her surprise when Mani introduced the thin, bespectacled man as Bala, the business manager for Olympic Constructions. Reva had expected someone more menacing than Bala, who was so frail that he listed slightly in the direction of his briefcase and seemed as if a strong gust of wind could pose serious challenges to his ability to stay vertical.

She got up to leave, but Mani waved his hand, asking her to stay, saying that this wouldn't take very long. Once Bala started talking, Reva quickly realised that his apparent harmlessness was perhaps the primary reason that he was chosen for this job. He spoke in a soft, conspiratory manner with Mani, explaining how the building would start becoming increasingly burdensome to him and that the construction company was actually doing him a favour by taking it out of his hands.

Mani merely flashed him a tolerant smile and asked him to help himself to some lemon juice.

Bala took a sip of the juice and contemplated for a moment, making a convincing impression of someone struggling to reveal something that they knew they shouldn't. 'I would strongly rec-ommend reconsidering the offer, Mr Mani. I don't think you have had much experience dealing with the likes of these construction companies. Who knows what sort of measures they would resort to.' He then shrugged apologetically before taking his leave, as if he also struggled under the weight of all this unfairness in the world and it was entirely coincidental that he derived a paycheck from it.

Once he left, Mani gestured to Reva to continue playing while making a smiling face, but Reva noticed that he missed a couple of easy shots that he usually would have made with his eyes closed.

She tried to come up with something reassuring to say but was interrupted by her phone. It was her mother trying to reach her for the third time that day. She was about to ignore the call, but the guilt in not calling her back the day before made her answer. The happiness in her mother's voice made Reva feel even more guilty for considering to ignore the call.

'Hi, Ma.' She mouthed her goodbye to Mani, miming that she was going to take the call upstairs.

'Tell your mother that I enquired,' he murmured formally before going back to playing carrom by himself.

'Toast with butter for breakfast, vegetable pulao from the canteen. Oh, and I am planning to make pasta for dinner.' Reva was reciting what she had eaten during the day in answer to her mother's first question.

'Make sure you add some vegetables to your pasta, Revathi. Add some tomatoes – you like them with pasta,' her mum instructed over the phone.

'OK, Ma, will do,' said Reva in a docile voice that both of them knew was fake.

'Why are you breathing heavily? Do you have a cold? Did you get wet in the rain yesterday?'

'No, Ma, I don't have a cold – I am just catching my breath as I am walking up the stairs to my apartment.'

She told her mother about the unfriendly visit from the construction company, which made her mother go on about a distant uncle who had started a property dispute with his neighbour regarding the ownership of a shared water well. Although it was several years since Reva had met these members of her extended family, she was quite familiar with every small disturbance in their lives that her mother narrated to her with unfailing regularity.

'He makes a steady income from simply suing other people – not everyone can be clever like that,' her mother remarked, somewhat defensively, although Reva hadn't commented anything to the contrary. Reva could then hear her mother blowing on the surface of the tumbler of hot milk that she usually drank at this time, after her dinner. She recalled how her mother would patiently wait for the milk to boil on the stove and bring her a glass of warm milk to her room every night, wearing one of her nighties printed with unrealistically large flowers. This memory made her feel a sudden wave of affection towards her mother.

'You were telling me that you had met Shreya. How is she doing?'

'She is good – in Chennai for a while waiting for her US visa. We ate dosas at Saravana Bhavan.' Reva balanced her phone under her chin while throwing away some mouldy vegetables from the fridge.

'Very good. Shreya's parents must also be looking,' her mother said, making the affection that Reva had just felt evaporate a little. She let the statement slide without a response, instead sniffing a cauliflower head to see if it was still edible. Even when she had picked the cauliflower aspirationally in the supermarket, she had willfully ignored the part of her brain that had told her that she would never end up cooking with it. She put it back in the fridge, knowing that she would throw it out in a couple of days anyway.

'– Her parents must be looking for a US alliance. All the good ones have settled abroad these days, anyways. You girls should learn from your friend at work – what is her name – Ranji?' her mother carried on without waiting for her acknowledgement, which was her default style of conversation. 'She listened to her parents and has done everything at the right time – you are both wasting your youth by working so hard and chasing careers. You can't be running around with babies and a nappy bag when you are forty, can you?'

Reva walked into her living room and started browsing for TV shows that she could watch once this call ended.

'– By the way, Revathi, did you see the email message that I forwarded? You should definitely meet Karthik. He is the nephew of Chinmayi – remember her? Her husband runs that mango export business? You may not. You were too little when they moved away to Bombay.' Her mother paused to take another sip of her milk before continuing, 'Anyways, this boy works for a big company in California and is in Chennai next month.'

Reva sighed. Back when Reva was twenty-four, her mother used to spend hours poring over online matrimonial websites for suitable matches for her and then mail profiles to her with added taglines – *Smart, handsome boy – studied at IIT + IIM!* or *US alliance – works at*

Goldman Sachs! Her emails always ended with an exclamation point, as if her inbox were a royal court where these men's presence was accompanied by liveried guards and blaring trumpets. Realising that these catchy subject lines were not tempting Reva to browse and buy any of these husbands immediately, she had then resorted to emotional blackmail in Reva's late twenties, but, by then, Reva had met Sebastian at work.

Sebastian had been kind and funny, with eyes that brimmed with the mischief of a joke waiting to be shared, and she had been carried away by the moored, yet unmoored feeling of being in love for the first time. He was also a Christian from Kerala, with a younger sister whose marriage prospects would be sullied if her brother married outside the community. They had worked out a plan for their future, though – they would wait for his sister to get married, after which they would brace themselves for the impact of telling their respective parents about their relationship. However, as with most well-laid plans, they didn't see a curve ahead – his sister had ended up falling in love and eloping with a Hindu, causing her to be renounced by her entire family. Watching his parents' anguish over their daughter's decision, Sebastian had refused to subject them to any further pain and stoically decided to fulfil the obligations that came with being a good son. Within three months of breaking up with Reva, he had married a girl from his native village. Admittedly, the fact that he had not been willing to fight for her had made getting over him a tiny bit easier, but not by much.

That was two years ago, and now that she was thirty-two and still unmarried, she no longer bothered with the pretence of being interested in the profiles of men that her mother sent but tried to be kinder to her in other ways to compensate for the fact that she had seemingly failed in one of her primary duties as a daughter. She still held out a little hope – that she would meet someone and fall in love again and this time it would all work out – but she also protected this hope fiercely from her mother.

'OK, Ma, I have to go.' Reva's voice held that particular tone that indicated that she needed to go because she wanted to be someplace else that was not this conversation.

'I have given him your phone number and email, by the way.'

'You did what?' said Reva, getting annoyed. 'What if he is a serial killer, or a stalker?'

'He will be nothing of that sort. Everything is a joke to you, Revathi. I don't know when you will stop finding fault with everyone you meet and finally settle down.' Her mother sighed grandly. 'Wait – before you go, have a word with your *paatti*. Let me put her on the line.'

'Hi, *paatti*,' said Reva, talking to her grandmother in the high-pitched, cheerful voice that people usually use to talk to children.

'Who is this?' shouted her grandmother into the phone.

'*Paatti*, this is me, Revathi. How are you?'

'She is a thief! Don't let her inside!' her grandmother screeched.

Reva could hear a mild scuffle at the other end as her mother took the phone back from her grandmother. 'Revathi, she is having one of her episodes. I will call you later.'

Reva felt relieved that this week's phone call to her grandmother was over quicker than usual, and then ashamed for feeling that way. Ever since Reva's father had passed away from a heart attack ten years ago, her mother had gone back to their village to live with her increasingly senile grandmother. Their phone calls would usually involve Reva introducing herself a few times, hoping for a rare moment of lucidity from the other end. In the rare instances that her *paatti* understood her, she would respond as if she hadn't spoken to Reva in years, 'Revathi *kanna*, how are you? How long since I have set eyes on you.' On hearing her soft voice suffused with affection, Reva would then get too emotional to respond.

Reva went back to her fridge and took out a half-empty bottle of white wine before settling back on the sofa. She gingerly picked up the phone as it pinged, mentally preparing herself for it to be from

Karthik, who now had her number. It was only Shreya, asking if she wanted to go to the beauty parlour together. She then poured herself a large glass of wine and sat down on the sofa. Seeking some escapist entertainment, she settled on a romantic comedy that started with the leading couple squirming in the therapist's room while being quizzed about their sex life. Halfway into the movie, when the couple inevitably started realising that they still loved each other after all, Reva fell fast asleep.

*

The next day, Reva was presenting her slides to a meeting room thick with the sleepy stupor that usually sets in after lunch. Her manager, Subramaniam, a short, portly man with an uneven moustache, was struggling to keep awake. She had seen him head out in the noon heat for lunch, and the cool air conditioning inside the room was now lulling him to sleep.

'So, Subbu, what do you think?'

Subbu's nodding head jerked up in surprise.

'We should assess any potential issues before going ahead,' he replied confidently. Reva thought that it was the kind of statement for which one didn't need to be a senior manager, or evidently, fully awake, to make.

'I completely agree with Subbu here. We should carry a more detailed assessment regarding the pros and cons of this new project,' Vijay piped up.

Vijay was Reva's colleague who had recently been transferred from the Bangalore office. Reva hadn't been impressed with his work ethic so far – he called for a lot of meetings and then simply distributed the work to the rest of the team without taking on much work himself. Just the day before, she had walked over to his desk to find him reading an article called 'Ten guaranteed ways to appear smarter than you are'. Noticing her, he had quickly closed his browser and opened a spreadsheet with a colourful graph. She had looked up the article later to find that building graphs had been number three on the list.

'What kind of issues do you anticipate?' she asked them both, trying hard to keep her voice neutral.

The speakerphone in the middle crackled with life, making everyone in the room sit up straighter. Subbu's manager had just dialled in from their head office in Mumbai. 'Do we have the marketing plan ready for the launch?' he asked, managing to sound authoritative despite the noise of traffic in the background.

'Yes, we do,' replied Subbu, rather eagerly. He then read the bullet points from Reva's presentation aloud, leaning close to the phone. Later that evening, when Reva microwaved leftovers in her kitchen, she would think that she should have spoken over Subbu with the answers, claiming credit for the three days of work she had put in to prepare this presentation. However, right then, in the meeting room, she just moved the slides back and forth to match the questions coming from the speakerphone.

After the meeting, Reva went back to her desk with a sense of mild relief that her presentation was over. However, something about the way that the meeting had unfolded made her uneasy, and she hesitantly ventured into Subbu's office. Subbu seemed surprised to see Reva but motioned to her to take a seat. His office was messy, and his desk was littered with papers stacked high enough to wobble dangerously if anyone sneezed in their vicinity. There was a copying machine at the corner of his table, with layers of dirt trapped in its plastic wrapper. The only colourful thing in his room was the enlarged picture of him and his wife smiling coyly from inside a pink heart-shaped frame. Reva sat on the swivelling chair in front of his desk, and although it was adjusted to be too high for a short person like her, she sat on it with her back straight, resting the tips of her toes on the floor.

'I wanted to ask about the promotion that we discussed during our last performance appraisal meeting,' she said, her voice sounding less assertive than she would have liked. She had been meaning to ask this during their weekly meetings, but it had just felt easier to postpone it every week rather than ask for something that she thought should have been given to her without any nagging in the first place. She had handled most of the complicated product launches in her team, and even though she didn't have any formal authority, all the other members of her team came to her for advice and help.

'Ah, yes. I have been meaning to speak to you about that myself.' Subbu gave her an oily smile that made her feel uneasy about what he was going to say next. 'I think you are a really valuable member of this team, and you are quite hardworking.'

'Yes?' Reva straightened her back further to brace herself for what he was going to say next.

'Well, while you definitely have the expertise to be the head of product management here, you lack the—' Subbu paused to wave his hand and look around as if her missing skill were to be found somewhere in the room if they looked hard enough '—leadership skills needed for the role.'

As she looked at him, preparing to say something in indignant denial, a small part of her thought that this was possibly true.

'Vijay, on the other hand, seems to be more well-rounded and also comes with a strong recommendation from upper management,' Subbu finished smoothly, almost as if he had practised this statement before.

'Really?' asked Reva. She couldn't think of anything else to say at that moment.

'I am sorry, Reva, my hands are tied.' He leant back as far as his chair would allow, clasping his hands over his round belly.

'You have a say in this decision, don't you?' She did not like the pleading tone that had now entered her voice.

'I will try talking to the head office again about your case.' He was looking down at his phone as a signal for her dismissal.

Reva went back to her desk and stared at her screen, unable to concentrate. The conversation had left her wondering about just how delusional she had been in her perception of her ability by her manager. She fantasised for a brief minute about quitting her job the very same day, leaving her team to struggle with her heavy workload. However, she knew that Subbu was capable of keeping things from derailing with some swift and haphazard reorganisation. She consoled herself by forwarding some of Subbu's emails marked urgent in red capitals to Vijay, typing, *FYI and action.*

Just as she had forwarded the third mail, she checked her phone and saw a politely composed message from Karthik, asking if she was available to meet for a cup of coffee or a meal, so that they could get to know each other better. She checked the email that her mother had forwarded from him – it introduced him by his academic merits, geographical coordinates and yearly salary in dollars converted into lakhs of rupees. Underneath this abridged CV, the message contained a low-resolution picture of Karthik in a business suit, where he looked cropped out from a group picture, with a glimpse of more black suits on either side.

She was distracted by Ranji's face popping up above her cubicle. 'Still on for lunch?' Ranji waved her lunch bag at Reva.

'Yes, let's go.' Reva got up from her desk with an exaggerated sigh. They reached the canteen on the floor above and Reva hastily loaded her plate with fried rice and dregs of a yellow gravy with unidentifiable vegetables and joined Ranji at a plastic table.

'I don't know how you manage to eat this nonsense from the canteen!' exclaimed Ranji, clicking open her tiffin box that transformed into flat-lay, photo-worthy individual containers of lemon rice, potato kari, pickle and fried pieces of appalam.

Reva simply shrugged and picked a piece of appalam from Ranji's box. 'I finally asked Subbu about my promotion today, by the way.'

'Oh, what did he say?' Ranji looked up from her lunch.

'Well, guess what?' Reva asked, not really expecting Ranji to guess. 'It sounds like he is going to promote Vijay instead.'

'What! That Vijay is a chameleon, I tell you – he should be head of acting, not head of sales!' Ranji replied with loyal indignation. 'Why don't you find another job with a better manager? You have an engineering degree from Anna University, for God's sakes. There will be plenty of other companies that would snap you up!'

'Not sure if that's entirely true,' Reva said, not in an effort to downplay the compliment, but because she genuinely wondered if it was true.

'Hundred per cent true. Let me send you the contact details of my friend who is connected to a few consulting firms.' Ranji immediately started tapping the cracked screen on her phone. Ranji's phone always had a cracked screen – she had no time to get it fixed, and even when she did, it wouldn't be long before one of her young boys dropped it again.

Reva thought about how they both led very different lives, although they were the same age. Ranji went home every day to a noisy household and contorted herself to the needs of her two kids, husband and in-laws. Reva went back to her one-bedroom flat and occasionally used paper cutlery to eat over her sink so that she would have less washing up to do. Ranji and Reva's friendship operated strictly within the parameters of the office – Ranji disappeared into the thicket of her life outside the confines of work and they never saw each other over weekends. Now that Ranji was newly pregnant with her third child, Reva wondered, somewhat selfishly, if she would be seeing even less of her.

'You tell me – how are things with you? How are things at home?' Reva asked, eating a spoonful of the rice and gravy. It tasted surprisingly better than it looked.

'I am not going to decide until next weekend,' Ranji declared without preamble.

'Decide what? What happens next weekend?'

'Decide whether to work or not, after the baby,' Ranji said, pausing to pick a piece of chilli out of her rice. 'I will be meeting Swami Dikshananda,' she continued, aimlessly dipping her spoon into her rice.

'Wait, you are going to let this Swami decide whether you should continue working or not?' Reva did not even make the effort to hide the incredulity in her voice. This was not the first time the Swami was featured in Ranji's life. Many of Ranji's important life decisions, including her choice of spouse, had been decided by the Swami. Reva had initially thought of the Swami as a therapist, helping his disciples lighten their worries by speaking to him. However, she soon learnt that all he did was place a flower in front of god's picture and provide his blessings if the flower fell down. Of course, the placement of the flower was done in exchange for a hefty donation, which meant that the only thing that got lightened was his disciples' wallets.

'Shouldn't there be an app or something that you could use instead?' Reva asked, unable to suppress a smile.

'Shh, don't be disrespectful,' Ranji begged. 'I knew you would be like this. I know it sounds, well, unusual, but it helps me to sleep at night knowing that the weight of the decision is not entirely on me.' She looked away from Reva and busied herself with separating more rinds of green chilli from her lemon rice.

'What is Siva saying about all this?' Siva was Ranji's husband, whom Reva discerned to be well-meaning enough, from the way Ranji described him. Their parents had arranged for their marriage after their horoscopes had matched and the Swami's flower had fallen, although the couple had spoken to each other just once before their wedding. Ranji seemed to be fine with the way things had turned out, though. Her only complaints were about Siva's idea of holidays, which involved visiting far-flung places of worship along with a noisy gaggle of aunts and grand-aunts.

'Siva has always been telling me that it would be easier to simply stay at home and help his mother with the kids, you know.'

'That's fine, Ranji, but do what you think is best. Just don't decide anything based on whether a bloody flower falls or not.' Ranji flinched on hearing Reva swear. 'Just do what you think is right at the end of the day for you, OK?' Even as she said it, Reva knew that one's belief was influenced by years of mental conditioning, and she was indulging in exactly the same thing that she was usually at the receiving end of – unsolicited advice from someone who thought they knew better.

'Why don't you wait till you have the baby to decide whether you want to continue working or not?' Reva asked, more mildly.

'I just like knowing these things. You wouldn't understand,' said Ranji defensively, her face starting to look as pickled as the lemon in her lunchbox.

'That potato kari looks really delicious. Can I try some?' Reva asked, making a blatant attempt to change the topic of conversation.

Ranji shrugged sulkily. However, within a minute, the part of Ranji's personality that hated conflict said, 'That's all you are having for lunch?' pointing at the half-eaten plate of food that Reva had now kept at a little distance from her.

'It was a very large helping of rice with small amounts of everything else – you know how the canteen is.'

'That's true,' Ranji replied absently, before paying attention to whatever her cracked screen had to say.

A small group of younger, better-dressed colleagues trooped into the canteen, accompanied by raucous laughter, and Reva waved at them. Although she usually had lunch with Ranji, she often joined these colleagues for after-work drinks, raising clouded bottles of beers to applaud the end of a work week, along with their own liberal mindedness. However, inwardly, she always felt like a little bit of a fraud when she acted like she was one of them.

What Reva had come to realise was that being a certain kind of liberal-minded person as an adult was usually the byproduct of having a childhood where mothers spoke fluent English and fathers ferried you around in air-conditioned cars to swimming lessons. This then manifested itself as online dating in adulthood, accompanied by complaints about old-fashioned parents who didn't approve of live-in relationships.

Reva had grown up in a lower middle-class family – and considered herself lucky when compared to the vast majority around her – but the religious rules had been tight, money even tighter. She grew up reciting the thousand names of Vishnu every evening with her mother, and commuted to secondary school on public buses, clutching a free bus pass along with an umbrella that served the sole purpose of fending off the leering hands that reached out however modestly she dressed.

She took pride in the fact that she had travelled far from her beginnings – her apartment had a well-stocked alcohol cabinet in place of a puja shelf, and she could afford to buy her own car with the softest of leather seats if she wished. However, she had also come to realise that however far you travel, you can never completely break free from the place you came from.

And this was how she found herself replying to Karthik and asking him if he had a preference for Italian, Indo-Chinese or North Indian for dinner.

*

The staircase of Grand Life Apartments ran along its sides, pausing at each floor to form a small, curved balcony. On Saturday afternoon, Reva stood on the balcony on her floor with a cup of instant coffee, unsurprised by the lack of breeze from the neighbouring mango and coconut trees that stood sullenly still. She perked up at the sight of a bird's nest at the corner of the wrought-iron railing and was taking pictures while thinking of playful yet profound captions for the ensuing social media post, when she noticed Jason pause hesitantly next to her.

'What bird is it?' he asked, inspecting the freckled turquoise blue eggs curiously.

'It's just the common crow. Surprisingly colourful eggs, though.' (*Don't judge a bird by its cover* would be a good caption, she thought, pleased.)

Jason unfolded himself from the railings, his head almost reaching the ceiling of the balcony. Reva appraised his appearance – he was wearing a T-shirt that was so faded that her mother would have taken it to use as a rag cloth when she wasn't looking, and shorts in that odd beige-yellow colour that she had only seen on foreigners. His long nose and the tips of his ears had turned bright pink in the heat of the sun, although he generally seemed to be more at ease now than he had been when he had first arrived.

'Didn't mean to intrude upon your afternoon,' Jason apologised, and Reva wondered if the clichés about the British existed for a reason. She stopped wondering when he asked about the weather.

'– This past week was especially hot, wasn't it? Is that normal for this time of the year?'

'It is always hot in Chennai,' she apologised in return.

The mango and coconut trees around them finally stirred, sending a gentle breeze their way. There was a lull in the construction site across the wall – the red bulldozer that usually roamed noisily across the rubble like a prehistoric creature was now resting its jaws on the ground.

'By the way, if you don't mind me asking,' Jason started, 'do you happen to know where the nearest high street is?'

'High street?' Reva repeated, cradling her phone instinctively for translation assistance.

'Department store? I packed lightly when I came, so I am just looking to buy clothes – some basics, really,' he explained, looking sheepish.

'I need to go shopping for a gift anyways – you can come with?' Reva found herself saying.

Jason accepted her offer with a ready eagerness that made her feel momentarily good about being charitable with her company. They stood there for a while longer, watching the bulldozer awaken and rent the air with its hoarse cry. The mother crow came flapping to its nest below their feet on hearing the noise.

Later that evening, Reva introduced Jason to her TVS Scooty, and gestured him towards the pillion seat. As she sat astride in front and swerved her two-wheeler onto the busy main road, she noticed Jason worriedly clutching the scooter's grab rails. She decided to distract him by pointing out the different landmarks of the city.

'This is the Gemini flyover,' she explained as she weaved through the maze of vehicles on the flyover propped by large billboards advertising deals on silk sarees, phone plans and life insurance policies. 'That is the Thousand Lights Mosque,' she pointed out later, momentarily admiring the cream-and-mint coloured building that she passed by without a second glance on her way to work every day. 'And this is the Express Avenue shopping mall,' she announced as they arrived at their heavily illuminated destination.

As soon as they stepped inside the entrance, they were enveloped in silky cool air conditioning, making Reva feel good about her decision to bring Jason here, rather than to the shops in T-Nagar that sold slightly misspelt versions of the brands found at the mall at a fraction of the price.

Reva thought that there was something about being reflected under the lights of shops called Armani and Calvin Klein that made people inside the mall behave differently than they would outside. Couples strolled about while lacing their arms around each other's waists, women wore low-cut dresses without protective dupattas or scarves, while men (mostly) walked around pretending not to stare. However, despite the modified perspective that the mall seemed to afford, her presence next to Jason elicited furtive glances that she pretended not to notice.

'You have all kinds of international brands here.' Reva waved her hand expansively around her. 'There are also shops where you can buy Indian attire if that's the kind of thing you are interested in?' she added, remembering the American colleagues from work who had looked around with wide-eyed wonder before urgently snapping pictures of everything. She had later looked at one of their travel blogs and found a selective slice of photos posted – of an entire family travelling on a single moped, the gap-toothed smile of a wrinkled flower-seller, a baby goat nibbling hungrily at a movie poster.

Jason's eyes didn't seem to possess that curious, questioning gaze that she had expected from a traveller, but had the overwhelmed look of someone who couldn't understand how he ended up somewhere that was so unfamiliar. A look of relief crossed his face when he spotted a sign he recognised. 'That should do it,' he exclaimed, sprinting towards the Marks & Spencers that occupied almost an entire floor.

After both of them finished their shopping, Reva suggested that they stop at the food court, noticing an air of interest around Jason for the first time. They walked around, the usually mono-syllabic men and women in uniform behind the stalls suddenly transforming into engaging salespeople who vied with each other to ask if Jason wanted a sample taste.

'People here are so friendly,' exclaimed Jason. Reva responded with a worldly chuckle.

She steered him towards a South Indian fast-food stall and ordered for both of them – an onion rava dosa for Jason and podi idlis for herself.

'Dosas and idlis are the basics of South Indian food. I grew up eating them almost every day,' she said, her voice taking on the extolling tone of a tour guide.

'So, you must be an expert at making them then?' Jason's voice was earnest enough to make Reva laugh aloud. She explained that although they originated from the same rice batter, the batter itself was quite laborious to make and could be bought in frozen packs from Diamond General Stores.

'So, how do you like living in Grand Life Apartments?' she asked, dipping her miniature idlis in sambar and eating them by the spoonful, like soup. She thought that it had the right level of spiciness when eaten that way but decided against recommending the same approach to Jason.

'It's a really charming place to live. I can't say the same thing about the one-bedroom flat that I left behind in London.'

Watching him gingerly approach the dosa with the tips of his fingers, Reva mused, 'You know, I quite admire what you have done – simply taking off from your life to transplant yourself somewhere that is so different. I wish I had the courage to do something like that.' She didn't mention that it currently took all her courage to simply defend herself from the societal outrage she caused for being single, with not much left over for sudden disappearances involving travel to far-flung places.

'Well,' Jason looked up at her quickly, his face momentarily losing its composure before he looked back down at his plate, 'I really needed to get away.' Although he was looking down when he said this, Reva could tell that he had a sad expression on his face.

After a moment, she added, 'Well, I am not sure if you know this already, but it is a local custom to have ice cream after every meal.'

'Well, if custom dictates, we simply have to, should we not?' he asked, a smile hesitating at the corner of his lips.

6

Jason

Jason woke up feeling the sun's warmth reaching him through the thin cotton curtains in the bedroom. It pulled his mind away from the haze of a dream that he couldn't recall in the few moments that it took to completely awaken. He pulled aside the curtain and squinted as the direct rays of the sun hit his eyes. He remembered that his shift at work didn't start until the afternoon, and he closed his eyes again to enjoy the gentle heat before it gained fierceness as the day went by. He then remembered, as he did every morning, that he was no longer with Emma, and felt that familiar weight lodge itself in his chest.

Unable to go back to sleep, he got up and opened the windows to his bedroom, which, unlike his flat in London, opened outwards, like the doors of a cuckoo clock. The neighbouring buildings were so close together near his bedroom that he felt like he could touch the neighbour's terrace if he stretched far enough.

He could see a short, lean woman hanging wet clothes to dry on the neighbour's terrace. She was wearing no jewellery apart from a cluster of glass bangles, and her saree, although hitched up, was tied into neat pleats. When she looked back at him, he lifted his palm to say hello, as he was unsure what else to do. She smiled back, but the softness of her smile belied the strength with which she then went back to wringing the clothes in her hand.

Thinking that it would be impolite to continue standing there, Jason walked over to his kitchen and started making his coffee in the French press that he had carried with him from London. As the sweet aroma of brewing coffee filled the room, the smell inadvertently took him to similar lazy, coffee-hazed mornings back at the flat he had shared with Emma. He checked his phone for the time, and although he had promised himself that he would not, he couldn't help checking Emma's social media profile.

Every time he checked, he felt a pang of sadness to see her life continue to unfold in all its normality without him. She usually posted a rotation of pictures not very different from those of her friends – of her cuddling a friend's tiny dog, pouting while trying on oversized sunglasses, eating a cupcake with some frosting intentionally left on her nose. Sometimes, she also posted pictures of her with groups of shiny people in dim-lit bars, with statements such as *Saturday night with my favs!* Jason would scrutinise the people in the picture closely with a feeling of mild dread, hoping to not chance upon someone new with an arm casually laid across Emma's shoulder.

He noticed that she had added a new picture since the last time he had checked, and he hastily clicked on it. It was a picture of her taken next to a single red rose, placed inside a glass flower vase that he didn't recognise. His mind raced as he wondered about its meaning. Who had given her the flower? Didn't the colour red have a special significance? In the deluded manner of unrequited love, he wondered if the rose was about him, and if it was a reminder of their last Valentine's Day together.

It had been one of those windy, cold days in London when everyone on the road walked just a bit faster so that they could get to some place warmer. Jason and Emma had agreed to meet at the closest tube to their house after finishing their respective shifts. Emma had been working part-time as a waitress and part-time as an aerobics class instructor, while her dream was to act full-time.

Many of her friends from drama school had managed to get minor acting roles, and although they all continued working multiple jobs, these small parts gave them the credibility to call themselves actors. When out for drinks, Emma's friends would complain about the insignificant roles they were playing – as the second female friend who recommends a new brand of tampon or as the understudy of a murderer in an off-West End Agatha Christie play, and Emma would laugh at their tales of woe. Later, though, when they were back home on their sofa, enveloped in the glow of their laptops, she would turn to him and ask, surely, she was prettier than Lucy? Jason would answer yes, of course, she was. He didn't say this just to make her feel better, but because he thought she was indeed prettier. In fact, perhaps too pretty to play the role of a supporting actress, he would say.

Where was her role as an extra in the cereal commercial, leave alone her big break then? she would then ask, to which Jason would close his laptop and counter her insecurities with an oft-repeated monologue about how perseverance was what mattered most in art and how her big break was just around the corner. Emma would sigh wistfully in response and then head to bed, forgetting to eat her dinner.

So, on Valentine's Day – the day that new couples baulked at the expectations placed upon them, and the day that single people felt the world at large sighing its disapproval at them, Jason and Emma had resolved not to fall for the hype fabricated by greedy consumerism – there would be no Lindt chocolates, flowers or overpriced restaurant dinner for two. Every day was a celebration of their love, was it not? Agreeing that it should be treated like just another day, they had bought chicken thighs from their local butcher and headed home. Their way home passed a bridge over a train track, and at the corner of the bridge, an enterprising man had set up a make-shift stall, selling red roses at five times their regular cost. Hassled looking men stood in line anyway, to buy bouquets of flowers wrapped and bow-tied into symbols of love.

Jason scoffed as he walked past the flower-seller, in the way that he usually did when he looked at the most expensive wine on the drinks list in a restaurant. They had crossed the bridge and passed their favourite Chinese takeaway when Emma said, in a small voice, that she was disappointed.

Startled, Jason had stopped walking and asked her what was wrong, but Emma hadn't replied and had continued walking further. A perplexed Jason had followed her, still holding her hand. Emma had then said in an anguished voice, looking down at the grey scarf that she had tucked into her bright blue peacoat. 'I know that we agreed not to do anything special. But I thought you would surprise me with roses anyway.'

'What?! Is that what this is all about? Let's go back and get those roses right now.' He had turned around, annoyed, inadvertently yanking her hand as he did so.

Emma had refused to move. 'No, I don't want them like this. And they are so expensive anyway,' she had said, a sudden defiance strengthening her words.

Jason had been conscious of the fact that they were making a scene. 'So, what do you want me to do then? How am I supposed to know that you secretly wanted them while saying that you didn't?' he had muttered in a low voice, gritting his teeth in a manner that he knew Emma hated. They had walked home and climbed the three floors to their flat in sullen silence.

Back at the flat, Jason had started grilling the chicken with rosemary and garlic, just the way Emma liked it, although he personally disliked the taste of rosemary. He had always believed that being in a relationship was less about grand gestures and more about these small acts of kindness, and Emma's anger had thawed over dinner as she tasted the herb. They had then huddled underneath a blanket and laughed over an episode of *The Office* before going to bed. But on days like these, he couldn't help wondering what he had missed – was there anything he could have done – a patch that he could have stitched to prevent the entire fabric of their relationship from unravelling? Should he have just bought those bloody roses?

All his memories of London, however, appeared surreal and grey when viewed under the exuberance of the Chennai sun. He sighed and put away his phone. He remembered that he had come to the kitchen to toast some bread for breakfast and opened the pack of perfectly square, white slices. As he threw one on a pan with some butter, he caught a quick movement from behind the red gas cylinder that was underneath the stove. It turned out to be the apricot-coloured cat from before, who jumped on top of the kitchen table and stared accusingly at him as if he were the real intruder in the kitchen.

Jason soaked a piece of bread in a bowl of milk and placed it close to the window. 'You're a hungry little fellow, aren't you?' he asked the cat as it started lapping the milk with rapid movements of its tongue, before burying its entire face in the bowl. Then, without a single ear-twitch of thanks, the cat swiftly jumped out of the window, vanishing from sight. Jason looked out to see where it went, but could only see Mani downstairs, patiently watering his plants with a hose that spluttered in moody bursts. Seized by a need for normal conversation, he picked up the standing fan that he'd borrowed from his neighbour and headed downstairs.

'Are you sure that you don't need it anymore?' Mani asked, shading his eyes with his hands while looking up at Jason carrying the tall fan gingerly down the steps.

'No, I ended up buying a portable air cooler.' Jason placed the fan down on Mani's porch, flexing his shoulder.

'Yes, those air coolers are quite popular these days.'

They both sat quietly on the armchairs facing the garden. The air was filled with the sounds that Jason now associated with a regular

Chennai morning – buses honking at a distance, dogs yelping, and a persistent drilling from the construction site.

The apricot-coloured cat made a reappearance on the porch, its tail held purposefully upright, and glided towards a plastic lid on which Mani had placed some yellow-coloured rice.

'This is Poons.' Mani scratched the head of the cat, the expression on his face turning gentle. 'Revathi named him after the Tamil word for cat, which is *poonai*.'

'Oh, is the cat Reva's then?'

'No, Poons is a free spirit. He likes to come and go as he pleases,' said Mani.

'Meow,' Poons agreed, licking the last speck of rice.

Noticing that the cat had temporarily dropped its cool act, Jason felt compelled to bend down and pat its soft back. It looked appraisingly at him before flopping down into a furry puddle against his legs and closing its eyes for a mid-afternoon snooze.

Jason gestured to the sheaf of papers that Mani seemed to be scribbling against the margins of and asked what he was working on. Mani explained that he was writing a book on the history of Madras, adding a little self-effacingly that people had no use for books these days, considering that all kinds of information was available on the internet anyway.

'Oh yeah, Chennai used to be called Madras, wasn't it? I've heard about the Madras curry,' Jason said conversationally, having skimmed the Wikipedia article on the city as part of his only due diligence before heading here.

'Madras curry?' Mani laughed as if the idea of combining the words Madras and curry together was rather hilarious.

'It is a famous spice blend,' Jason added rather ineffectually.

'I am sure it is,' Mani observed in a way that implied that the world was ridiculous enough for anything to be possible. He leant his head closer to Jason, a smile still creasing his face. 'So, tell me, Jason, what made you decide to become a chef?'

Jason rifled through his memories to see if there was any specific incident that propelled him towards a career in the kitchens. All he remembered was the feeling of familiarity and comfort when he cooked, knowing that there was at least one thing in the world that he was good at. He explained this to Mani who nodded approvingly.

'That is actually very good that you realised it so young. I worked as an accountant for quite a while before I finally turned my hand to writing.' Mani bent down to scratch Poons' neck before looking up at Jason. 'Since you like cooking, I may have something for you,' he said, getting up from his chair and motioning Jason to follow him.

Jason nodded agreeably and carried the fan inside. He followed Mani's lead and removed his slippers, and walked inside the flat, the red cement floor feeling cool to his feet. Mani's living room was large and airy and, in the centre of the room, a mahogany swing hung low to the ground and swayed gently in the breeze. The walls were painted a crisp white and the lack of any photos of gods, or any other pictures at all, in comparison to Kamala's house, was quite conspicuous. There was a large stringed musical instrument in one corner, and a wooden desk on which there was a typewriter that looked like it was actually in use.

As they walked further into the house, they passed a kitchen from which Jason caught a whiff of the distinctive smell that he now associated with South Indian cooking – the smell of mustard seeds, chillies and curry leaves being tempered in oil. He saw the profile of a woman who looked somewhat familiar, bent over the stove.

'That is Fatima. She helps around the house,' said Mani. The woman briefly looked up from the pot and smiled at him, and

Jason recognised her as the one he had seen drying clothes on the neighbour's porch earlier that morning. She turned away to add the tempered spices to a pan with a sharp sizzle.

Mani kept on walking further into the house, and Jason quickened his pace to keep up with him. They finally reached something that looked like a storeroom. It was musty, with a small circular window close to the ceiling, through which sunlight streamed in, catching dust motes on the way. It was filled with the randomness of things found in any attic or basement – copper cauldrons, cardboard boxes, rolled-up mattresses and several rows of books. Jason placed the fan next to a case of books preserved carefully with covers made from old Tamil newspapers.

Mani seemed to be inspecting another shelf nearby, and when he walked towards Jason, he was holding a book held together with thick swathes of brown tape. 'It used to belong to my sister,' he said. From the way Mani used the past tense without meeting his eyes, Jason decided not to enquire further about this sister. Instead, he accepted the book, carefully wiping away the light layer of dust that had formed on the covers of the book with the edge of his T-shirt. The original title of the book was written in the mellow curls of Tamil, but there was a small translation printed on the side that read, *Cook and See*.

'I will definitely cook and see what happens!' He laughed weakly at his own joke. Mani tilted his head back and also laughed, with unexpected loudness, although Jason couldn't tell if it was because of his comment or some distant memory that this book had brought.

*

Jason went down to Diamond General Stores, intending to buy more milk and sugar. He passed the jackfruit stall in front of the shop, usually operated by a young man who would shout, 'JACKFRUIT,

SAAR? GOOD PRICE!' every time he passed by, at which Jason would mumble, 'No, thank you,' and quicken his pace. This day, however, he found an old, wrinkled man at the stall, sitting quietly and staring morosely into the distance with such an inexpressible sadness that he slowed down. He pointed to the fruit, and the old man benignly patted it and handed it to Jason without haggling for the price. Only when carrying the hefty fruit back did Jason realise that he could have simply bought some of the smaller pieces of fruit that were already sliced and sold by the dozen.

Back in the kitchen, he gingerly stroked the fruit's green exterior that seemed to spike with goosebumps at his touch. He pierced it with his knife and hefted it apart, the fruit feeling surprisingly supple despite its hard exterior. It opened to reveal cavities containing pieces of bright yellow flesh that glowed with the importance of a highlighted sentence. He tasted its sticky sweetness, enjoying the foreign sensation of savouring a new fruit – something he could not recall doing since becoming an adult. Jason had never really travelled far in his life and had not taken a gap year to Thailand, India or Indonesia, as some of his friends had. The holidays he had gone on with his parents were to all-inclusive beach resorts in Europe, which were usually so full of British tourists that it had just felt like home, except with more pale knees and pink elbows exposed. So, nothing in his life had prepared him for the assault on his senses of everyday living in Chennai – the relentless heat, the noise and diesel smoke in the streets and the constant hustle that was part of getting anything done. All this would have bruised him enough to pack and go back home if he hadn't been numbed by Emma already.

He did not need the friendly reminder from his social media account to remember that it was Emma's birthday that day. He had been checking her account constantly through the day, reading the wishes being posted, which were all unsurprising variations of the words happy, wonderful and lovely.

Jason washed the jackfruit pulp off his hands and sat in front of the laptop to type something that he had been rephrasing in his mind all day. *Happy Birthday*, he typed, and then made his keyboard eat up the bland phrase letter by letter. He then went and poured himself a mug of coffee and sat back on the sofa.

Happy birthday. Hope you are having a good one, he typed and then examined his words. Thinking that it didn't sound cheerful enough, he added two exclamation points at the end, just in case, and then pressed Send.

He could immediately see that the message came up with a little tick mark that gave away the fact that it had been read. He breathed heavily, weighed down by the power imbalance between the person initiating a conversation and the person taking their time to respond. He then mindlessly clicked through Emma's online posts again, and then again, although he now knew every one of them as familiarly as his own memories of her.

He looked to see if any of his friends were online – these friends, who would have tried to comfort him through awkward thumps on his back and copious amounts of alcohol in the neighbourhood pub, now sent him one-line messages such as *How're things mate?* accompanied by a thimble-sized beer. He noticed one of his friends, Chris, surface with a variation of this question, to which Jason gave his practised response about the hot weather. *Cheap beers though?* Chris responded back. Jason was about to give up on the conversation when Chris surprised him with, *You take care, Jase*, which he knew was the closest that his friend would come to a commiserating virtual hug.

Emma finally sent a response after fifteen excruciating minutes. *Thanks so much! How've you been?*

He read the reply, then again. It was exactly what she typed in response to friends who surfaced once a year to wish her a very happy birthday on social media. It hurt him to realise that he meant nothing more to her than any of these so-called friends now. He left her message unanswered and went back into the kitchen, feeling a little bit like the jackfruit that waited for him on the kitchen table, its heart dismembered into tiny little pieces.

*

By the time Jason's auto reached Anna Salai, it was afternoon, and the boiling sun had bled all the blue from the sky. Jason had broken into a sweat, but he knew that he just needed to cross the road before he would be enveloped in the air-conditioned coolness of the hotel where he worked. He glanced guiltily at the people whose livelihood depended on operating in this heat – women selling snacks heaped in paper cones, barebacked men ferrying boxes on rickshaws, young children begging from cars at the traffic signal. A young girl with torn clothes and sandy hair returned his glance and continued staring at him with unabashed curiosity, seemingly forgetting to ask him for money. Jason gave her some anyway but then had to quicken his pace in order to avoid the gaggle of children who noticed this and were now headed towards him.

With its soft music and plush air-conditioned interiors, the lobby of his hotel felt far removed from the heat and grime of the city, although it was just a sliding glass door away. He nodded to the black-suited staff at the front desk and headed towards the back entrance to the kitchen. He stopped in his tracks when he noticed the profile of a blonde girl seated on one of the black leather sofas in the lounge. He turned to look at her face, his heart suddenly beating faster, although he knew that the chances of it being Emma were next to none.

When he had just landed in Chennai, he had been hopeful that Emma would follow him all the way here and had often imagined how he would react on bumping into her, probably in a surrounding like this. He would say that he had never been better and that coming to India was the best thing to have ever happened to him. He would even conjure up a new girlfriend – possibly a journalist he had met at the hotel or a fellow chef whom he would concede to be even better than him. 'Wait, you didn't really come back here thinking that I would be waiting for you, did you?' he would say, his voice filled with concern and just the right touch of incredulity. Even in this imaginary narrative, he knew that this act would soon give away to a feeling of immense relief and happiness that Emma had finally come to her senses and was here, looking for him.

The girl turned to look at him, and he released the breath that he didn't realise he had been holding. She was around Emma's age and returned his intense stare with an uncertain half-smile. Jason quickly rearranged his face to match her smile before rushing past into the corridor that led to the kitchen, feeling rather foolish.

The kitchen at The Tamarind Room was gleaming and shiny and much more expensive looking than those in any of the restaurants that Jason had worked for in London. It served Indian cuisine with a Western influence and had dishes like raw mango soup, tamarind glazed cod, and idli-sandwich on the menu. Jason thought that the head chef was quite intense but talented, nevertheless.

During last week's group huddle with the team, the chef had started the meeting by asking, 'You've seen your neighbourhood *maamis* going for their morning walk wearing Nike shoes and sarees?' and looked around, making eye contact with everyone in the room, making sure that they registered his words.

'That is what our food represents – the amazing taste of Indian cuisine, after removing all the stuffiness that goes behind its preparation,' he declared, and some of the younger chefs had actually broken into applause at this little speech. Aneesh, a fellow chef, had winked exaggeratedly at Jason, and Jason had raised his eyebrows back in response, although he had had absolutely no idea what this chef was going on about.

That day, Jason was covering for the sous-chef who was on holiday, and making what went on the menu as 'South Indian sushi'. It involved rolling pickled lemon and cucumber onto seasoned sticky rice and serving it with a yoghurt dip tempered with mustard seeds and chilli flakes. Although he had considered the idea preposterous when he first heard of it, he had to admit that the flavours seemed to work well together. The restaurant was usually frequented by business types who stayed at the hotel, although they did have the occasional couple coming in to celebrate a special night, feeding spoonfuls of heart-shaped mango tart to each other.

Aneesh was covering for the dessert chef that day and was folding chocolate delicately into cones of dough, making bite-sized chocolate samosas. Even Jason knew that samosas were not originally meant to taste of chocolate. He remembered eating his first samosa in school, when he had gone to the house of one of his Indian friends. The mother, whom he had always seen in traditional Indian clothes, had barged into his friend's room without knocking and placed a plate that was generously heaped with warm samosas in front of them. He couldn't recall whether he had been in year ten or eleven, but he could recall exactly how that samosa had tasted – the outside pastry crumbling satisfyingly to give way to soft potatoes, which had then surprised him with a hard kick of chilli. When he had just started working in The Tamarind Room, he had asked Aneesh, 'So where can I get a proper samosa around here?'

'I guess Gangotree would have some, but you do know that samosas are essentially a North Indian dish, right?' Aneesh had replied, stretching the word 'North' as if it were a part of the country that existed on another planet.

Aneesh was now looking at him across the table while his hands continued to work on expertly folding the samosas. 'Want to grab a beer after our shift?'

'Yeah, OK.' Jason shrugged. His only other plan had been to go home and check if more pictures of Emma's birthday celebrations had been posted online. Aneesh winked at him before going back to sealing the edge of his samosa cone.

After their shift, they sat on the plush leather seats of the bar downstairs, sipping their discounted Kingfisher beers in companionable silence. From the corner of his eye, Jason spotted the blonde girl from the lobby seated at an adjacent table, leafing through a magazine. Noticing him at the same instant, she smiled and, after a moment's hesitation, walked towards their table.

'You look awfully familiar. I feel like we've met before, perhaps?' She wrinkled her freckled nose at Jason, smiling hesitantly in a way that made her look quite pretty. She was wearing loose, billowy cotton trousers with an elephant print and a black top that was submerged under a cluster of colourful beaded necklaces.

Jason admitted that he couldn't recall meeting her before, although he was also, indeed, from London. Meanwhile, Aneesh had drawn a chair for her from a nearby table and was offering to buy her a drink on Jason's behalf. She thanked Aneesh profusely for the chair but perched herself at the edge of it, perhaps to indicate that she wasn't planning to stay at their table for long.

'So, have you travelled around much?' she asked Jason but continued without waiting for his answer. 'I started with the golden triangle up North to see the Taj Mahal, but then my friend Eva,' she paused here to roll her eyes at both Jason and Aneesh as if they were all common friends with this Eva, 'had to get back to her boring banking job. I am planning on just chilling in the South for a few more weeks, though.'

Seeing that there was no similar explanation forthcoming from Jason, she continued with the practised enthusiasm of someone who had said that statement a few times before, 'This country is pretty amazing, isn't it?' and looked at them for confirmation, her eyes wide.

Aneesh gave her a quick glance, seemingly to look for any signs of sarcasm. 'Most definitely is,' he told her, not bothering to hide his amusement.

'Such lovely people, too.' She nodded earnestly. Aneesh nodded his head solemnly in acceptance of the compliment, as if he were singularly responsible for making all the people here so lovely.

'So, how about you? How long are you here for?' she asked, tilting her head towards Jason.

'I'm actually working as a chef in the restaurant here. Staying put for a while.' Jason raised his beer for a sip.

'Oh, how cool!' she exclaimed, clasping her hands together. 'This one here is a proper traveller, isn't he?' She looked at Aneesh for confirmation.

Aneesh winked at Jason before responding to her. 'So, have you tried the food at this restaurant? Jason here makes the best mango tarts you can find on this side of the country.'

'As if they can be found anywhere else,' Jason said lightly.

'I usually try to eat at the non-touristy places, you know.' She tossed her sun-bleached hair from one side to another. 'I am just staying here as a little treat after weeks of backpacking,' she added, a little defensively.

'So,' she looked first at Jason and then at Aneesh, 'I'm thinking of heading down to Pondicherry this Friday with a friend. Do you guys want to come?'

'I would love to, but my missus may not be very happy about that.' Aneesh continued in an obviously teasing voice, 'But I don't think my friend here has other weekend plans.'

Jason politely shook his head, explaining apologetically that he wouldn't be able to come. The girl shrugged and said, 'No worries, see you around then,' with awkward cheerfulness and left their table, the anklet that she was wearing on one leg chiming as she walked away from them.

'*Dude*, what was that about? I thought that was going so well!' Aneesh exclaimed, gulping the last swig of his beer while his eyes continued to pin Jason accusingly.

Jason shrugged. Aneesh got up to go to the bar again and came back with two pints of beer and a question, 'So, you have a girlfriend back in London then?'

'Yes,' answered Jason, surprising himself with the ease at which he lied.

'A-ha,' Aneesh exclaimed loudly, thumping the table and displacing some of the peanuts from their bowl. 'So, what does she do? And what are you doing here without her?'

'She is an actress,' replied Jason.

Aneesh did not say anything but made a slack-jawed expression with his mouth to show how impressed he was that the likes of Jason had ensnared an actress, whose good looks were implied in the mere mention of her profession.

'You lucky bastard! Is she good? Is she in anything famous?' He whipped out his phone, ready to open the white rectangle through which you could see pictures of anyone with the wave of a finger.

Jason recalled Emma posing a similar question to him not too long ago. It had been an autumn evening, austere sunlight filtering through the window into a time when his opinion had still mattered to her. 'So, what do you think? Am I good?' she had asked, peering over his shoulder while he watched one of her audition videos. The video's storyline was nothing new – a series of scenes through which a wife discovers that her husband is cheating on her and, after a teary confrontation, decides to leave him. Emma was playing the wife, dressed in cardigans, aprons and varying expressions of concern. Jason had always thought that she had great screen presence, but there was something about the earnestness with which she acted each scene – the very intense anger at which she discovered another woman's message on her husband's phone or the immense sadness with which she left a goodbye note – which made him feel as if he were watching an actor playing a character, instead of getting lost in the story being narrated. He remembered her shocked face when he had told her this, her cup of tea stopped mid-air as she tried to process his statement. Emma had then started crying inconsolably while Jason tried to explain that he had only been trying to help.

Back in the emptying bar of the hotel, Aneesh grabbed a handful of peanuts in his hand and funnelled them one by one to his mouth expertly while still eyeing Jason, waiting for an answer.

'So, how did you become a chef then?' Jason asked, keen to change the topic.

'Well, actually I studied engineering and have an MBA,' Aneesh added conversationally and Jason looked at him in surprise. 'I come from a normal middle-class Indian family, man – first you study engineering or medicine as a default and then think about what you want to become in life.' Aneesh signalled for more beer, his previous pint having disappeared into the gap between his two sentences.

He continued, 'I worked for a couple of years as a consultant before starting my own restaurant – it was called Many Biryani Stories – and it filled the niche for an upmarket biryani restaurant in Chennai. Anyways, long story short, it did well for a while, but I had to close down because my investing partner left.'

Jason nodded, drawing mental parallels to his life, as one did in such conversations. He had always wanted to open his own restaurant but lacked the confidence, as well as resources, to quit a salaried job and take the plunge.

'– By then, I had realised that cooking and being in the restaurant business was what I really wanted to do. So, I travelled to Europe, got a diploma from Le Cordon Bleu and when I returned, I heard about this place opening up. And here we are.'

'Impressive.' Jason was genuinely impressed.

They were now the only customers left at the bar, and Jason knew Aneesh well enough to know that subtle hints such as looking at the time on his watch would not work. 'Hey, we should really get going. Early shift tomorrow and all that.' His voice was uncharacteristically firm.

Aneesh hesitated for a moment, perhaps wondering if he should stall Jason, but ended up asking for the bill.

They walked to the hotel gates, and the hotel's night security guard, a short moustached man in a starched white uniform, observed Aneesh's loose-limbed demeanour with narrowed eyes.

'Looks like we need to get an auto for Sir.' He motioned Jason to follow him.

They walked to the auto stand behind the hotel, where a bunch of auto-drivers stood in a huddle, smoking bidis. They perked up at the approaching business and started surrounding them with an eager interest that made Jason a little uneasy. However, Jason noticed that the security guard's demeanour had changed from the token servitude that he usually displayed while opening doors inside the hotel to firm authority in the auto stand. He negotiated the fare with a driver, bundled Aneesh inside and rapped the top of the auto authoritatively for it to start moving, as if it were one of many carriages that belonged in his kingdom's stables.

Another driver, in the meanwhile, swerved his auto near Jason and asked, 'Where do you want to go, sir?' Jason bent down and asked politely, 'If you don't mind, could you switch on the meter?' The driver nodded his head vigorously and made a big show of putting on the meter that showed the base fare as Jason got inside.

There was less traffic at this time of day, and Jason felt the wind whip pleasantly across his face as the auto sped across the road. Occasionally, supersized lorries thundered past, jostling the auto in their wake. Sodium vapour lamps illuminated the streets with their burnt yellow glow, and the tea shops along the roads were bright and busy, heaping biryani by the plateful for workers who were finishing a long day.

'Sir, where is your house in T-Nagar?' asked the driver. The driver's voice had a certain imperious authority, which was further emphasised by his grey-speckled hair and gold-rimmed spectacles.

'It is near Srinivasa Theatre. Next to the entrance near the main road.'

'OK, OK. I know the place.'

A minute later, the driver asked, 'So, when are you giving back our Kohinoor diamond, sir?'

'What?' Jason exclaimed, feeling like an unsuspecting puddle that was suddenly stepped into.

'The Kohinoor? The one that your great-grandfathers stole from under our very noses?' The driver raised his eyebrows at Jason through the rearview mirror.

If someone had predicted three months ago that he would be discussing the Kohinoor with an auto-driver at midnight in India, he would have laughed incredulously. But then, here he was and having this surreal conversation. And anyway, if it really came to it, Jason's great-grandfather had been too busy running a tailoring shop in Hastings to be pilfering diamonds anywhere.

'Look, not in my pocket.' He turned his shirt pocket inside out and laughed, a little bit more nervously than he would have liked. He saw a few brightly lit gas stations pass by but couldn't recognise the area and wasn't sure how close they were to his apartment.

Thankfully, the driver laughed along with him. 'Don't forget to bring it back next time you visit, sir.' He glanced at Jason's nervous reflection with considerable satisfaction. The auto swerved sharply towards a bridge, and Jason heaved a sigh of relief when he recognised the underpass lined with political posters that glowed fluorescent yellow in the dark.

'Right there – please stop at the house next to the black water tank,' said Jason as the auto puttered to a halt.

He reached for his wallet in his jeans pocket, and his heart tripped when he found nothing there except his keys. He furiously searched all his pockets, hoping that his wallet would magically appear if he searched hard enough. He had paid for the last round of drinks at the bar, but he had been too distracted at the auto stand to have noticed anyone slip a hand into his pocket.

The auto-driver was beginning to piece together what was happening and said, 'It's two hundred rupees. By the meter,' sternly, spectacles lowered on the bridge of his nose to accentuate the effect. A thin dog with black patches around its eyes had come to watch what was going on and wagged its tail at both Jason and the driver.

'Sorry, I seem to have lost my wallet,' Jason said in his best apologetic voice. 'You could wait here for a couple of minutes, and I could go and get the money from my apartment? It is right there, on the third floor.' He pointed towards his kitchen window. The driver squinted up at the uniformly dark windows of Grand Life Apartments and gave Jason a disdainful look.

'What is going on?' Jason heard the voice before he saw Salim descend expertly from a bicycle that was much too large for him. He bent down to the driver, and they exchanged a few brisk sentences, the driver checking on Jason periodically as if he was going to run away without paying him. Salim then produced a roll of money from his pocket and counted out the notes with the expertness of a card dealer while Jason shuffled his feet uncomfortably next to him. The driver restarted the engine with a splutter, but not before darting a parting glare at Jason.

'Thank you so much for that, Salim,' Jason exclaimed, opening the iron gates so that Salim and his cycle could enter.

'No mention. Good thing I was working late today,' Salim replied, as he filled a plastic mug from the garden and placed it on the ground for the dog that was still hovering near them. It lapped up the water gratefully.

'Let me pay you back right now? Stop by for a second?'

'No hurry to pay me back. It is fine,' the boy insisted, but as Jason started walking upstairs, Salim parked his cycle and followed him.

Salim waited in the living room, as Jason returned with the money and a plate of home-made biscuits. 'I bought an entire jackfruit,' he said, by way of explanation.

'So,' Salim examined the chunky, rectangular biscuit with forensic attention, 'of all possible things you could make with a jackfruit, you decided to make this?'

'Have you not had a jackfruit biscuit before?'

'No. I don't think *anyone* has ever had one before,' Salim replied, a smile playing at the corner of his lips. He bit into one contemplatively and ate an entire biscuit before announcing his verdict. 'These are good.' However, he shook his head in a rather baffled manner that indicated otherwise. A moment later, an inspired look crossed his face and he asked Jason enthusiastically, 'Have you eaten Bourbon chocolate biscuits, sir? They are costly but very tasty.'

'I have, actually. These biscuits are different – they are called shortbread biscuits –' Jason started explaining.

Salim, however, had lost interest in the biscuits and was leafing through the pages of the *Cook and See* book that Jason had kept on the coffee table.

'Mani gave this to me,' Jason explained the book's possibly incongruous presence in his house.

'This is fancy Iyer cooking, sir,' Salim declared, as if that was all that needed to be said about the book before closing it. He then glanced at a notebook that was left splayed open next to the cookbook.

'I've been writing down recipes ever since I started cooking,' Jason explained, a little self-consciously. 'My handwriting may be a little difficult to understand, though.'

Salim contemplated the contents of the notebook for a minute. He then shook his head gravely at Jason. 'I cannot believe that you leave so many empty lines on every page that you write. What a waste, sir. My mother would hang me from my ears on the clothes-line if I did this.'

7

Kamala

Kamala was not looking forward to going to the wedding. Even on normal days weddings disagreed with her, but now, the thought of fielding a series of repeated small talk enquiries about Lakshmi made her head ache, as if there were hundreds of tiny wedding bands marching around inside.

The day after Lakshmi had left for the UK, Kamala had sent her daughter a message asking whether she had reached safely. Lakshmi had sent a terse, one-word response: *Yes*. A couple of days later, Kamala had asked if Lakshmi was busy studying for her exams, to which she received the same response, written with presumably the same sullenness. She sent a few more messages, which Lakshmi had then proceeded to ignore, perhaps feeling uncharitable in sending even these one-word responses her mother's way. Kamala could have called Lakshmi, but one could say that Lakshmi didn't just inherit her stubbornness from nowhere.

'I have a migraine again, Sundu. I don't think I can make the early morning muhurtham for the wedding tomorrow.' She rubbed her forehead with a herbal balm that smelled pungently of menthol while waiting for her friend's response.

'You need to get these headaches checked – you have been having too many of them lately,' Sundu reprimanded.

'What is the point of going to see the doctor for something like this? He will pocket my money and prescribe more aspirin, that's all.'

'Anyways,' Sundu replied in a tone that implied that she didn't quite agree but was going to move on for purposes of expediency, 'about the wedding – Aruna came all the way to our houses to invite us. Maybe we can just go show our faces at the wedding reception in the evening?'

'Yes, let's do that. I have a pair of silver lamps that came free with my jewellery chit-scheme subscription, so we can take that as a wedding gift.' There had been a necklace with a peacock pendant Kamala had set her heart on for buying this year. Before Lakshmi had turned her life upside down, that is.

After the call, Kamala checked her phone to see if a message from Lakshmi had somehow made its way to her during the five minutes that she was speaking with Sundu. It hadn't.

The event was one of those elaborate weddings where a giant heart-shaped flower arrangement spelling the bride and groom's name loomed at the entrance of the hall. The reception area was teeming with well-dressed people – all the women looking uniformly resplendent in silk sarees and gold jewellery, and the men trying to keep up with their women's shininess in silk kurtas and veshtis.

'Come on, let's find Aruna and mark our attendance,' Sundu muttered as they walked past the entrance staffed by giggling girls, who were sprinkling rose water on the guests in welcome.

They found Aruna hovering inside, giving instructions to the musicians who were nodding their heads half-heartedly to whatever she was saying. On spotting Sundu and Kamala, she exclaimed, 'Hello, hello! Hope your children are all doing well? Please make sure you eat well as soon as the food is ready.'

She had the expression of tired happiness that came from the stress and relief of seeing her only daughter get married, and

Kamala felt her migraine throb harder. Sundu assured Aruna about everyone's well-being and exclaimed that the colour combination of light green and pink on Aruna's silk saree was particularly flattering. They all then exchanged notes on each other's sarees before leaving Aruna to deal with the musicians who had taken this opportunity to drift away from her.

The bride and groom stood on a stage decked with velvet-and-gold thrones, and there was a long queue to go up to the stage to congratulate them. 'Let's sit for a while and see if the queue gets shorter,' Kamala suggested. They sat down on a pair of empty plastic chairs next to a middle-aged couple who were fanning themselves with the wedding invites.

'– The girl is dark-complexioned, but, at least, she seems to come from a well-to-do family. That silk saree alone must have set her father back by thirty thousand rupees.' The wife passed on her astute observations to her husband.

'If it is really silk,' countered her husband. He had a surprisingly squeaky voice for someone with such a serious, well-oiled handlebar moustache. 'These days, they make such convincing polyester sarees that you cannot tell a real one from a dupe.'

'It looks real. You can also tell by the jewellery that the bride is wearing. They are all the latest designs advertised on the billboards outside Pothys.' The woman touched the cluster of gold necklaces around her own neck protectively in case their authenticity might be called into question. She then took out something that looked like a prayer book from her handbag and used it to fan herself instead of the flimsy wedding invite.

'This heat is killing me. Can someone increase the speed of the fan?' She snapped her fingers at a young man distributing tumblers of grape juice from a tray. He replied that he needed to check with his supervisor about adjusting the fan speed and disappeared with a smile that was more smug than apologetic.

She turned to Kamala and asked, 'It is so hot in here, isn't it?' while fanning her prayer book more vigorously to emphasise her point. 'We are just returning from the US after visiting our son in Minneapolis. It was so cool and comfortable there, just like a hill station. It was as if the entire city were permanently air-conditioned!' She punctuated the end of her sentence with a high-pitched giggle.

Kamala gave her best approximation for a smile. 'Sounds very nice.' She craned her neck to see if the queue to the podium had become shorter.

'Our son works for Deloitte there. He is also due to get his green card anytime now,' her neighbour added brightly, basking in her son's cleverness.

'How about your children? Are they all doing well?' her husband asked, sidling closer to his wife, while turning towards Kamala.

'I have one daughter. She is studying in the UK.' At that, Kamala turned to Sundu, hoping to put a stop to this bothersome conversation. Sundu, however, seemed to be engaged in some work-related tussle with her Blackberry and didn't look up.

'What is she studying? Our son did his master's in economics in the US.' The woman eyed the empty chairs next to Kamala and Sundu, perhaps wondering where their husbands were.

'She is doing her master's in computer science at Oxford,' Kamala replied.

'Oho! Well done,' the man squeaked. Kamala acknowledged his enthusiasm with a smile, as she was also one of those people who judged parents by the calibre of their children's education. 'How old is she?'

'She is only twenty-three.' Kamala used the word 'only' pre-emptively, knowing what was to follow.

'She is still young. I think twenty-five is the right age to start looking. Although, from our experience, we find that girls have become too picky these days, so you shouldn't delay too much beyond that. They become too opinionated on what they want as they become older,' he declared authoritatively, as if he were quoting a recent research article that he had read about the gender-age matrix for marriage in the *Economic Times*.

'Right.' Kamala's voice wavered a little. This made Sundu look up from her phone and at the couple, her forehead furrowed. She then cleared her throat and announced a little loudly that it looked like the dining hall had opened for evening tiffin. This made the couple next to them confer with each other briefly before making a beeline for the dining area.

Kamala and Sundu went through the usual motions of attending a wedding – they went up to the podium, congratulated the couple and got blinded by the flashlights when they posed for the official photograph. They ate the evening tiffin of pongal, vadai and sweet kesari, which, Sundu observed, was made with cheaper oil substitute instead of ghee by the crafty catering company which should be blacklisted. They had just picked up their favour bags containing fried snacks and blouse pieces and were a few minutes away from exiting the venue when Sarasu accosted them.

A friend of Aruna's, Sarasu had the unnerving habit of towering over someone and staring intently without smiling. Conversely, her husband was short and plump and always had a ready smile that matched his relentlessly pleasant expression. Kamala and Sundu, perhaps unimaginatively, referred to them as Laurel and Hardy between themselves.

'We were just wondering where you were,' Sarasu said, eyeing both women rather accusingly. Sarasu had always been jealous of the close friendship between Kamala and Sundu and had made many unsuccessful attempts to ingratiate herself with them in the past. Since that hadn't worked out very well, she now simply acted a little put out whenever she saw them together.

'We came a while ago, back when that nice young man was play-ing the violin – I forget his name – what is it?' Kamala turned to Sundu, not really expecting an answer, then turned back to Sarasu. 'In fact, we were just about to leave.' She knew that saying this statement now would lay the groundwork for their exit later into small talk.

'Where is Lakshmi? I heard she was in town. Did she not come with you?' Sarasu asked, casting her quick eyes around Kamala's shoulders.

'Why are you hiding your daughter from us? It has been so long since we set eyes on her. I don't think she will even remember who we all are, now that she has gone to a foreign country,' Sarasu's husband added jovially, looping his thumbs around the belt that was stretched tight across his round belly.

'Nothing of that sort. Lakshmi was asking after all of you,' Kamala protested weakly, her headache pulsing. 'Anyways, it was a short visit this time. We will organise for a meet-up the next time she comes.'

'How is that son of yours doing, Sundu? He has been married for nearly three years now, hasn't he? No good news yet?' Sarasu cast her intense gaze on Sundu.

'Good news is that he is not yet divorced like his mother,' Sundu replied in a merry voice, enjoying the look of immense awkward-ness that came over both Sarasu and her husband's face.

Kamala threw Sundu a furtive chastising look. 'I think we need to get going before the traffic gets too congested – it is an auspi-cious day, so there are too many weddings adding to the regular traffic, don't you agree?'

'Yes, yes, of course.' Sarasu's husband nodded quickly, relieved at the change in topic. He then spoke to them in length about various short-cuts that they could take to get to their side of the city quicker. Sundu did not disagree with him, but with the uncharacteristic meekness with which she was nodding her head, Kamala knew that she had no intention of following his directions.

On the drive home, Sundu commented, 'Well, of all the four hundred people at the reception, I don't know why we had to bump into that Sarasu. Do you think she is tracking us with a GPS?' She chuckled at her own joke and looked over at Kamala, who was pensively staring out of the car window, her mind weighed down by thoughts about Lakshmi.

'Why are you so quiet?' Sundu asked as she swerved to avoid a rogue van that was travelling in the wrong direction. The driver lowered his window and shouted at her.

Sundu was about to respond in kind when Kamala placed a restraining hand on her elbow. 'My head is still aching, that's why.'

'You will never listen to my advice about seeing a doctor. There is paracetamol in my handbag if you want a tablet,' she said, pointing her thumb to the back seat. Sundu had still not removed the plastic covers from the seats of her car, although it was over three months since she had bought it. A leather briefcase stuffed with papers had been tossed in the back, and next to it sat a bright red lunch bag, which rumbled like an empty stomach every time they hit a pothole.

'No, I don't think a paracetamol will help.'

They sat in silence as Sundu tried to find a radio station for them to listen to. She settled on one that played Carnatic music interspersed with advertisements for turmeric antiseptic creams.

'So, tell me, does Lakshmi have a boyfriend in the UK?' asked Sundu in a matter-of-fact tone as she swerved her car into a quieter street off the main road.

'Why do you ask that?' Kamala exclaimed, unable to hide her surprise.

'I saw that pickled look on your face when that moustached fellow was talking about Lakshmi's marriage prospects. I had half a mind to interrupt him and say that it was none of his business, though, mind you.'

'Well, I wish she had a boyfriend,' said Kamala, more dramatically than intended. She turned to look out of the window.

'Really? You do?' asked Sundu, now looking back at her worriedly.

Kamala's headache was now intolerable, and she closed her eyes and groaned.

'Kamala, are you OK?' Sundu parked her car under a tamarind tree on the road and turned to Kamala, looking concerned. 'Wait, here drink some water.' The radio had now stopped at a station where there were two zippy youngsters enthusing about how Coca-Cola was the answer to every teenage problem. Sundu switched it off.

'So, when Lakshmi was here, she told me something—' Kamala started into the silence.

'What did she tell you? Is everything all right with her?' Sundu interrupted, sounding genuinely concerned. She checked if Kamala had a fever by placing her palm against her forehead.

'Her health is fine,' Kamala said, hesitating before she continued. 'She told me that she doesn't want to marry a boy. She wants to marry a girl.'

Sundu raised her eyebrow but spoke evenly. 'She specifically told you that she wants to marry a girl?'

'No, not like that. She said that she just likes girls that way,' Kamala finished in a frustrated voice, and her frustration soon dissolved into tears. She started sobbing softly.

Sundu offered her a neatly pressed handkerchief with embroidered flowers from her handbag.

'She has always liked rebelling against everything I say. But this is really, really quite something,' sniffled Kamala.

The two friends sat there quietly, without speaking to each other. A few tamarind leaves fell on the windshield as tiny yellow flecks.

'Obviously, you wouldn't mention this to anyone, right?' Kamala murmured. 'I can't even imagine what people would say if they knew. They would probably think this is all because I didn't raise her properly.' Kamala had always overcompensated for the lack of a father's presence in Lakshmi's life and had been conscious about society's perception of her as a single, and therefore, potentially inadequate parent.

'People who like wagging their tongues are going to talk about one thing or the other. We should only care if Lakshmi is happy at the end of the day, shouldn't we?' Sundu said firmly.

'That is easy for you to say. You have a son who has married a suitable girl,' Kamala commented churlishly.

Sundu sighed. 'Well, this suitable girl you speak of doesn't want my son to have anything to do with me, if she can help it.'

'Oh! I didn't realise it was that bad.' Kamala dabbed at her eyes with the scalloped edge of Sundu's handkerchief.

'Well, I guess I was a little ashamed to admit that I had raised a son who had ended up taking the side of his wife over his own mother.' Sundu shrugged.

'Just give him some time. He will come back to you once the new wife loses her shine.' Kamala patted Sundu's arm as her friend shrugged again.

They continued to sit in contemplative silence. 'I don't know why God is testing us like this,' Kamala added.

Sundu nodded her agreement. 'I am sure it will all work itself out,' but she said this in the tired, knowing voice of someone who has seen and done it all before. She then started her car again but didn't switch the radio back on.

*

The day after the wedding, Kamala still woke up with a headache, but it felt just a bit lighter for having shared her worries with Sundu.

She decided to get on with the chores that she had postponed for a while. She went to the tailor's to collect the blouses she had given for stitching, stopped at the Ramar temple right next door to say a quick hello to the resident deity and then carried on to the bank to deposit a cheque. She was walking back home, when she noticed Mani outside the gates of the apartments, having an altercation with a tall, burly man who had his lungi folded up around his waist. Kamala wondered if he was the same man she had noticed running a funeral business outside their gates, his garlanded white van advertising transportation to heaven for a discounted fee.

She couldn't hear what Mani was saying, but she could tell that his voice was raised, and his hands were gesticulating a little too wildly. Mani was mild-mannered in general, but on occasion, she knew that everyone had to act tough to get by – as her mother used to admonish her shy nature as a child, if she didn't learn to raise her voice, other people would swallow her for lunch and burp to everyone else that she had wanted to be eaten.

She reached the gates of the apartment block and could now hear the man speaking in the menacing tones of someone straight out of her TV serials. 'One of these days, you may be walking on the road, and a lorry may not see you. Do you really think this house is worth it?'

'Please take these empty threats back to where you came from. Don't for a minute think that it will work on me,' Mani responded in a voice that sounded like it had been raised and angry for a while.

The man responded by stepping threateningly close to Mani, making Mani flinch reflexively and take a step back. The man laughed, much too unkindly, and Kamala's breath shallowed with fear. Her shouting experience was limited to raising her voice at the auto-driver who demanded an exorbitant fare, or at the repair fellow who claimed that it was entirely her fault that the internet stopped working overnight. However, looking at Mani's face, drawn with distress, she decided to intervene.

'Listen, Mister . . . ?' She paused, as if she was waiting for him to fill the gap with his name. The man hadn't noticed her until then, and he cast his eyes over her frail frame clad in a cotton saree, looking confused at first, and then annoyed.

'*Maami*, I know who you are. It is better for you if you do not intervene,' he warned.

'This is indeed my business, too. If you have finished what you have come to say, you should leave,' she said, speaking with a calmness that surprised her.

'You don't know the kind of people you are dealing with.' He wagged his finger at both Kamala and Mani. However, by his furtive glances towards the gates, she knew he was preparing to leave.

'Well, we do now, thanks to you,' she continued as the man plucked a rose roughly from a bush and threw it on the ground on his way out.

'I will file a complaint to the police if you show your face here again,' Mani said to the back of the retreating man. He turned to look back at Mani as if this was the most absurd thing he had ever heard in his life and clanged the metal gates of the apartment loudly shut.

Mani took strident, angry steps to the porch and Kamala trailed after him, tucking her saree into her waist.

'I am guessing this thug was sent by the construction company? He seemed very different from the other man with the briefcase.'

'These rascals send different people to do their dirty work. Bala is the business manager who cleans up after,' Mani said, the anger in his voice tapering away to despair as he looked in the direction of the garden. 'I don't think they will stop harassing us, Kamala. They seem to want this place at any cost. I don't want you and . . .' Mani waved his hands upstairs to indicate Reva and Jason, 'to get into any kind of trouble.'

'As the saying goes, "barking dogs seldom bite".' She quoted the English proverb in an assuring manner but wondered how true it was even as she said it. She recalled an incident where a stray dog had nipped at Sarasu's ankle, requiring her to take a series of rabies shots, but she wasn't sure if the incident had involved the dog barking its intentions first. Sundu would know, she thought, making a mental note to ask her about the dog – and also about men who barked louder than dogs.

8

Revathi

'Gobi Manchurian, Schezwan Fried Rice, American Chop Suey –'
Reva was reading the menu inside the Chinese Dragon restaurant
located on the sixth floor of a multi-storeyed hotel. It was decorated
expensively in black marble, and its walls were covered with Chinese alphabets emblazoned in gold. Reva had suggested this place
to Karthik because of her fondness for fiery Indo-Chinese food, the
kind that made your eyes water with chilli and your senses swim
in soy. She now realised that it was quite pointless, as she felt too
nervous to enjoy the food.

Karthik was sitting across from her and examining the menu
carefully. He was tall and dressed neatly in a T-shirt with a
crocodile logo and fashionable tortoiseshell glasses. His hair was
ruffled carefully to appear flouncy rather than neatly parted. His
appearance was similar to the sentences in his emails – deliberate
and carefully arranged so that he didn't come across as being too
serious. Reva had also spent some time deliberating on her appearance and wore a simple, embroidered black kurta that didn't give
away the fact that she had tried on three other outfits before
picking this one.

They discussed the logistics of ordering in a somewhat formal
way – they were both vegetarian and Karthik suggested that Reva

ordered for both of them since she was familiar with the menu. When Reva explained to him that some of the dishes could be quite spicy, she liked that Karthik was able to openly acknowledge that his spice tolerance was no longer what it used to be.

Once Reva placed the order, the waiter, a young man dressed in a black and gold waistcoat, turned to Karthik, and asked, 'Anything to drink, sir?'

'A beer for me, please.'

After a brief pause, during which Reva's thoughts travelled to her mother and back, she said, 'I will have the same.'

Once the waiter left, there was an awkward silence during which Reva sipped some water and Karthik straightened the paper place-mat with bamboo motifs.

'So, which school did you go to in Chennai?' Karthik tilted his head attentively in anticipation of her answer. Unsurprisingly, within a few minutes of discussion about schools and tuition classes, they were able to find three acquaintances that they had in common.

'That Raghav from your college is quite successful in the Bay Area now – his start-up was acquired for close to two million dollars, you know?' Karthik widened his eyes at Reva to show how impressive that was, before cautiously dipping his fried paneer in a radioactive looking red sauce. She could see that he found the food spicy by the large gulps of beer that he took after every mouthful, but he continued to eat it uncomplainingly.

'So, is that something you want to do at some point as well – start up on your own?' she asked, covering her mouth with her hands as she chewed on her food.

'The visa situation ties me to my company, and I can't really quit until I get my green card, which could take several years. Even when I do, I am not sure I would have the guts to do something on my own, though,' he admitted rather wistfully. She could imagine his regular middle-class upbringing in Chennai, his parents praising him for dreaming pragmatically even as a child – he would have been one of those kids who really liked playing cricket but was instead taken to music classes to learn an instrument, a violin possibly. He would have worked hard to excel in all subjects at school and not just the ones he liked while being disciplined enough to play video games in moderation. Now, in the US, she imagined that he would stop for only one or two beers with his colleagues on weekdays and buy cartons of buttermilk from the supermarket to make curd rice to eat with pickles on Sunday nights.

'How often do you visit Chennai?' she asked.

'I try to visit at least once a year. Although last year, my parents came to the US and stayed for two months over the summer. I started getting used to having a hot three-course meal waiting for me when I came back home from work.' He paused, perhaps contemplating that his statement could be misunderstood for wanting a wife for that reason, and added, 'Although I am not a pretty bad cook myself,' with a self-deprecating laugh.

Reva could have continued the conversation by commenting on her cooking skills, or rather, the lack of them, but decided that it was perhaps too soon. 'What do you usually do on weekends?' she asked instead.

'I've started taking flying lessons, actually.' He raised one brow in anticipation of this statement surprising her.

'What do you mean by flying? You mean skydiving?' she asked, her eyes drawn to the flying bird drawn on her Kingfisher beer glass.

'No, flying an actual plane.' He immediately started digging up photos on his phone to show her.

'Wow, that's really cool. Must be a great feeling to fly your own plane!' she exclaimed with appropriate enthusiasm.

He showed her a picture of him in the cockpit, signalling an excited thumbs-up, while the actual pilot behind him gave a canned smile for the camera. 'That is my instructor, Jake. I have gone for only three lessons so far, though,' he added truthfully.

'My hobbies are pretty lame, comparatively. I like reading, but it has been hard to make time for it these days.'

'You need to make time for things that you really like.' He pointed his fork at her. 'Have you read *Thinking, Fast and Slow* by Daniel Kahneman? It is quite a dense read but totally worth it.'

'I am not that much into non-fiction. I need a story to follow.' She shrugged. Both of them concentrated on rolling the fat strands of chop suey on their forks.

Karthik continued earnestly, as if her preferences could be changed if she just happened to meet the right book, ' — You should really read this one. In fact, I brought it with me here. I can lend it to you if you like.'

As the evening went on and another pair of beers made their appearance, Karthik became more talkative, and Reva's laughter became a little more high-pitched.

'I need to be honest with you about something,' he said seriously, his words sobering Reva's laughter. 'I am here for less than two months, and we want to figure things out before I leave.'

'Oh,' was all that Reva could come up with, imagining the other half of his 'we', presumably his mother, maintaining a neat to-do list titled 'Wedding Stuff', with 'Find a girl' as one of the items to be crossed out, just below 'Book a venue' and above 'Get gold jewellery from locker'.

'So, let's meet a few more times before I leave,' he suggested, in a very non-casual manner.

'OK,' was the only answer that Reva could think of saying at the moment.

'I know this entire thing is slightly awkward,' Karthik continued, sensing her hesitation. 'However, I really enjoyed dinner, and it would be great to see you again.'

Reva nodded, withdrawing into herself and smiling politely at him. They were both quiet as they scanned the restaurant for the waiter at the same time. Reva glanced at the family of four seated next to them – two young boys fighting with each other while their parents looked absorbed in the glow of their phones. Her current situation made Reva wonder if the couple had got married after a five-minute perfunctory discussion over filter coffee and fried refreshments, or if it had been one of those drawn-out love marriages and whether, in either case, it had eventually made any kind of difference.

Once the bill arrived, they split it without arguing about who was going to pay.

*

The next day, Reva washed her scooter in the walkways of the garden, trying to unearth its original silver colour from beneath a thick layer of dust. As she rinsed soap water next to the guava tree, she found herself mentally replaying the conversation with her mother the day before.

'My astrologer has predicted that this will be the year you will finally get married!' her mother had announced ebulliently after Reva had described the dinner with Karthik as being 'all right'.

Reva had enquired if this prediction had been obtained by calling the astrologer's hotline that cost nineteen rupees per minute, but by then, her mother had moved on to lamenting about Reva's so-called modern values that prevented her from marrying Karthik in the very next available auspicious hour.

She took a break from being annoyed with her mother to join Mani and Jason on the porch. They seemed to be in the middle of a conversation that involved Mani nodding his head with exaggerated seriousness to whatever Jason was saying.

'—I think I have a bit of a problem with the boiler. The red light doesn't come on, and it doesn't heat up the water.' Jason then added after a pause, 'Oh, and by boiler, I mean the thing that heats water in the bathroom,' and then, 'I worked the afternoon shift, you see, so I need to shower in the evening.'

'Why do you need to work the afternoon shift?' Reva enquired in an inscrutable voice.

'Because the kitchen is really busy during . . .' he replied automatically before trailing off as he noticed Reva watching him with an amused expression.

Mani pursed his lips disapprovingly at her and turned to Jason. 'You mean the geyser isn't working? Let me call the electrician.' He pulled a chunky mobile phone out of the front pocket of his shirt.

Reva exchanged a this-will-take-a-while shrug with Jason as Mani engaged in a convoluted conversation with the electrician. Mani first discussed the electrician's daughter's scores in the board exams, then proceeded to discuss the mileage issues of his new motorbike before arriving at the immediate matter of the geyser.

'—So, Nandu, can you also get a packet of milk from Diamond General Stores on the way here?' added Mani before ending the call. He then looked at his phone closely to make sure that he had pressed the correct button to end his conversation.

'Did he just ask the electrician to buy milk?' Jason whispered to Reva doubtfully.

Reva nodded, smiling. Back in her village, she remembered the time when their electrician, Kasi, had actually stepped in to milk their cow because the milkman's wife had been taken to the hospital. She looked at Jason and tried to imagine the kind of childhood that he might have had – rollicking in the countryside while eating jam-filled scones and impossibly red apples if any of those Enid Blyton books were to be believed.

'How are things at the restaurant? What's new on the menu these days? Avocados on dosa perhaps?' She was continuing their conversation from the last time they had crossed paths on the walkway. Jason was the only person in her social circle who was a chef, and unlike other jobs such as consulting or banking, she thought that talking about food actually made for reasonably interesting conversation.

'Actually, that's not a bad idea,' Jason replied with immensely English politeness. She now knew that that implied it was a terrible one.

There was a loud bang on the road, accompanied by a puff of smoke and Nandu, the electrician, emerged from the white fumes like a magician's illusion. Mani went to admire his new Enfield bike and instructed him to park it inside the gates of the apartment block so that it did not get stolen.

'Hi, you are Nandu. Sorry, sir, *I* am Nandu,' gushed the electrician to Jason, flailing under the pressure of trying to make a good impression on the foreigner in their midst. He then cleared his throat and said, 'Good to meet you, sir. How can I help you today? I am Nandakumar. You can also call me Nandu.'

'Nandu is also a Tamil word that means crab,' chipped in Mani, addressing Jason.

'What? No, I was named after the great Lord Krishna, not a crab,' said Nandu, looking quite offended, while scuttling towards the staircase and following Jason in a rather crab-like manner.

'Our electrician Nandu is such a character.' Reva shook her head, smiling.

'Wait, did he forget the milk?' asked Mani as Reva's phone buzzed with another message from her mother. It was a fifteen-minute video of a puja being performed at a temple where the god specialised in providing marriage expediting services. Reva pressed the mute button harder than necessary on her phone.

Her mother somehow seemed to sense Reva's intentions and escalated her messaging to a phone call. 'So, when are you meeting Karthik again?' she asked as soon as Reva picked up.

'Soon,' replied Reva, in an exaggeratedly bored voice that was intended to ward off her mother's tone of intense interest. Mani handed her the post and she waved him goodbye before starting to walk up the stairs.

'—Listen, Revathi. You should meet him a few more times and then go ahead in marrying him even if you like him only around sixty or seventy per cent. You cannot simply keep on acting choosy like this,' her mother admonished. Reva kept quiet, not wanting to start an argument about the incredulity of using a passing grade for the decision to marry someone.

Her mother continued, 'Remember Sarala, who had just got married less than two years ago? She came home yesterday with her little baby. It is a girl, and she had given the baby one of these fancy modern names – Ahana, Ashita, something like that. The baby was so well behaved and didn't cry even once.'

'That's nice,' replied Reva absentmindedly. She paused in the balcony of the first floor and tilted her chin towards the breeze that teased her and then disappeared.

'Don't you remember her?' her mother persisted. 'You two used to be constantly playing hide and seek around the haystacks when you were younger. She has a younger brother who got married last year into the family that owns a big eye hospital in Trichy?'

'Yes, I do remember her. I haven't seen her or her brother for several years now, though,' Reva replied patiently. Although she didn't care for this kind of gossip, it brought upon a sense of guilt upon Reva, even though her mother's tone was not really accusatory. This time.

'So, this Karthik, I hear, is in town only for a couple of months.' Reva's mother deployed her characteristic disregard to conversational continuity.

'Enough about Karthik, Ma. I have met him only once.' Reva found herself starting to get annoyed earlier than usual in her conversations with her mother.

'What to do? I have started becoming repetitive in my old age. It is just that I worry about you,' her mother replied in a mollifying tone. She paused significantly, and Reva knew that she was going to follow-up with another change of topic. 'I made palkova with milk that was starting to turn yesterday. I thought of you and ate it all myself!'

'I see,' Reva answered, somewhat passive aggressively.

'How is work going? All busy-busy as usual?' her mother asked, unwilling to end the conversation without eliciting a normal response from Reva.

'Yes, same as always. I need to go finish some work now, though, Ma. Bye!' Reva adopted a preoccupied voice, although her plans for the evening involved nothing more than numbing her brain with some reality television.

'OK, Revathi, remember what I said, and I hope you come to a good decision quickly. Also, don't forget to eat properly for dinner,' her mother continued, even as Reva kept repeating her goodbyes to end the call.

*

Sorry, it looks like I can't make it today, Shreya had texted, followed by a crying face that gushed a waterfall of tears. Reva felt more disappointed than Shreya perhaps intended her to be – she had spent the whole day running errands by herself and had been looking forward to the walk by the beach, going as far as imagining some of the conversations that they would have once they met.

She decided to go by herself anyway. As she headed out, she saw Jason leaning across the balcony, drinking a bottle of beer while waiting for a breeze that had no intention of arriving.

'Heading out for a run?' he asked. Reva was confused by the question until she remembered that she had pulled on exercise clothes to give a sense of purpose to her stroll.

'I am heading to the beach where it should be cooler. Want to come?' she asked, jangling the keys of her scooter to punctuate the end of her question. Jason replied that it was the best idea he had heard all day.

'Ah, do I need my swimming trunks?' asked Jason when they were halfway down the stairs. Reva assured him that there was definitely no swimming involved at this time of day, and they would just be walking alongside the beach on a concrete walkway.

The walkway that curved along the shores of Besant Nagar Beach was brightly lit and bustling with activity, although it was almost nine p.m. on a Sunday. Jason and Reva walked slowly, weaving their way through middle-aged men on power walks and groups of yelping teenagers, while getting periodically engulfed by waves of large families trailing balloons, strollers and grandmothers.

'What tree is that?' Jason pointed at some trees with large, waxy leaves, planted evenly along the sides of the walkway.

'Just because I live here doesn't mean I am personally acquainted with every plant that grows here,' Reva laughed. 'Let me take a picture, and we can ask Mani Uncle.'

They walked far enough to reach a spot that had less footfall and sat down on the low wall facing the ocean. The night sky stretched endlessly into the horizon and the ocean roared loudly beneath it like an animal unafraid of the dark. The sea breeze felt cool and silky against the skin, and they closed their eyes, glad to have found this little pocket of calm.

The whispers and giggles reached her first, before Reva noticed the couple sitting on an adjacent wall. They looked younger than twenty and were gazing at each other with the kind of manic smiles that only young love can elicit. The boy was surreptitiously grazing his fingers against the girl's, who was responding by playfully making her fingers dance.

'I used to have one of those.' Jason tilted his head towards the couple.

'What? A struggling beard?'

'Ha ha, very funny,' Jason mocked, although he smiled. 'I meant a relationship. A girlfriend.'

'What happened?' Reva asked, sitting up straighter. Jason told her about Emma, and although he didn't say when exactly it had all transpired, she figured it was quite recent from the care he took to sound very detached.

Reva, in turn, told him about Sebastian to show that she understood. 'You will get where I am very soon. The point of not caring.'

'I know.' He glanced at the couple, then back at her. 'I just want to get there now.'

They walked further along the beach past brightly lit food and drink stalls, the recent exchange of confidences inducing a comfortable silence between them. Jason stopped at a juice cart to scrutinise the list of drinks that Reva thought to be more numerous than the ticket combinations available for worship at the Tirupati temple. A young, saree-clad woman behind the cart called out, 'Pineapple juice, sir? Made with fresh pineapples.' After performing an instant customer analysis, she added, 'We have piña colada also.'

'What do you think? Pineapple or watermelon?' Jason asked Reva. 'Or should we be adventurous and go for Cool Cool Cool?'

'That is juice made from saathukudi.' The juice-seller pointed at the round, leaf-coloured fruits. After an industrious pause, she added, 'Sweet lime in English.'

Reva tried to tug him away from the stall murmuring, 'Well, we don't really know what kind of water they use in the juice in these stalls,' in a low voice, which turned out to be not quite low enough.

'Everything here is made only with bottled water, madam,' the juice-seller told Reva in an injured voice that was matched with an equally injured expression. She then straightened a handwritten sign hanging by the side of the stall that declared, *MADE WITH 100% MINERAL WATER*, to further emphasise her point.

Jason asked her for pineapple juice, and the woman multitasked between juicing neatly sliced pineapple chunks and reprimanding three kids seated on the sand beneath the stall whom Reva hadn't noticed until then. They were two boys and a girl, all aged under six, who had decided to ignore the notebooks sprawled around them in the sand in favour of taking turns to poke each other and giggle convulsively.

One of them, a girl with braided hair looped in a red ribbon, looked up with wide eyes at Jason, and then at Reva before proceeding to make a big show of counting something in her fingers and then carefully writing down her discovery in her notebook with a rather professorial air. Reva smiled encouragingly at the girl, but she didn't look up again to notice.

Jason drank the juice appreciatively as they continued on their walk. They passed by a brightly lit police lookout station where two men in khaki uniforms were seated reclined on chairs, slurping juice loudly through straws while several CCTV monitors flickered around them.

'Hey, look, there's a guy selling soan papdi.' Reva gestured towards a cart with a glass globe, filled with snow-coloured flakes of sugar candy.

She explained to Jason that the ringing of the bell from these carts as they passed through the roads was a relic from her childhood, comparing it with the ringing of ice cream vans in Jason's. As she brought up this reference with ease, she realised how much she knew about life in the UK from just reading the books that had filled the library in her school. She had pieced together clues along with Enid Blyton's intrepid investigators as a child, swooned in the countryside in the arms of Georgette Heyer as a teenager and, as recent as the month before, had inhabited the world woven by Zadie Smith for an entire weekend. She was certain that Jason would not have encountered as many stories from India and wondered, in a slightly alarmed manner, if his entire frame of reference for the country came from watching *Slumdog Millionaire*.

The man with the soan papdi cart moved purposefully towards them.

'Go on, then, have some.' Jason nudged her, and before she could respond, waved at the man who smiled obligingly back. He gave her a generously heaped paper cone, which she carefully held in her hand, the silvery sugar strands pulled in different directions by the breeze.

They sat back on the wall, this time facing the road ahead, next to a parked truck that had the words *World's first 6D experience* written underneath a picture of a T. Rex that had a moustache drawn on its face.

Reva let a sugary strand dissolve in her mouth and was surprised by how plain it tasted compared to its preened, pistachio-bedecked counterparts that she had grown accustomed to eating now, sold in the air-conditioned sweet shops. She hesitated before she reached for more.

'Not as good as you remember it, huh?' Jason asked with a wry smile.

Reva nodded and raised her eyebrows in an expression that meant, unfortunately, yes.

'That's usually the way with these things,' Jason said matter-of-factly as he reached out to pick a strand for himself.

*

Reva was not sure what the trigger was – whether it was her mother and her constant disappointment in Reva's personal life, or if it was

Vijay, who was reading an article called 'What happens when you eat only carrots all day, every day' when she had walked up to his desk to enquire about a project deadline. She somehow felt emboldened to bring up her promotion with Subbu again. She knocked on his door and walked in stridently, although he didn't answer her.

Subbu was at his desk, leaning as far back as his chair would allow, thumbing through his phone. He looked up at her with an expression of annoyance, as if she were a buzzing fly that had somehow managed to enter his tightly shut, air-conditioned room.

'I wanted to discuss the topic of my promotion again.'

'Yes?' Subbu asked, the briskness in his voice indicating that he didn't have much time for this conversation.

'I am unhappy with your decision. I think I deserve it as I am more effective than anyone else in the team,' Reva said. She had wanted to sound calm and confident, but somehow, an inflection had crept in at the end of her sentence, making her statement sound more like a plea.

'I mean, a lot of us are unhappy about a lot of things.' Subbu leant forward and clasped his hands on the table. He peered at her through his bifocal spectacles that magnified the lower half of his eyes. 'Take me, for example – I have been waiting for a promotion for five years now. But I understand that we should all believe in the system.'

Reva wanted to ask, 'What system?' but she knew that the system was essentially a huddle of middle managers who promoted employees based on their chest-thumping capabilities.

She would have normally retreated from the conversation at this point, but there was something about the way in which Subbu was now running a fat finger over his printer and staring closely at the dust on his hand with interest that made her continue.

'You know, I have worked here for seven years and given it my best. Maybe it is time that I start looking at other options,' she said, sounding as if this was something that was just dawning on her.

He looked back at her, a little surprised, but then cleared his throat to sound more authoritative. 'We don't encourage ultimatums here, Revathi. Remember, everyone is replaceable, so think carefully before you say anything else.'

'You may also need to think carefully whether you are motivating and rewarding your employees fairly.' She walked out of the room, her heart beating rapidly at having worked up the courage to say these words. She was usually the kind of person who would think of an appropriate response to level someone's scathing comments several hours after the conversation was over and was glad that she had held her ground with Subbu this time.

However, by evening, the adrenaline rush of having confronted Subbu soon gave way to severe self-doubt. 'I might have just made things worse with my manager, Ranji. I don't know what made me say that I am considering leaving my job,' she said morosely, sipping ginger chai from a flimsy white plastic cup. They were seated on one of the fake leather chairs in the office canteen, under a motivational poster that said: 'If you can dream it, you can achieve it.'

Ranji listened to her while making appropriate clucks of sympathy and outrage. 'You know you can always find another job easily enough.'

Reva wondered for a moment if it was insensitive to continue talking about her career, considering that Ranji had decided not to work after the baby was born.

'Look, don't worry about me, OK?' Ranji said, reading into Reva's hesitation. She smoothed her flowy white kurta over her small baby bump affectionately, emphasising her point. 'I don't expect you to completely understand, you know. We are just at very different points in our lives,' she explained softly. 'You tell me, how's it going with Karthik?' she added teasingly and nudged Reva with her elbow, as if they were eighteen and discussing their favorite crush.

'I have met him just once, so let's see.' Reva shrugged.

'Are you meeting him again?' Ranji asked with interest before arranging her face to be as neutral as possible. In Ranji's case, both their families had met in her house for coffee, and the prospective couple had been given a few minutes to talk with each other in private on her balcony. 'What did you two talk about?' Reva had asked with amusement when she had first heard the story, unable to imagine a topic of conversation that could have convinced Ranji to marry him in under five minutes. 'Oh, I can't even remember. I remember liking that he was very tall, though!' Ranji had giggled in response.

Reva nodded now. 'Yes, we have made plans to meet again,' she said lightly, moving the plastic cup to her left hand and flexing her right wrist.

'Very good!' exclaimed Ranji and looked at Reva as if she was proud of her. *If I were one of her boys, she would have patted my head now,* Reva thought petulantly, gulping down the last sip of her chai.

9

Jason

Jason liked going up to the terrace of Grand Life Apartments at dusk when the heat of the day relented to give way to a cooler evening. The terrace was large, and colourfully punctuated by the residents' clothes that hung limply from the clothesline without so much as a single flutter. A cylindrical water tank painted a bright candyfloss pink stood next to a mangled mass of television antennas and cables at the back. Jason sat down on a block of concrete next to the water tank and was about to open the book he had carried with him when he noticed a movement behind one of the towels hung to dry. He walked towards the clothesline and found Kamala doing something that could only be best described as poking the towel with a wooden stick.

'Hello,' said Jason, bemused. 'Have the clothes been misbehaving lately?'

'Oh, hello,' Kamala replied distractedly. 'These clothes are for tomorrow's prayer. They need to remain pure – so I am not touching them by hand,' she explained, removing the towel with her stick and deftly depositing it in her bucket in one practised movement.

After she finished with her clothes, she came and sat next to him, pressing her hands on her knees. 'These knees are not what they used to be.' She exhaled. They both sat in silence for a while, watching the sun disappear behind the minaret of a mosque in the distance.

'Hope you are doing well? Is your daughter still here?' asked Jason politely, looking sideways at Kamala. Her greying hair was held together in a bun, and she was wearing a cream saree with a matching blouse that hung loosely around her shoulders. She also wore an air of unmistakable sadness that he couldn't recall noticing before.

'No, she left three weeks ago.' A hissing sigh emanated from Kamala, reminding Jason of his mother's old tea-kettle.

'Ah, I didn't know that she had left already.' He tried to sound as commiserating as he could. He had met Lakshmi briefly when they had crossed paths on the staircase and murmured perfunctory hellos to each other. Although she didn't bear any obvious resemblance to Kamala, she had walked with the same gait as her mother; her back stooped as an apology to the world for being tall.

'Yes, she did.'

The wistfulness in Kamala's voice made Jason wonder if this all-consuming obsession with their children was something that he had missed noticing in his parents back home. The last time he had seen his parents was a week before he had left for India. They still lived in his childhood home up in Liverpool, but every time he went, the house felt smaller and mouldier than he had remembered it being while growing up. During a dinner of overcooked shepherd's pie, he had explained to them that he was going to be working in a restaurant in Chennai. 'Where is that? Is that near Mumbai?' his father had asked. 'Why couldn't you just work at one of the many Indian restaurants here – like that place next to the post office? Even Shabnam said that their chicken curry was as good as anything you can get in India.' Jason had thought that this would have been a very valid endorsement if you discounted the fact that Shabnam, who was a teacher at the school that his mother worked in, had been to India just once.

His mother had sat next to him on their sofa covered with frilly cushions and talked about their upcoming yearly holiday to Spain, the terrible weather and their cat's digestive problems. His father had watched football on the television and occasionally grunted whenever his mother called out to him during the conversation. The television volume had been so loud that Jason asked his mother if his dad was starting to lose his hearing. This had led to another one-sided rant from his mother about the long list of health problems between them, which ended with Jason pretending that he was following the football on television as well.

On the terrace, Kamala now stared at the darkening horizon without quite looking at it. It made Jason say, 'I have made carrot cake downstairs. Would you like some?'

His head chef had asked him to make a dessert that would resemble the carrot cake served in European cafés but taste like the carrot halwa here. He felt that his version, made with the addition of cardamom and saffron to a cake recipe, was a rather feeble first attempt but quite edible, nonetheless.

'I don't eat cakes as they usually contain eggs. I don't eat eggs because I am a vegetarian,' Kamala explained, apologetically.

'Oh, you are a vegan?' Jason asked.

'I don't know what that is. Maybe that's another new thing these days. We have been strict vegetarians here for generations, and none of us eat eggs also.' Kamala stretched her legs as if she was preparing to get up but then folded them back again.

'So, you wouldn't have to worry about over-egging the pudding then!' Jason quipped and Kamala looked at him as if he might be a little slow and confirmed again, 'No, no egg in any pudding.' Jason smiled to himself and they both stared at the sky as it turned a deep brownish red, the colour of bricks heaped by the roads here after a night of rain.

*

On Sunday morning, Jason examined the *Cook and See* book closely, thinking that he had never come across a recipe book quite like it. It contained no glossy pictures, and the recipes were written with the sparse, precise air of someone who took the task of fixing an afternoon snack with as much seriousness as a surgeon performing open-heart surgery. It had no preamble on how a particular ingredient had a personal connection to the author and did not even have a cursory 'enjoy' at the end, as if any doubts cast on the enjoyment of these recipes reflected poorly on the person involved in the questioning.

He turned to the back of the book for a picture of the author – Meenakshi Ammal – a bespectacled woman who looked to be in her seventies, her eyebrows captured mid-raise, as if she had a further instruction or two to impart to the photographer taking her picture. As he flipped through the book, and mulled over the names of the dishes – banana flower curry, gooseberry pickles, tender pumpkin milk koottu – he felt overcome by a compelling need to create something from scratch, a feeling that he couldn't recall having in a long time. Urged by this sense of purpose, he placed the book in his bag and headed to the nearest vegetable shop.

It was still early in the day, and the sky was unusually cloudy as he headed to the shop on the road that tilted away from Diamond General Stores. The shop had a name that he couldn't pronounce, but he knew that it sold vegetables mainly because of the words *Fresh Fruit and Vegetables* written in English underneath its name board in Tamil.

As he searched for specific ingredients in the shop, it struck him that the vegetables arranged neatly in individual piles didn't come pinned with little name tags like their counterparts in the UK. He had previously laughed at these tags back home – if someone couldn't tell the difference between broccoli and beans at Tesco, one had to assume that they had bigger problems than simply not knowing what they were cooking for lunch, didn't they? Here, he squinted around, trying to match his Google search for 'bitter gourd' with one of the piles of lumpy-looking vegetables that all sat identically dressed in green. He heaved a sigh of relief when he spotted Kamala standing at the far corner of the shop, inspecting each baby aubergine with intense scrutiny before placing it in her basket. Jason walked over and interrupted Kamala's examination, admitting that he needed help.

Kamala introduced him to the vegetables as if he were a late arrival to a party currently in full swing.

'This is chow-chow,' she said, pointing to a pear-shaped, light-green vegetable that appeared to be friendly at first glance but later barbed him with tiny spikes when he ventured closer.

'This is kaaramani.' She indicated to the lanky cousins of the bean family and, after staring at a cluster of them studiously, added, 'Also called valve-tube beans.' If he hadn't known Kamala better, he would have thought that she was having a laugh with these names.

'This is called butter fruit.' She gestured to what he knew was an avocado. She waved her hands dismissively, adding, 'They are a new addition here. Not used for normal cooking.'

As they walked back home together, Jason asked almost play-fully, 'So, what are you planning to make with the chow-chow?' just so that it gave him a chance to make the satisfying sounds that comprised the vegetable's name.

'Just a thogayal. A thogayal is like a chutney.'

'Oh, nice. I want to learn to cook these dishes from you one of these days.' He smiled at her in a manner to indicate that he was only half-joking.

She looked up at him seriously, shielding her eyes from the sun that was now back to blazing the sky. 'I was planning on making lunch now. If you are free, you can come.'

Kamala got flustered with Jason's presence in her kitchen and appointed him to a chair that was temporarily separated from the dining table. Jason insisted that Kamala should at least let him help chop the vegetables.

'Nothing to chop,' she assured him while simultaneously bringing out a plastic cutting board and a knife. She tamed the bristles of the chow-chows with her knife, and expertly chopped them into small pieces quicker than he could have done.

'So, we are having chow-chow chutney for lunch today?' Jason enquired, crossing one leg over the other and looking around. Kamala's kitchen had rows of shelves arranged neatly with un-labelled plastic and stainless steel containers, and pots and pans of varying sizes accommodating each other in the crannies of the others' shapes. The smell of roasted chillies hung in the air, although Kamala had not started cooking yet.

Kamala paused, taken aback at his seemingly foolish question. 'Just eating thogayal is not a meal,' she explained in a voice still recovering from its astonishment. 'I will be making a kozhambu and a kari as well.'

He opened the *Cook and See* book from his bag, and it took him a while to find what she was cooking next – mor kozhambu – which was filed as a 'seasoned buttermilk soup'. The recipe, before it even got into the list of ingredients, started by admonishing, *Use only thick sour buttermilk*, as if to warn that if he didn't have this at home, he had no business reading any further.

Kamala started making the mor kozhambu by mixing buttermilk with rice flour and kept calling out the ingredients she added as she went along. The warm spices from the dish travelled towards Jason, making him suddenly hungry.

'Lakshmi likes mor kozhambu as well, but I didn't get to make it for her while she was here,' Kamala said to the bubbling liquid on the stove.

Something in Kamala's voice hinted to Jason that there was more to her sadness than just the loneliness from missing her daughter. 'How is Lakshmi doing?' he asked.

'I wish these children never had to grow up.' Kamala sighed, not exactly answering his question. She seemed to want to say more but stopped herself and focused on stirring the cooking vessel. A few moments later, she added, 'Sometimes, I think I made a mistake sending her to the UK to study. She seems to have changed completely.'

'Sometimes change is not entirely a bad thing, is it?' Jason ventured, wondering if Kamala's definition of complete change involved something literal like Lakshmi dyeing her hair a hot pink.

'Well, I just don't understand what's going through her mind these days,' Kamala said, casting her eyes towards her gods in the cabinet, as if they were going to imminently chip in with their explanation.

'I don't think parents can ever completely understand their children?' Jason ended the statement with the inflection of a question. In the way one brought their own personal experiences to prop such statements, he added, 'My parents needed to be brought around to my choice of profession, too. They would have much rather I found a respectable desk job.'

'Are you happy that you chose to become a cook?' Kamala looked at him quizzically, as if she really doubted such a possibility.

Jason didn't even have to contemplate his answer. 'Oh, absolutely. I don't think I would have lasted more than a few weeks punching things into a computer.'

'Well,' Kamala said in a tone that showed she disagreed, 'I'm sure you can do whatever job you set your mind to.'

She turned to the stove. 'I am also going to add some sundakkais in the kozhambu. You can add any vegetable you like – brinjals, ladies' finger,' she explained. 'Sundakkais are . . .' she started, and, seemingly tired of trying to translate everything into English, admitted, 'I don't know. Why don't you search on your phone?'

Jason took out his phone and exclaimed, 'Ah, they are called turkey berries,' and started reading out its origin and uses in medicine in the newscaster's voice that one used when reading out information from a phone.

'I already know what it is,' Kamala waved her hands at him impatiently. 'And now you also do.'

'All done,' she finally declared, finishing the dish with the tempering of the lemon-yellow kozhambu with specks of mustard seeds and curry leaves.

Jason rushed to help Kamala bring out all the dishes to the dining table, but she shook her head vigorously to indicate that she didn't need his assistance and walked out to the living room with the stainless steel dish held in her hand. She instructed Jason to sit at the dining table and switched on the ceiling fan above to ensure that he didn't follow her again before retreating into the kitchen to get the rest of their lunch.

Kamala ate on a stainless steel plate with her hands, while giving Jason a porcelain plate with a spoon. He mixed the rice and kozhambu with the spoon, deciding against using his hands, although the thought briefly crossed his mind. The mor kozhambu was tart and spicy, and the rice soaked it up swiftly as if it had been waiting for this encounter all its life.

'You should be the one who should be a chef,' he announced graciously to Kamala while helping himself to another serving using the heavy ladle.

'A chef?' she asked him incredulously as if he had suggested that she should have made a career out of flying frisbees. 'Becoming a chef was not something that women from respectable families even considered,' she told him emphatically.

She made a hole in her rice into which she poured the kozhambu before mixing it with her hands. She then crushed a piece of appalam and mixed it with the rice and koottu. 'In my generation, and especially my mother's, the ladies of the house just cooked well. If you had tasted my mother's cooking, you wouldn't even touch mine.'

She paused, and Jason waited, guessing correctly that she was going to talk about her daughter again. 'Every younger generation obviously thinks that they know best. When Lakshmi was younger, she wouldn't like to take my kozhambu in her tiffin box to school – she wanted me to make sandwiches, with the edges cut out and filled with strawberry jam.'

Jason could remember a lot of sandwiches in his life, most of them quite undesirable – Christmases at home when there were turkey sandwiches for three days in a row, summer holidays when they ate sandy cucumber sandwiches by the beach and later, as a harried student, those soggy ham and cheese sandwiches from the discount aisle.

He voiced this aloud and Kamala replied, 'We all want what we don't have, don't we?' in a rather world-weary manner before ladling a third helping of the kozhambu onto his plate, despite his protests that he had eaten enough.

As recommended by Kamala, Jason finished his meal with curd rice accompanied by a mango pickle. Kamala nodded at him encouragingly as he ate and brought out a procession of other side dishes – curry leaf powder, fried vadams, crisped sun-dried chillies – which he eagerly ate because he was curious how they would all taste together.

After dinner, she went into the kitchen and came back with a daffodil-coloured, perfectly shaped mango. 'I bought these

Banganapalli mangoes for Lakshmi because she used to really like them as a child. She didn't eat much while she was here. I will give you some to take back – they are going to get rotten soon anyways.' She sliced the mango with a small knife and gave a bowl of evenly sliced fruit to Jason. She then proceeded to slice the slippery flesh around the seed for herself.

Jason ate the sweet pieces of fruit while sitting reclined on Kamala's sofa with his legs outstretched, feeling dosed with the momentary contentment of having an unrestrained, decadent lunch. He lazily flicked through the *Cook and See* book again, and asked Kamala, 'So, do you follow any recipes from a cookbook, or do you have your family recipes secretly stashed away somewhere?'

'Family recipes?' she asked, furrowing her brows as if it was a concept unfamiliar to her. 'I know the recipes for most of the dishes by heart. For some dishes or snacks that I don't make regularly, I just search on Google. You know that you can find all these recipes,' she pointed at his well-thumbed book, 'on YouTube, right?'

Jason confirmed, laughing loudly, that he was indeed familiar with the concept of the internet. Kamala looked unsure as to what had been so funny but leant back on the sofa with a rare smile on her face.

*

Later that week, Jason came home from work to find Bala from the construction company sloping away in his tilted gait from Mani's porch. On his way out, he smiled at Jason, and it was only later that Jason wished he hadn't returned his smile.

He came to the porch to find Mani slumped in his chair, its candy colours looking incongruous against his defeated expression. He eyed a large envelope that he fiddled listlessly in his hand.

'Those bastards,' Mani said, staring into the distance, moment-arily forgetting that he was speaking to Jason, 'claim that the land on which this apartment is built actually belongs to the temple.'

Jason sat down next to Mani on the wall, giving him his complete attention.

'What's even more convenient is that the temple is willing to hand it over to Olympic Constructions. In exchange for a generous donation, obviously.'

'Are these documents even real?' asked Jason quietly, eyeing the envelope that had now been dropped to the floor.

'Even the god inside the temple knows that it is not.' Mani leant his hand against one of the pillars that held up the porch as if he had a sudden need to be supported by the solidity of his home. 'This house has been in my family for three generations. That guava tree there,' he said, casting his eyes towards the garden, 'was planted by my mother. She used to even whisper to the tree during her last days.' He smiled softly at the tree as if they shared a common secret with his mother that they had promised not to disclose to anyone else.

Jason sat silently, not saying anything for a long time. His eyes took in the rose bush that had just started to flower; its tiny pink buds yet untouched by the dust from the road that covered everything else. A squirrel that lived on the guava tree scurried past his feet, and he felt a wave of empathy towards it, thinking that they were not too different. They had both made a temporary home for themselves here, after all.

'If I don't sell the house, the only option we have is to contest them in court.' Mani sighed, leaning back to close his eyes.

'Maybe we should contest them if they are simply making things up?'

'I don't think we stand a chance against these thugs with bottomless pockets, Jason,' Mani said in a defeated voice that indicated that he didn't quite expect him to understand how things worked here.

Jason didn't know how to respond to that. He was familiar with the concept of money elbowing out old establishments that fostered a sense of community back home – pubs, bookshops, council houses giving way to glossy new buildings – but he had accepted that this was simply the way life marched on ahead. As if this needed confirming, he heard the drone of construction start again from the neighbouring plot accompanied by the blinding glare of newly installed night floodlights, signalling the rush to replace the old with the new.

10

Kamala

Kamala had just started her evening prayers when there was a startlingly loud crash downstairs. She wrinkled her brows and paused her prayer recitation to wonder aloud to her gods, 'What is all this commotion?' before heading down to investigate.

When she reached downstairs, she saw Mani inspecting one of the windows close to the porch, his hands on his hips.

'I hope you aren't hurt?' she asked, tripping a little against the last steps of the stairs in her hurry to reach him. Mani shook his head, saying, 'No, I'm fine,' and turned his gaze towards the window that had its glass broken, leaving behind a large starburst-shaped hole.

'You should have added metal bars on the windows like I've asked you to,' she chided, and looking at Mani's eyes dulled with worry, regretted saying it. She thought that the breaking of glass was a very inauspicious omen, but hid this thought, although she couldn't hide the anxious expression that accompanied it.

'Mani, your feet!' she exclaimed, noticing that he was standing barefoot in the remains of his window, the sharp glass pieces drawing blood. He waved his hands away at her to show it was of no consequence but flinched a little as they both walked towards the porch.

Reva came down, followed by Jason, and they all inspected the large red brick thrown at the window. Although the brick didn't come accompanied with a note of explanation, they all understood the message it carried, apart from Jason, who enquired if this could perhaps be the result of a drunken night out that had got a bit out of hand. (*What are these young people in the UK really up to?* Kamala wondered worriedly, her mind reaching for Lakshmi, although there were more immediate concerns lying in broken shards around her feet.)

'We should have CCTV cameras installed around here, Uncle,' Reva said in a rather adult-to-adult voice to Mani. 'And let's file an FIR with the police also.'

Mani nodded at her, although he didn't seem to be really listening. 'I had told Bala yesterday that we will be contesting the ownership of the construction company in court. And now, this.' He tilted his head towards his injured window.

'Well, this is just plain bullying.' Reva squared her shoulders towards the brick, which stood mutely at the centre of the porch after calling them all to this meeting.

'Be careful – they can get through to your feet even if you are wearing slippers,' Kamala warned Reva and Jason as they helped to clean up the broken pieces with sturdy brooms made from the spine of coconut leaves.

When Mani started exclaiming to Reva and Jason about how incredible it was that something as delicate as glass was made from something as mundane as sand, she knew that he was trying to hasten a sense of normality to their disturbed evening. 'Yes, there is a big glass factory in Sriperumbudur if you want to visit.' She nodded towards Jason, trying to do her bit to help Mani. Reva and Jason nodded at them in feigned amusement to show that they appreciated the effort.

As soon as Kamala went back to her apartment, she called Sundu, reporting this incident. Sundu surprised her by asking if Mani had given serious thought to handing over the house to the construction company.

'The law doesn't mean much to these sorts of people, Kamala,' she warned, and instead of feeling reassured as Kamala usually did, she was left feeling more uneasy after speaking with Sundu. For the first time, it began to sink in that she might need to find a new place to live soon, and she looked around her living room with a renewed sense of awareness of all the memories that it held within its faded cream walls.

It was only when she sat down to eat her dinner in front of the television that she remembered she hadn't finished her evening prayer. She went back to the altar with her hands folded, and questioned her gods, 'Is this all part of your bigger plan for us?'

In their characteristic stiff-upper-lip manner, her gods didn't say anything back.

*

Kamala expertly side-stepped the parked motorbikes and stray dogs on the pavement as she made her way to the temple. As she walked, she thought about the threat to Grand Life Apartments, and her heart sank a little at the prospect of her home of over two decades ceasing to exist in a matter of a few weeks. She also thought about one of her younger patients she had seen the day before, a well-behaved boy wearing vibhuti on his forehead, who had called her 'Paatti' instead of 'Doctor Aunty' and giggled his apology after. The sound of the young voice claiming her as a grandmother had made her heart bloom with joy, before deflating in disappointment in almost the very same instant.

Preoccupied, she had walked well past Karuthamma's flower stall before she remembered that she had forgotten to buy jasmines for her worship, so she retraced her steps. She must have crossed this busy road, weaving through oncoming traffic, a thousand times before, but all it took was one distracted moment that day, and a man arguing with his wife on his motorbike. Before she could register her surprise, she heard the heavy screech of tyres and found herself hurtling onto the road with a force that she couldn't ever recall experiencing in her life. In what seemed like a fraction of a second, she was laid unfurled on the tar road, facing the blindingly bright noon sky, wondering if this was the one moment her entire life came down to. As her eyes fluttered, she thought of Lakshmi, the one person who mattered more to her than her own life. The image of her daughter that came to her mind was the young girl that she used to be – the girl who would run circles around the kitchen in delight when she agreed to fry her favourite plantain chips, the girl who would hold on to Kamala's saree pallu while she fed crows on the terrace, the girl who would hug her tightly at night even when Kamala's blouse was drenched with summer sweat. As she tried to move her hands and legs, feeling an urgent need to say something to her daughter, she found her thoughts slowly becoming speckled before they swirled and closed in on her.

*

For what seemed like a very long time, Kamala felt surrounded by darkness. Her head hurt to think and her mind felt completely blank. She heard a few voices around her which seemed very distant. One of them, a soft female voice, came close to her and asked, 'Can you tell me your name?'

She wanted to open her eyes to look at where she was, but her eyes refused to follow her instructions.

'Lakshmi?' Kamala asked. The voice didn't respond, and she said, 'Lakshmi,' definitively before getting submerged in darkness again.

The next time Kamala came to, a few flashes of memory came to her – the beep of the motorbike's horn that arrived a little too late, the acrid smell of hot melting tar on the road beneath her as she fell, the all-consuming need she had felt to hold Lakshmi in her arms. She managed to flutter her eyes open, and the world rushed to her in all its brightness, although it took her a while to make out its distinct shapes. She realised that she was in a dim hospital room, next to a faintly beeping machine.

As she looked around the room, she felt a wave of relief to see the familiar profile of Sundu sitting on a chair next to her. She looked at Kamala and said, 'Good, you are awake again. The doctors have left for the night. I decided to stay, just in case.'

Kamala wanted to ask 'Just in case of what?' but didn't say anything. Sundu continued, 'How many times have I told you to take an auto instead of walking in the noon heat? You never listen.'

Sundu removed her spectacles and rubbed her eyes, 'Thank goodness it was only a lightweight TVS-50 that this man was driving. The doctors said that you escaped lightly with a mild concussion and a fracture.' Kamala looked down at herself and noticed the bandages that covered her arms, although her entire body felt quite numb. She found herself drifting off to sleep again.

Close to midnight, the time spelt out by a big clock on the wall, Kamala was wide awake again. It was extremely quiet except for the gentle noise of the air conditioner vent rustling the window blinds. Sundu was still propped up in her chair, wearing a saree in a colour that she liked to call parrot green, reading something on her phone.

'Sundu,' Kamala murmured. 'You know, when the bike hit me, all I could think about was Lakshmi and how angry she had been with me when she left home.'

'Lakshmi is not angry with you,' Sundu responded gently. 'She just called me while you were asleep, and I told her that it was nothing to worry herself about in the middle of her exams.'

'I need to go see her,' Kamala spoke urgently.

Sundu eyed her friend with concern for a minute, but with the twitch forming in the corner of her lips, Kamala knew that she was going to say something that she considered to be funny. 'Too bad that you needed a literal knock in the head to see some sense.' Sundu quipped.

She then looked down at Kamala with more seriousness, 'In that case, you should definitely go see her. Take some time off from work.'

'Will you come with?' asked Kamala. Usually, she hated doing what she thought of as imposing on other people, even when it came to Sundu. But something about this accident had made her feel different, almost as if it had cleared some congestion between her mind and her throat.

Sundu looked surprised but openly pleased at being asked for help. 'Yes, I think I can come with you. I haven't taken any holidays since the beginning of the year anyway. Let me speak to my assistant about it.'

Kamala wanted to protested that Sundu should let her arrange and pay for it all, considering it was her request, but she felt too tired to argue, and it felt good to let her friend take care of things.

She thanked Sundu, who simply swatted her phone in her direction.

*

'Hello, hello, hello,' Kamala greeted Reva and Jason, the second and third hellos added by the heavy dose of painkillers she had just been administered.

'I am so glad that you are OK,' Reva exclaimed, dragging a chair to sit closer to her bed. 'We just met Sundu Aunty on the way here. She said you should be out of here in no time.'

Jason, who stood with his hands in the pocket of his shorts, eyed the various apparatus around the room studiously before asking, 'Hope you're feeling better?'

'Fantastic. First class,' Kamala said grandly and, in the chance that she hadn't managed to entirely convey how she was feeling, added, 'Fit as a fiddle.'

Kamala felt pleased with herself for being so witty when she noticed Reva and Jason exchange amused glances with each other.

'I am practising my English because I am going to your country very soon,' Kamala announced to Jason.

'Oh, are you visiting Lakshmi?' Jason asked, as Reva added, 'That's great!'

The mention of Lakshmi's name made Kamala wrinkle her brows. Her head was feeling fuzzy, and she had a feeling that she was forgetting something – a puzzle, or a riddle that she had needed help solving. 'Lakshmi is a lesbian it seems,' she remembered. 'She told me when she was visiting me.'

Jason opened his mouth to say something, but Reva spoke first. 'Aunty, it is a really good thing that she trusted you enough to tell you. My friends from college, now in their thirties, have still not told their parents.'

'There are so many of them these days?' Kamala marvelled, with wide-eyed surprise.

A nurse in a white saree came in carrying a meal tray containing idlis and sambar for Kamala and, noticing that she had visitors, came back with a cup of coffee just for Jason.

'This food is from the hotel next door. Who knows what kind of oil they use for cooking,' Kamala said, eyeing her very red sambar disapprovingly.

'I actually brought mor kozhambu for you,' Jason announced, but the way he pronounced it, Kamala wondered how he had somehow managed to pack the capital of Sri Lanka into the small Tupperware container that he produced from his bag. She nodded in recognition as she smelled the distinct aroma of tempered curd and spice. She would have usually insisted that all this fuss over her was unnecessary, but that day, she felt openly delighted that someone had taken the trouble to cook something for her.

'This is very good, Jason,' she said, eating some of the mor kozhambu with rice, while gesturing to Jason and Reva to eat the idlis and not waste any food. 'A gold ring for the hands of the chef who cooked this,' she murmured in Tamil, which Reva translated, making Jason's cheeks turn the colour of the pumpkins that he had added to the kozhambu.

As Kamala reclined back on her bed after eating, she felt the world pleasantly come in and out of focus, as if it were playing hide and seek with her.

'Lakshmi and I used to play hide and seek when she was younger,' she recalled aloud. 'She would always hide behind the well at the back of Grand Life Apartments, and I would pretend to have a tough time finding her.' She giggled aloud at the memory of Lakshmi's disappointed face at being found. 'Well, the apartment and well may not be around for much longer, I suppose.' She sighed.

'You shouldn't be worrying about all that now, Aunty. You just take rest.' Reva leant forward to place her hand on Kamala's shoulder but stopped herself on seeing the bandages on her arm.

'Anyways, everything is in God's hands,' Kamala said, closing her eyes in prayer. She thought of the beatific smile of her favourite god, the one who played mischievous pranks to steal butter from milk-maids, and fell into the deepest sleep she could ever remember having.

*

Kamala was discharged after two days in hospital, with instructions to rest for a few weeks until her elbow healed. It was her first week of being stuck at home, and she already missed the purposefulness of going to work and the daily social interactions that entailed. There were only that many soaps that she could watch on the television and so many games of Solitaire she could play on her laptop while waiting for the day to go by. Whenever she felt guilty for whiling her time away with what she considered as empty pastimes, she would virtuously switch on religious TV channels that showed live coverage from temples and let the sounds of chanting hymns and bells make her drift off to sleep on the sofa.

A few visitors apart from Sundu dropped by – relatives, colleagues and acquaintances – to whom she kept repeating the story of how the accident happened ('Two-wheeler drivers on the roads these days are crazy-o-crazy,' everyone gave their uniform pronouncement) and how she escaped with minor injuries through god's grace ('We are just on our way to Tirupati next week – we will thank the Lord at his abode personally,' more than one person had offered).

Lakshmi had called her a couple of times since the accident, and her voice had been concerned enough to show that she cared but also withdrawn enough to indicate that she did not want to engage in topics of conversation outside of her mother's health.

Kamala, on her part, also replied carefully, as if she were reading out a typed medical report. 'The swelling on the left ankle has subsided briefly, but the right elbow requires immobilisation from a sling for three weeks,' she had last confirmed. She didn't mention anything about her migraine, which still announced its loud presence in her head at regular intervals.

Downstairs, she heard a clanging of the front gates, and she walked over to the kitchen window to see who it was. It was Salim, rolling a gas cylinder inside the gates of the apartments, closely followed by a tailless brown dog. He bent down to give the dog something from his pocket before shooing it out and closing the gates from inside.

'*Maami, sowkiyama?*' he greeted her in the exaggerated brahminical Tamil that he used with her, which Kamala gathered to be less for her benefit, and more for his entertainment. 'I heard you recently knocked down a two-wheeler.'

'No, the two-wheeler knocked me down,' she corrected him, and Salim responded by smiling impishly at her.

'Thank you for bringing this over so quickly, Salim. I had missed the last delivery while I was in the hospital.' She ushered him inside. He wheeled the red cylinder along the floor of her living room and into the kitchen, his hand making quick circular motions as if he imagined himself to be nearing the finish line at a car race.

'How is your mother doing?' she enquired. She had known Salim and his mother from when Salim was still a toddler running around Diamond General Stores with nothing but a thread around his waist. His mother used to manage the till while also trying to teach her son to count by pointing out the numbers on the measuring scale.

'She was not keeping well but is fine now. She asked me to bring this for you,' he said, bringing out two bars of peanut candies in see-through plastic packaging – the kind Kamala had added unfailingly to her monthly orders at the store for the last decade.

She was touched by the thoughtfulness of the gesture. 'Wait a minute.' She walked purposefully into the kitchen. She had set aside some of Lakshmi's foreign chocolates – the cheapest ones for Salim and his mother – but she changed her mind and brought out the nice ones that came in a pink clasped box decorated with delicate gold trimming.

'This is very nice, *Maami*, thank you,' Salim exclaimed, his affected dialect slipping in surprise.

'By the way, *Maami*,' he hesitated as he was just about to leave, 'my mother and I were passing by the apartments when we saw a man throw something against the window below.'

'Oh, you did?' Kamala asked, looking up from the TV remote that she was about to press.

'Yeah, my mother asked me to be quiet and not act like a hero when I said I will go stop him.'

'Your mother is correct. You should always listen to her.' Kamala nodded. 'No point in getting involved with these thugs.'

'Well, unless you are Rajni.' Salim shrugged, as if he was stating the obvious. 'Then you can fight them all away single-handed.' He then moved his hands and elbows to mimic fending off an attacker in a hero-like way like the famous actor.

'All that fighting in the cinemas is staged. It is not real,' she said worriedly, wondering if the violence portrayed in lamentable new Tamil films was putting ideas into young boys like Salim.

'No, it is real,' Salim insisted.

'What nonsense are you saying? It is not,' Kamala argued, and they went back and forth like this for a while until Salim chuckled.

'You little rascal,' Kamala chided him. She paid him a little extra for the cylinder and candies and asked him to spend it on books for school, but she knew very well that it would go towards the cost of an overpriced movie ticket for the new Rajni movie on release the following week.

Around seven in the evening, Sundu came by with dinner, thinking that Kamala was still out of cooking gas. 'You wouldn't believe the amount of water that the tenant living downstairs consumes every day,' Sundu complained, unpacking the idlis that she had bought at Saravana Bhavan on the way to Kamala's house. 'I have to switch on the motor twice a week to fill up the water tank. If he gets to know that I am going to be away, he will squander away the water from the entire tank in a day, as if his forefathers' money paid for it.'

'Doesn't he just live by himself? What does he need all that water for?' Kamala asked in outraged solidarity, although she knew that Sundu could be quite peculiar when it came to certain aspects of money. Although she owned two houses and drove an expensive car, she still took care to turn off the power switch of her microwave and television every night before going to bed.

'Heaven knows.' Sundu shrugged, mollified briefly. 'So, are you sure you are managing all right by yourself and don't need a full-time nurse at home?' she asked, looking at Kamala while also arranging the idlis on a stainless steel plate.

'Yes, I am. I don't want a stranger poking around the house when I am not looking,' Kamala replied. 'Why are you eating only one idli?'

'Oh, I told you about my new diet, did I not? It is called intermittent fasting. I can't eat anything after five in the evening. However, today, I thought I would give you company and have just one idli.' She clutched the plate with the precious solitary idli in her hand and added brightly, 'I think this diet really works. I have already lost two kilos!'

'Yes, I can see that your salwar is a little loose around your waist,' Kamala lied kindly.

Sundu picked up an avocado from the vegetable basket in the kitchen and held it up in her fingers. 'What were you planning on making with this?'

'Not sure. Jason gave it to me, asking me to try it.'

'I have never eaten it either, although I have noticed that it costs even more than an Alphonso mango. Let's see what all the fuss is about,' said Sundu, picking up a knife and running it through the avocado's middle. Kamala thought her culinary curiosity might have something to do with the fact that she was still hungry from eating just that one idli.

'Is it supposed to be eaten as a sweet or savoury?' Sundu raised her eyebrow questioningly at the avocado, which was in no position to answer primarily on account of being sliced into two.

'Jason said it could be eaten either way.' Kamala shrugged.

They both agreed on an experiment where Kamala would eat her half with a seasoning of chilli powder and salt, while Sundu would eat hers with sugar, and they would then judge which one tasted better. Sundu sliced the avocado into green cubes and popped a couple of pieces in her mouth before dividing it into two bowls.

'So, about this apartment,' Sundu spooned a generous helping of sugar into her bowl, 'is Mani planning to contest the case in court?'

'Yes, he is. Although I think it's a lost cause trying to go to court against these politicians, don't you think?' Kamala ate a spoonful of her spiced avocado and made a face to show mild disappointment. 'I have been meaning to ask you about the court case — '

'Yes, I can represent the apartments.' Sundu answered the question even before Kamala could complete her sentence.

'Mani will be glad to hear that.' Kamala nodded, knowing that it was implied that she was glad to hear that herself. 'Aren't you already very busy, though?'

'Well, I can hand over something else to a junior lawyer, I guess.' Sundu shrugged.

Kamala reached for a spoonful of sugared avocado and contemplated for a moment before pronouncing, 'You know what we should make with this? A chutney.'

'Yes, I think that will be best,' nodded Sundu approvingly. 'By the way, for our London visit, I asked my assistant to arrange for our visas. She said that it will make the visa application easier if we get an invitation letter from Lakshmi,' she continued, deploying her brisk work-voice.

'Actually,' Kamala started bravely but soon lost courage for what she was about to say next. 'I am not planning on telling her that we are coming.'

She took their empty dishes towards the sink without looking at Sundu. She didn't want to tell Lakshmi about her visit because she was afraid of her daughter's reaction. What if she asked her not to come, or worse, ignored her message and stopped talking with her again?

Kamala walked to the sink and started washing the piled dishes awkwardly with one hand. Sundu stared at her, her eyes looking enlarged through her bifocal glasses. Kamala waited for Sundu to berate her, but Sundu simply said, 'Why are you washing these dishes now? Let me help you wash and clean up everything after the TV serials are over.'

11

Revathi

Do you want the rose or the regular facial, *akka*?' the girl at the beauty parlour asked Reva.

'The regular one, please,' said Reva, mainly because it was five hundred rupees cheaper and she knew that she wouldn't be able to tell the difference.

'You should get the rose facial,' the girl continued, standing very close to her and inspecting her face. 'It will help to whiten your dark skin colour.'

'No, that's OK, my complexion is fine,' said Reva defensively.

The frail girl, who could hardly be fifteen, stepped back from Reva and hopped from one foot to the other in a sparrow-like manner while continuing to look at Reva's face disapprovingly. Her hair was tied up in a high knot held together by multiple pins and decorated with plastic pearls. It was a hairstyle for a much older person, and Reva guessed that someone in the parlour must have attempted practising bridal hairstyles on her. Her neck and hands were as dark as Reva's, but her face looked pale with a thick layer of make-up.

'The rose facial comes with an extra massage for your head and neck, *akka*. Very good if you are sitting in a chair all day,' she continued mulishly, disregarding Reva's answer.

'Fine. The rose, then,' Reva relented. Noticing the gleam of victory in the girl's eyes, she knew that she should have agreed to the facial in exchange for a discount like any other sensible customer would have done.

'Ah! You got suckered, too. That is how I ended up getting some coconut deep-conditioning hair treatment when all I wanted was a pedicure,' laughed Shreya. She was sitting on a tall chair facing a mirror, her hair swallowed by a giant helmet.

'Treatments here are still a fraction of the cost in the US, you know?' continued Shreya. Reva nodded and pulled a chair next to her so that they could both now face the silver-flecked mirror and watch their reflections speak to each other.

They were approached by another young girl with a mop who smiled shyly at them and asked them to lift their legs so that she could drag the grey confetti strips of her mop underneath their chairs. Reva noticed her glance admiringly at Shreya and her outfit – white jeans and a sleeveless green top that skimmed her lean frame. Shreya gave the girl a quick, confident smile, and in her smile, she seemed to acknowledge this appreciation as something that happened to her every day.

Although Reva had always admired Shreya's air of confidence, this smile made Reva recall a specific moment from several years ago. They had both travelled to Goa as part of a girls' trip and were sharing a room when Reva inadvertently walked into Shreya scrutinising herself in the mirror. Not realising that the door was open, Shreya had been pinching the part of her stomach above her jeans' waistline and looking into the bathroom mirror with an expression between self-loathing and disgust. Reva had been surprised, and even strangely comforted, to realise that even obviously beautiful women were plagued by a sense of unhappiness over the way their bodies looked.

'A penny for your thoughts,' Shreya asked.

'I was thinking about our Goa trip, many years ago,' said Reva, not entirely lying.

'Yes, it was so much fun! We should go on a girls' trip again!'

'We totally should,' Reva agreed, although she knew that they wouldn't, considering that all the girls from that trip would need to be uprooted from their families across various corners of the world in order to make it happen.

The sparrow-like girl had quietly flitted under Reva's legs and placed her feet inside a large blue plastic tub. She filled it with hot water. 'Too hot?' she asked Reva, watching her toes curl in discomfort.

'Yes, please add some cold water.'

'It has to be this hot – otherwise, it will become cold very quickly,' the sparrow-girl dismissed her request. She then picked one of Reva's legs and started rubbing it vigorously, in the manner of someone washing a cooking vessel with stubborn burnt bits stuck at the bottom. Reva was about to protest, but both the heat of the water and the rubbing started feeling pleasantly abrasive and so she leant back in her chair.

Shreya's phone chirped for her attention and, from the way Shreya smiled indulgently at the message, Reva guessed that the message was from her boyfriend. Shreya took a photo of their reflection in the mirror, peered closely at her phone and then chuckled. Conscious that she was having a conversation with her thumbs, she showed Reva her phone – in reply to her photo, her boyfriend had sent an emoticon of a blonde girl sitting under a hair helmet.

Reva laughed on cue, although what she really wanted to do was roll her eyes. This was exactly the sort of thing that the two of them would have rolled their eyes together at before. Although they had been friends for over a decade, they had been closest when the two of them had been the only single ones left from their large group of girls from high school. Before Shreya had left for the US, they would spend entire weekends together, browsing in second-hand bookshops that smelled of naphthalene balls, and watching movies in heavily air-conditioned theatres where they would need to wrap their dupattas around their shoulders for warmth. Reva's mother would ask in frustration, 'Why don't the two of you spend more time looking for suitable boys instead of spending all this time together?' Once, she had even added hopefully, 'Does Shreya have an older brother?'

'So, you never gave me the detailed debrief after meeting Karthik,' Shreya's reflection asked Reva's. Her tone of voice was conspiratorial, rubber-banding to its previous closeness whenever they were both in the same city.

Reva raised one shoulder at the mirror. 'I am going to meet him again. Get to know him better.'

'What were your first impressions, though?' Shreya pressed.

'He is nice, and also quite normal compared to the really weird guys in their forties that my mum has been sending my way recently,' Reva admitted.

'So, how about Jason?' A teasing note entered Shreya's voice.

'What about him?' Reva raised her eyebrows, although she knew exactly what Shreya was asking.

'Well, you've been spending a lot of time with him, haven't you?'

'I do like him—' said Reva and watched a triumphant expression cross Shreya's face in the mirror '—as a friend.' Shreya's expression turned into an overdone sad face, making Reva laugh. Reva realised as she said this, that Jason exuded an air that was the equivalent of an all-caps 'UNAVAILABLE' sign hanging around his shoulders, which had made her fall into an easy friendship with him, and not consider much else.

'Well, friendship can change into something else very quickly,' said Shreya with the encouraging optimism that dragged a chair and joined the conversation whenever two friends speculated about dating prospects.

The sparrow-girl, whose name turned out to be Chitra, was now showing Reva a large tub of nail polish bottles to choose from. She inspected the bottles, feeling like something other than the light pink colour that she usually chose for her feet. She picked a light blue, the colour of a swimming pool floor after its water had been drained.

'That's a cool colour.' Shreya nodded approvingly.

With the open nail polish bottle in hand, Chitra peered around Reva's legs to stare at someone behind her. She then leant forward and whispered to them, 'Look at the two ladies there?'

Reva turned first, followed by Shreya. There were two salwar-kameez clad, middle-aged women with their heads covered, sitting underneath a shampoo advertisement featuring a bare-shouldered woman with lustrous brown locks. They were browsing through film magazines while giving occasional instructions to the ladies working on their feet.

'They are married to the same guy. One husband, two wives,' Chitra continued whispering conspiratorially.

'What?' asked Reva, and both she and Shreya turned back to look in unison. It was perhaps not very uncommon for someone to have two wives, but both wives being close enough to spend quality time together, getting pedicures together, was certainly peculiar. Reva began to suspect that Chitra was making all this up, but this didn't stop them from bursting into giggles.

Pleased that she had made them laugh, Chitra continued making gleeful comments – 'The husband will need a lot of headache pills!' or 'They look like sisters – do you think they are sisters with one husband?' – until Reva asked her to stop, mainly because of the suspicious glances now being directed at them from that corner.

'Are you married, *akka*?' Chitra looked up from Reva's feet, revealing a gap in the front of her mouth where a tooth used to be.

'No,' Reva replied, busying herself with inspecting whether her nails had dried or not.

'Not sure if you are interested in applying for the position of the third wife?' Shreya joked, and all three of them burst into laughter. Although Reva laughed the loudest, the fact that Shreya's statement applied only to Reva and not to both of them stung her just a small, tiny bit.

*

'Whatever we decide, the buck stops here,' Subbu said to his team of five, jabbing his ballpoint pen on the table for effect. Reva's manager had just returned from a trip to their head office in California and, in the way that some people brought back souvenirs, he brought back new catchphrases from his meetings abroad and flaunted them. Reva checked the time on her phone to see how many more minutes of the team meeting were left to endure.

'Rightly said, Subbu,' Vijay piped up. 'Ajith,' he swivelled his chair sharply and addressed one of the junior employees in their team, 'do you know why we have seen a decline in the month-on-month sales of our B56 software?'

Ajith, a spectacled, cherubic twenty-two-year-old who had been in their team for less than two months, looked distraught to be questioned and directed befuddled eyes towards Reva for help.

'It is the seasonality in procurement by businesses,' Vijay explained before Reva could say anything. Reva rolled her eyes – it was just like Vijay to ask a question so that he could give the answer himself.

'Well spotted, Vijay,' Subbu said. This seemed to be the pattern of their weekly meetings – Subbu and Vijay generally agreeing with each other on every topic that came up for discussion. Reva started answering her work emails on her laptop as they continued talking.

'And you, Revathi,' Subbu now addressed her, which made her look up with a start.

'I want you to hand over the new product launch to Vijay.'

'What? But why?' she asked, picking up her coffee mug instinctively as a crutch to continue this conversation.

'We can discuss the particulars later,' Subbu dismissed her as Vijay gave her a simpering smile.

Back at her desk, Reva wished that she had come back with a sharper retort to challenge Subbu rather than a weak 'but why?'. Subbu was making her give away one of the projects that she had spent the last few months toiling over, and now Vijay was going to take all the credit for it by just moving it over the finish line.

Around half an hour after the meeting, Vijay slinked to her desk and sat on the chair next to her, leaning it back as far as it would allow. He then opened a pack of Lay's crisps that he had carried in his hand and started crunching loudly.

'I thought we could discuss the project handover if you have time, that is?' He dug his hand into the crisp packet and brought up two crisps stuck to each other. He examined the stuck crisps with interest before looking up at Reva for a response.

'We can actually discuss it now. Let me open the last presentation that I had made.' Reva clicked her mouse furiously, staring at her screen.

'I know you think that I don't deserve this promotion,' Vijay continued, rolling his chair closer to her.

'Well, I don't think that exactly,' she started, although that was exactly what she thought. 'But yes, I was under the impression that I would get promoted this quarter.'

'You know what, maybe the stars will align for you next quarter,' he said in a manner that was almost sincere, and Reva wondered for a short minute whether she had judged him too harshly.

'Hey, listen,' he continued in the same easy, friendly tone. 'Do you want to continue managing this project so that you can build your profile for your promotion? I can speak to Subbu about it. Or wait, here's an idea – why don't we work on it together?'

He said it so smoothly that her instinctive reaction was to agree with him. She then looked at him, reclined with the relaxed air of someone on a deck chair by the beach, and knew that it was a terrible idea. In reality, she would probably continue to do all the work, as she had been doing so far, while Vijay would most certainly swoop in at the end and take credit for it.

She translated what she really wanted to say into office-speak. 'Thanks for offering, Vijay. However, it may be better for our clients to just have one point of contact leading the project,' she said, shrugging, her voice matching his light and friendly tone.

'Cool, no issues. Think about it and let me know,' he replied, although Reva had just let him know.

As she watched him walk away, leaving his empty crisps packet casually at an unmanned desk so that it would be somebody else's problem, she knew that he would be the sort of person who would continue to get rewarded for building the right connections, and she would not be able to catch up with him, however hard she worked.

When she relayed this conversation to Ranji over lunch, Ranji responded with appropriate sympathetic clucks. 'You know, I saw him around the office recently. He carries a comb around in his pocket and uses it whenever he comes across a reflective surface, right?'

'Yes! The very same,' said Reva, laughing. 'There is a rumour that someone actually saw him use the back of a spoon once.'

Ranji chuckled loudly in response. 'You are still going to look for a new job, right? How is that going?'

'I am going to start applying today,' Reva said, realising, even as she said it, that she had been foolish in waiting and hoping that things would work out in her current situation, rather than make the temporary bruising effort to change things.

'That's very good.' Ranji proffered her encouragement while opening her tiffin box, which had two rotis neatly folded into triangles in one container and potato curry in the other. 'I have been thinking that maybe once I stop working, I can start one of those food blogs that contain healthy, colourful recipes for kids, you know? I have always wanted to make lunches of the kind that I've seen on these mummy blogs – like quinoa upma or spinach macaroni – but never had the time.' She looked down at her lunchbox reproachfully for not containing any ingredients with bloggable health benefits.

Reva had seen these websites, written and forwarded by friends, containing painstakingly prepared lunches for kids who would probably try to stuff them in their mouths in under five minutes so that they could go out and play during their lunch break. The thought of applying Ranji's analytical mind that could dissect and recompile a balance sheet in a morning's work to arranging a coriander sprig with the right amount of artfulness on top of an idli, slightly bothered her. But she knew that it was impossible to insert oneself into another person's reality and assume things on their behalf. 'I am sure if you do decide to write a food blog, it would be a pretty awesome one,' she said instead.

Later that evening, Reva wrote the cover letters for the jobs that she had been interested in and reached out to a few ex-colleagues who had left to join tech start-ups that were growing in strength in the city. Once she made the headway she wanted to make that day, she walked around the house and uncharacteristically folded her clothes, cleaned the fridge and reviewed the large stack of post that she had ignored for a while. She then opened her laptop again and re-read the entire message trail between her and Karthik over the last week – they had been talking almost every day, and the most recent messages were regarding the logistics of their next in-person 'catch-up', as they called it. Karthik had asked whether she wanted to come with him for a Carnatic music concert, and she confirmed that she was free. After a moment, she added that she was looking forward to it, in order to compensate for the fact that she had taken almost the entire day to respond, while he always made it a point to respond to her messages immediately.

*

Later the next evening, Reva and Kamala were seated on Jason's sofa, the sweet smell of boiling sugar wafting in from Jason's kitchen.

'I am just adding the finishing touches now.' Jason peeped out of his kitchen for a moment before disappearing again. He had called them both to ask their opinion on a dish that he was planning to share with his head chef at the restaurant, and just from the fact that he had mustered the courage to ask them for feedback, Reva gathered that this was quite important to him.

She looked around his apartment as they waited – his apartment was sparsely decorated and laid out very similar to hers, with mosaic flooring and rust-coloured ceiling fans. However, there were touches of foreignness in the room that caught her eye – a strappy athletic backpack of the type that she usually saw friends elsewhere on social media strike heroic hiking poses with, an expensive laptop covered carelessly in faded stickers and black outdoor sandals left askew in the middle of the living room.

Jason came out of his kitchen with two small glass bowls and an expectant smile. Kamala sat up straighter on Jason's sofa taking on the air of scrutiny that surrounded judges in reality cooking shows.

'It is my take on the rava payasam, or should I say Indian pudding?' Jason grinned.

'Indian pudding,' Reva repeated, bemused. She knew payasam as the sweet and creamy dish with the simple aftertaste of cardamom that her mother made every year for her birthday, irrespective of whether she was around to celebrate it with her or not. She had a spoon of Jason's payasam, and while it tasted nothing like her mother's she had to admit that it was surprisingly nice. It was silky and intensely milky and carried a whiff of something flowery.

'Is this flavoured with . . . ?' She trailed off, taking another spoonful to help complete her sentence.

Jason nodded encouragingly, and when she tilted her head at him questioningly, said, 'Lychee. The fruit has overtones of rose, so I thought it would work well in this dish.'

'It's actually really good.' The taste of lychee was subtly woven through, and it tasted even better once she managed to suspend her memory of what the original payasam tasted like.

Kamala, whose left arm was still in a sling, held the bowl on her lap and ate a few ruminative spoonfuls. 'Payasam doesn't taste like this,' she said, her usually gentle tone becoming assertive when it came to talking about food she knew. 'This tastes like ice cream.' And as if that comparison wasn't specific enough to show how far from a payasam it was, she added, 'Like tutti-frutti ice cream.'

'We are probably not Jason's restaurant's target audience, you know,' Reva replied jokingly, using the term 'we' generously, as she mainly meant Kamala. She was glad to notice that Jason hadn't quite heard Kamala's feedback and was distracted by the ringing of his phone. He mouthed an apology in their direction before picking up the call.

Reva watched the easy smile on his face get replaced by a look of shock. She heard him mutter a quiet, terse 'bastard,' before dropping his phone on the sofa in a daze. He then blinked a few times and turned to Reva and Kamala in surprise, as if he couldn't understand what they were doing in his apartment.

'What's wrong?' Kamala asked immediately.

Jason walked purposefully into his kitchen without replying. Reva and Kamala exchanged a concerned glance and, after a moment's hesitation, followed him into his kitchen.

Jason was standing at a small dining table in the middle, chopping potatoes with all his strength, as if slicing them were the only thing that mattered.

'You need to wash them first here,' Reva said, feeling the compulsive need to say something. She didn't know why she added the 'here' – potatoes presumably grew under the soil everywhere in the world.

'Everything all right with your mother and father?' Kamala was looking concerned.

'Yes,' he replied tersely. 'Yes, they are fine.' He took a deep breath and picked up an onion.

'So, I just heard that Emma is getting married,' he continued, peeling the onion with a furiousness that belied the steely politeness of his voice. 'To one of my best friends,' his voice finally losing its politeness as he spat out the name, 'Chris.'

'Oh, Jason, I am so sorry to hear that.' Reva remembered how much it had hurt when she learnt about her ex-boyfriend Sebastian's wedding, even when she had thought that she was over him.

Kamala's brows were furrowed in concentration as she tried to comprehend what Jason had just told them. For a while, both Reva and Kamala didn't say anything, but simply looked at Jason warily as he continued chopping potatoes with the furious energy that came with misplaced anger.

'This Emma is a donkey,' Kamala suddenly declared, making both Reva and Jason blink at her in surprise.

'She is like a donkey that doesn't know the smell of camphor,' Kamala further explained, and Reva nodded in comprehension. She told Jason that he was being compared to the complex, woody perfume of camphor, the value of which was understood by only those refined enough to appreciate it. She didn't add that whenever her mother used this Tamil phrase with her, Reva was the donkey.

Jason seemed to be at a genuine loss for words, but Reva was glad to notice that he had at least given the chopping of potatoes a rest.

'Don't mind me. Sometimes, I don't know the right things to say.' Kamala sighed and looked out the window, where the sun was setting behind the mango tree, giving the leaves a golden halo.

'No, no.' Jason stared at Kamala, then said slowly, 'That was *exactly* the right thing to say.'

12

Jason

Jason had not been able to sleep all night. The thought of Emma and Chris together, delighting in the newness of their romance, sent a sharp stab of pain into his chest. He was glad that he was at least far away in India, as all his immediate instincts propelled him to land on Emma's doorstep and demand some kind of explanation.

He knew that he might have at least felt better if Emma had downgraded to someone smarmy and inconsiderate – someone who would have been a much inferior replacement to him. Chris, on the other hand, was actually a half-decent person, or at least had been.

Chris and Jason had become unlikely friends after a combined internship in a coffee percolator factory during high school – Chris's family owned the business and his internship had been a rite of passage for him, whereas Jason hadn't needed a reason beyond the hourly wage. Although Chris came from money, he was always careful to speak self-deprecatingly about his privilege. They had lost touch until a couple of years ago when Chris had moved to London after selling his family's factory. He now worked in banking and owned a penthouse in Notting Hill – all dark wood floors and bay windows. Jason recalled how he had introduced Emma to Chris at Chris's housewarming party, and how, later on the way home, Emma and Jason had laughed excessively while mimicking the posh accents at the party discussing holidays in summer homes and perils of expanding business ventures to Africa.

Like dregs in wine glasses caught in the bright glare of morning, his open laptop reminded him of his unnecessary online excesses of the night before. He had been looking at Emma's photos on her social network, bracing himself for photos of her and Chris – the first one would probably be cute but not too heavy – a sun-dappled selfie over brunch, possibly.

Noticing that there was nothing new on her profile, Jason had started looking at the photos that he had carried with him here on his laptop, ones that went all the way up to their initial months of dating, when they had taken that first giddy trip to Paris, when everything about each other had appeared new and shiny and exhilarating. Now, looking at how happy he had looked, even when completely drenched in rain, made him feel first sad, then angry. Angry at Emma for giving him this happiness, then wrenching it away. Fuelled by righteous anger, he had started typing, *Congratulations. So how long was I a fool for?* But, thankfully, the flaky internet connection had started acting up again, forcing him to restart his laptop. A few minutes later, he was glad that he hadn't sent that message and at least preserved a little bit of his dignity.

Now, he closed all his open photos and checked his email. A new email from Chris had made its way to him overnight. The email asked him, in colourful italics, to save a date in July the following year for the wedding of Emma and Chris. The first thought that came to Jason's mind, ironically, was that the loopy font of the email was the exact opposite of Emma's childlike and straight handwriting, pen pressed hard against the paper.

He swiftly got up from his laptop and got ready to go to work, not giving himself pause to further wallow in sadness. The auto that he took that day to work was even more old and rickety than usual, and the driver gleefully overpriced the trip, mainly due to the logistical convenience of Jason being from another country.

'Three hundred rupees, saar,' he said with a straight face, for a trip that the security guard at the hotel had negotiated for half the price just a few weeks ago.

This happened often with Jason, and he would usually let it slide, not wanting to haggle for what he thought translated to just a pound here or there. Today, he felt something like anger surge within him, not directed towards the driver, but towards himself for being such an easy target. He took out two hundred rupees: 'I think this is a fair price for this trip. Is it not?' He held out the notes and looked evenly at the driver.

'Not at all, saar. This much money will only get you to City Union Bank. This hotel is fifteen minutes away from there,' the driver, a short, balding man with a moustache, insisted righteously.

'I paid this just yesterday, and you have not even switched on the meter. Let me take down your vehicle number to report.' He was repeating something that he had heard Aneesh say.

The driver looked surprised and squared his shoulders in preparation of saying something indignant again. However, seeing the resolve on Jason's face, he changed his mind. 'Fine, saar.' He quickly took the money from Jason's hand, wished him a good day genially and went on his way, leaving behind a cloud of exhaust smoke and dust.

As Jason waited to cross the road at the traffic signal, he was approached by an old woman begging for some money. This was also a daily occurrence, and Jason would usually relent – there would always be some characteristic that would tug at his heart – a mother who looked too tired to even swat the flies that swarmed her baby's face, or a young girl standing barefoot on the melting hot tar road. He would find himself compelled to give them some money, feeling guilty for having so much more and not having done much to have deserved it. Now, he ignored the pleading eyes and voices. He didn't awkwardly shake his head as he sometimes did, but walked unapologetically, matching his gait with everyone else who behaved as if these beggars were invisible.

When he finally reached his corner of the kitchen, he was glad to start working and simply concentrate on the task at hand. He was making a lentil soup topped with foam, to be served in a cappuccino cup to locals who would sip it with a look of mild incredulity. He simmered, puréed and frothed on repeat, and the methodical act of cooking helped him to focus on the present and distracted him from thinking about anything else.

The head chef, a short, wiry man with salt-and-pepper hair, was making his rounds in that energetic, springy way of his that usually made Jason nervous. He stopped by to take a sip of Jason's soup.

'Good, I like the consistency, but it is a little blander than my original version,' he said, raising his eyebrows critically at Jason. He didn't wait for Jason to explain himself. 'Don't be stingy with the dhania – I mean coriander powder,' he explained as Jason nodded as attentively as he could. By now, he knew that the chef was only looking for acknowledgement of his instructions and not for any collaborative discussion on evolving his dishes.

The head chef clapped his hands to get everyone's attention for a team meeting. He wanted to talk about their new menu that was going to draw focus to local ingredients sourced from various parts of India.

'We want the best, most interesting ingredients for our food – even if that means we need to get mud crabs from Kerala or herbs all the way from Leh.'

Jason was standing at the back of the circle of chefs, distractedly staring into the distance. When he focused back to the present, his eyes met Aneesh's across the kitchen worktop. His friend mimed the act of sipping a beer, and Jason nodded back at him.

Later, when they were at their usual seats in the hotel bar, Aneesh declared, 'I think we work for a complete nutcase.' In a rather exaggerated imitation of the chef's nasal voice, he continued, 'We need to source the finest ingredients, even if it means flying to the moon and hand-picking the greyest rocks that we can find.' He chuckled and looked expectantly at Jason to contribute his share of rants.

'Yeah,' replied Jason absent-mindedly.

'*Dude*, what's up with you?'

'Nothing.' Jason rotated his pint of beer listlessly.

A waiter arrived with Aneesh's burger and fries. 'You must be homesick,' pronounced Aneesh, picking up a thin fry and rolling it in a spicy cheese gravy. 'How long have you been away from your family, girlfriend and the rest? Three months? Four months?'

'Yeah, I suppose.' Jason shrugged. He then said the next statement so softly that he could have been mistaken for speaking to himself. 'Well, my girlfriend and I actually broke up.'

'I am sorry to hear that. What happened?' exclaimed Aneesh, returning the burger that he had just picked up back to its plate.

'The usual story,' Jason adopted a casual tone. 'Emma felt that the relationship had run its course. But in reality, there was someone else. And this someone else also happens to be my close friend.' He lowered his head, unable to maintain his casual tone till the end.

'That sounds tough. Long-distance relationships are hard, dude.' Aneesh nodded commiseratingly.

'I guess.' Jason shrugged again. He watched Aneesh eye his burger hungrily before adjusting his face to an appropriately serious expression that fit their topic of conversation.

'Dude, it's OK – you can eat your burger.' He was half-smiling at Aneesh.

Aneesh grinned back and took a large bite of the burger, which oozed with very yellow cheese. With his mouth half-full, he muttered, 'Let's get out of here and get you a proper drink.'

They went to a smoky, dim-lit place near Anna Nagar that called itself a resto-pub. It played loud hip-hop music to which a group of young teenagers danced on world-unweary feet.

The waiter, a young man with a struggling goatee, seemed to recognise Aneesh and exclaimed excitedly, 'Mr Aneesh! We haven't seen you around for a long time. I thought you had left town without telling us.'

'What to say, the missus keeps me on a tight leash.' Aneesh mimicked cracking a whip, making the waiter laugh loudly.

'So, how did you meet this missus of yours?' Jason wanted to steer the conversation towards something other than Emma.

'We met through family. That, translated into Indian-English means that we had an arranged marriage.'

'Oh really! How well did you actually know each other before you got married?'

'We met in person only a handful of times, as we were working in different cities, but we did call each other almost every day for three months. We used to keep talking for hours through the night.' A soft look came over his face at the memory. He took a large gulp of his drink. 'Well, looking back, I have to admit that we clearly didn't know each other well when we got married. I knew some random facts about her – that she liked Ilayaraja's music and liked reading *Harry Potter*. In fact, I even read my first ever fiction book to impress her. It was one of those Chicken Soup ones – ?'

'A recipe book for chicken soups?' offered Jason, although that sounded a little improbable.

'No, dude, this was not about real soups . . .' He stared hard at his empty glass of rum, seemingly to help him jog his memory. 'It was called *Chicken Soup for the Ghost* – no, of course, I meant *Soul*, not *Ghost*,' Aneesh snorted. 'Anyways, it was all great until we got married. It was only after we started living together that I realised that she was completely mad,' he finished, although the statement was not made without an undertone of pride.

After sharing four more drinks, a few life philosophies on marriage and several ideas for restaurants that the two of them should start after quitting their current jobs (definitely not Indian fusion, both of them had vehemently agreed), they said their good-byes and Jason headed home.

It felt like a very natural extension of the evening to pick up the phone and dial Emma's number. She picked up on the fourth ring.

'Hello.' He could hear the lightness in her voice, as if she had just finished laughing before picking up the phone. The very sound unsettled him.

'Hi, Emma.' He spoke in the most normal tone that he could muster.

'*Jason!* Hi! How are you?' Caution now clouded Emma's voice.

'I just got your wedding email.' He inhaled to maintain a sense of calm. 'Congratulations.'

'Why, thank you!' she exclaimed. 'I am sorry that you had to hear about it this way. Chris must have just sent his entire email list to the wedding planner,' she added, a little nervously.

Jason's mind blanked in response.

' – You know how Chris likes planning in advance. He is a Virgo, after all,' Emma rambled on. This sort of statement about star signs that he would have thought to be endearing earlier, now struck him as being plain airheaded. He realised that he didn't want to hear any more about Chris, or rather, anything more from Emma at all.

'Well, congrats again, then,' he said, ending the call.

He sat down on his bed in a daze, unable to reach beyond the numbness that he had felt since morning. With the drowsiness and tiredness brought upon by life and alcohol, he fell asleep in a curled position on the bed, the phone still not far from his hand. However, even heartbreak had not numbed him enough for the mosquitoes that woke him up in the middle of the night, delivering painful bites around his exposed elbows and ankles. He got up to switch on the electronic mosquito repellant in the bedroom, feeling as if he were a passerby watching someone else's life unfold in a house that he hardly recognised. Engulfed by this surreal feeling, he fell into a deep, dreamless sleep.

13

Revathi

Reva slid Kamala's post underneath her door, taking care not to disturb the ants attracted to the flour kolam drawn outside. Kamala's door was unlocked, which she thought was rather surprising, considering that one of Kamala's favourite pastimes was regaling Reva with stories about robberies in their neighbourhood.

'Aunty?' she called out softly, walking inside the living room where a fan stirred the air overhead. She noticed Kamala seated in the corner of her sofa with a book on her lap, her head nodding gently in sleep. Reva's voice made her wake up with a start and look at her in wide-eyed surprise.

'Aunty, your door was left open,' Reva said in the reprimanding tone that the young used with the old once they had reached a certain age.

'I must have forgotten to close it.' Kamala sighed, placing the large book down on the sofa gingerly, as her left arm was still on a sling.

Before Reva could ask about her injured arm, Kamala answered, 'All recovering along well. Nothing to worry about,' and beckoned Reva to take a seat next to her. Reva noticed that the book was actually a photo album, with faded red poppies printed on its cover. Reva was familiar with these old albums, which were different from the bottomless photo reels of today. There were no please-like-me selfies, no peace signs flashed with two fingers in jubilant group pictures and no pictures of landscapes just because the sky looked moderately pink. These were carefully posed photos economised to capture as many memories as possible within a thumb-sized photo reel.

Kamala picked up the album and opened it with her right hand. Reva placed it across both their laps so that they could view it together.

'Lakshmi had just turned three here.' Kamala pointed to a photo by the beach where Kamala looked startlingly pretty in a green saree that billowed all around her in the sea breeze. Lakshmi was seated on her lap and smiling broadly, her chubby arms raised with a greater sense of victory than someone who had just won first place in the Olympics.

Adjacent to this, was a picture where Lakshmi was toddling her way towards a cat lying on the floor of the very same living room they were in now. 'Wait, don't you think that cat looks like Poons? Do you think it could be Poons' grandfather?' Reva asked, smiling. The cat had the same orange patches as Poons, apart from one large white patch across his nose, which made him appear as if he had just surfaced from burying his face in a carton of vanilla ice cream.

'Could be. Lakshmi used to call this cat Mum-mum, the same phrase that I used to tell her that it was time to eat.'

'My mother also used the same phrase to make me eat!' Reva laughed. They continued looking at more photos in the album, and Reva noticed that most of these sepia-tinted pictures that captured Lakshmi's growing-up years were taken in and around Grand Life Apartments. The garden in the pictures appeared lusher and wilder than it was now, and the garden was an unruly thicket of plantain leaves instead of concrete.

Kamala paused to point at a picture of a woman posing serenely on the building's terrace, where a badam tree lent its shade. 'That's my mother.' Reva noticed that Kamala's mother was dressed in the way widows were expected to, in a nine-yard ochre saree draped around a face that wasn't centred by a pottu, or framed by earrings, as Kamala's was.

As if she could read Reva's mind, Kamala said, 'My mother was actually very modern for her times. She insisted that I don't dress like that when I lost my husband.' She looked down at her bangles, and her voice sounded a little clouded when she spoke again, 'You know, once you no longer have a mother, nobody asks you the question, "Have you eaten?", with as much concern or care.'

Reva felt a sadness for the inevitable loss of her own mother rise within her, even though her mother was, at the very moment, inundating her phone with gifs of birds that chirped at her to have a lovely day.

Reva leant towards Kamala and asked in an exaggerated imitation of her own mother's admonishing tone, 'So, Kamala Aunty, have you eaten your lunch?'

'I have, *kanna*, thank you,' Kamala replied, pressing Reva on her head to bless her, but stopped just in time from saying the words of her prayer aloud.

Reva turned the album to the next page. 'Wait, is this Lakshmi dressed like a, er . . .' She stared at the picture of Lakshmi with what looked like flower cut-outs sprouting out of her head. 'I want to say, a bouquet, or is it a flowerpot?'

'Yes, flowerpot. I have to say that was not the best fancy dress costume I have made. She hated it!' Kamala laughed extra hard to recover from her previous emotional moment.

'I can see why.' Reva nodded solemnly as she turned to the next page.

*

'So, when are you meeting Karthik next?' Reva's mother asked almost immediately after answering her call. The conversation with

Kamala the day before had made Reva resolve to be more patient with her mother, but the patience was quickly giving way to the annoyance that crept in during every phone call.

'He is actually coming to pick me up in an hour,' she murmured, somewhat impatiently. She didn't want to let her mother know any other details about where she stood with Karthik, as it would most certainly be used as leverage for future conversational pinpricks.

'Good. I am glad that you are continuing to meet him, Revathi. Hope you come to a good decision quickly.' She was repeating something that she had said multiple times recently. Reva's annoyance threatened to flare into something bigger, but she reminded herself that her mother meant well and changed the topic of conversation to the rain that was predicted for later that day.

'If those good-for-nothing weather reporters on the news predicted rain, it means that the sun will shine brightly,' her mother declared with considerable authority. Reva had sensed the perceptible shift in the air that indicated the onset of rain earlier in the day, but she felt like agreeing with her mother on at least one thing and let it slide.

An hour later, the skies opened, sending down loud, noisy torrents of rain that shook the trees like rag dolls and turned the roads into muddy rivers. From her window, Reva watched Karthik jump out of an auto and place his hands uselessly above his head to protect himself from the rain. He took long strides towards the gates of the apartments and surfaced at her door moments after, stooping down to enter inside. He looked different from Reva's one-week-old memory of him, appearing taller and leaner. He was also dressed differently, wearing a green kurta that looked freshly creased from its recent memory of being folded on the shelves of Fabindia.

'I couldn't bring the car as our driver had gone to pick up my mum from work. We, unfortunately, need to take an auto from here to the concert,' he apologised.

'Sorry that the apartment looks a little messy,' Reva apologised modestly in return, gesturing towards the living room that she had spent two hours cleaning in anticipation of his visit.

'Come on, it's not messy at all.' He looked about him with interest.

Although Reva had thought she had tidied up her apartment satisfactorily, she now found herself critically eyeing the haphazard piles of magazines that could have been arranged neatly and the old fuzzy cactus by the windowsill that she suspected was no longer alive. Karthik walked towards her bookshelf as Reva knew he would. She had gone to the effort of rearranging her books so that the paperbacks with their candyfloss covers were at the back and those that reflected a discerning taste – the Zadie Smiths and the Murakamis – were at the front.

'Here, I got something for you,' he said, rifling through his bag and bringing out the book he had mentioned during their dinner. 'I am looking forward to hearing what you think,' he said, looking at her earnestly.

'Ah, my next favourite read,' she said in a light tone, which was meant to be sarcastic, but the sarcasm seemed to get lost by the time it reached Karthik.

'Would you like something to drink? Juice, coffee?' she asked, walking into the kitchen.

'Coffee is good.' He hesitated before following her inside.

It was a sparse room, with a mixer-grinder that her mother had bought with considerable money and hope standing unused in a corner, while the microwave stood importantly in the middle. She got out her bottle of Nescafé and shrugged. 'Got to go basic, unfortunately.'

'Sure, Nescafé is great,' offered Karthik solicitously.

She took out a sachet of milk from the fridge, poured it into two cups and placed it in the microwave. She stood next to Karthik by the window and watched the rain turn the dusty brown leaves of the mango tree into a bright, glossy green. Karthik stepped back in startled surprise as Poons jumped onto Reva's windowsill, twitching his head to shake water off his soaked fur.

'Karthik, meet Poons. Poons, meet Karthik,' Reva introduced the two of them with mock-formality and they both eyed each other with supreme wariness.

'Poons is our apartment cat, but he doesn't really live here,' she explained, placing cat food onto a fish-shaped ceramic bowl, both of which she had bought just for the occasion of Poons' visits.

'He is your version of the Schrödinger's cat then,' observed Karthik.

Reva narrowed her eyes and smiled, thinking that it was not exactly comparable to the physics thought experiment where a cat could be considered both alive and dead at the same time. At least a point in his favour was that he didn't try to explain the experiment to her.

'So, you are a cat person then?' asked Karthik, eyeing her while taking a sip of his coffee.

'I like animals in general. We were surrounded by all kinds growing up in the village, and my *paatti* used to make it a point to feed them all.' Although Reva pretended that this was all normal small talk, she knew that even seemingly harmless questions such as preference of pets, or references to quantum mechanics, took on the loaded meaning of a compatibility test in this fast-forward courtship.

'I never understood cats – I feel that they are always thinking about something sinister.' As if to support this observation, Poons gave Karthik a cold, unblinking stare until he averted his gaze from the feline.

'Poons is usually quite friendly, but then, he is also a cat,' laughed Reva.

As Karthik murmured appreciatively while drinking what Reva considered pretty mediocre coffee, she thought about a question that Shreya had asked her recently. 'So, do you *fancy* him or not?' she had asked in a teasing voice. Reva had shrugged evasively in response, although Shreya couldn't see her shrug over the phone. She now appraised Karthik as he continued to closely examine the things in her apartment as politely as possible – the books on her shelf, the Frida Kahlo print on her wall, the half-eaten pack of Krackjack biscuits next to her coffee. She liked that he didn't try to impress or flirt – at least not in the obvious way that some men did, either by inflating stories of their achievements or by moving their eyes furtively towards a bra strap that strayed away from her blouse. He just seemed to be interested in knowing more about her, and that, if not attractive, was at least endearing.

The rain was still pouring violently when they headed out for the concert. They continued getting wet inside the auto as well, although the protective plastic sheets draped on the sides flapped valiantly against the onslaught of the water pouring inside.

'So, you must be a fan of Carnatic music then?' Reva curled her toes so that her feet didn't get completely wet in the water pooled underneath.

'Yes, I am,' he answered, in that considered way that she came to identify as his natural manner of speaking. 'I learnt to play the flute growing up, and I enjoy listening to all kinds of classical Indian music. My mother still posts Carnatic music CDs to California, although I tell her repeatedly not to bother, as everything is now available online.' He smiled at her. 'How about yourself?'

'Well, I have never been musically inclined, unfortunately, but that's not for lack of trying on the part of my mother, though.'

Karthik looked back at her with a slightly horrified expression and apologised gravely, 'I am so sorry. I was just looking for company – in fact, this concert we are headed to is a flute recital by my old music teacher, and I just assumed that you would have liked to come. I should have really asked – '

'Don't worry about it! I can handle being exposed to a little bit of culture now and then.' She watched with amusement as Karthik clutched the side rails of the auto as its tyres sunk and emerged out of watery potholes.

Once they reached the Sabha, Reva started arguing with the driver who demanded an increased fare to what they had agreed upon. 'You only mentioned Nilgiris. This road is much farther from that. And driving through all this rain is not easy, madam.' The driver gave Reva a look of studied disdain. Reva sighed and paid him the extra money, not wanting to prolong standing in the rain. Karthik watched this exchange quietly, trying his best not to interfere.

The concert hall was not one of the fancy venues in Chennai with plush velvet seats and air conditioning, but a smaller affair with cream coloured cane chairs and slow-circling Khaitan fans on the ceiling that generated more noise than breeze. The rain seemed to have kept many of the concert-goers away, and there were hardly a dozen people in the hall.

Reva saw a familiar face from the corner of her eye and tried to duck into a seat quickly. However, before she could nudge Karthik towards a seat, Nataraj Uncle walked purposefully towards her and spoke in his booming voice, 'Hello, is that you, Revathi?'

She turned around and pretended to be taken by surprise. 'Hello, Nataraj Uncle! Been a while since I have seen you. How have you been?'

'All of us are doing good. I could barely recognise you – you have become so thin that you are soon going to vanish into nothing one of these days!' He rubbed his belly and laughed juicily, making her retreat a little. He looked at Karthik and then back at her and beamed. 'Revathi, you didn't tell me the good news! When did you get – ?'

'This is Karthik and he is a friend visiting from the US.' She interrupted Nataraj Uncle before he could finish his question.

'Oh, is that so?' asked Nataraj Uncle, looking sincerely confused at the concept of friendship between the two of them. In an effort to stop him from asking more questions, she asked about his daughter. 'How is Kavya? When is she visiting Chennai?'

'Kavya is doing good – you heard that she just finished her PhD in the US, didn't you?' Nataraj Uncle said, clapping Karthik on the back for no reason, making him wobble a little.

Reva nodded. She hadn't heard from Kavya, as they had drifted apart with the distance and now evolved into friends who caught up with each other once a year to exchange superficial updates about their life. She had, however, scrolled through the pictures of her graduation ceremony on social media, and noticed the scarlet graduation gowns, bubbly champagne flutes and the comment from Nataraj Uncle underneath the twenty-five odd pictures of his daughter: *Send more pictures. Regards, Nataraj.*

'She is also not yet married. You girls should get married, you know. Settle down. Career is important, but personal life is even more important at this age,' he said, with a sigh of frustration that she gathered was directed more towards his absent daughter than at her.

Reva was used to such statements by now and was usually capable of taking the leap of imagination to place herself in the parents' shoes and say something light-hearted – 'Kavya and I have to get married only to each other, Uncle! Where are all the eligible bachelors lining up at the doors?' or something to that effect. But now, she felt herself bristle at how someone who had not seen her for several years found it perfectly acceptable to lecture her on the shortcomings in her personal life.

Karthik coughed when he realised that Reva was taking too long to reply. 'Looks like the concert is going to start – we should get to our seats before the music police catch us.' He added a weak laugh at the end that made both Reva and Nataraj Uncle also laugh and nod in agreement.

'You should drop by our house when you are around the Kilpauk area.' Nataraj Uncle wagged his finger down at Reva before heading to his seat at the front of the Sabha.

'Definitely, Uncle,' nodding her head in acknowledgement, although she knew that she would definitely not.

Later, when they were in their seats, waiting for the faded crimson curtains to open, Reva whispered, 'Sorry you were caught in the middle of that. He means well, but you know how nosy people of that age usually get.'

'It is OK – we have all been there, and that's why we are here, aren't we?' Karthik smiled at her briefly before turning towards the opening stage.

The artist playing the flute, an old man in a flowing white beard, was seated cross-legged on a mat and flanked on either side by a violinist and a mridangam-percussionist, who both looked bored even before the concert had begun. Reva became restless less than five minutes into the concert. Karthik alternated between nodding his head in tune to the music and glancing at her guiltily.

All around her, there were middle-aged men and women attentively patting their thighs in rhythm to the music, some of them even looking up at the ceiling in rapture, as if this music opened some gateway to the heavens above. All Reva felt was an uncontrollable urge to check her phone. Her phone buzzed tele-pathically in response, eliciting a disapproving scowl from the old woman next to her. For the rest of the concert, Reva pretended to sit attentively still, feeling as if she were back in the classroom of a particularly strict maths teacher who used to throw well-aimed pieces of chalk at students who appeared distracted in class.

After the concert, they went backstage to say hello. The backstage area consisted of a single, large room where the musicians stood packing up their instruments into velvet-lined cases. Up close,

Karthik's flute teacher looked even older and walked with a slight stoop that wasn't evident when he was on stage. However, he recognised Karthik almost immediately, which made Reva think that Karthik probably came often to his concerts, perhaps every time he visited Chennai.

'Karthik! Been a very long time! Do you still practise the flute in America?' His teacher looked openly pleased to see Karthik.

'A little out of practise right now, though, I must admit. Wonderful concert – such a flawless rendition of Thyagaraja's *Endaro*. It was a pleasure to listen to,' enthused Karthik.

Reva observed Karthik with interest, as this was the most excited that she had seen him so far. Apart from knowing the fact that Thyagaraja was a famous composer of Carnatic music, Reva didn't know much else about the songs, and wisely refrained from adding anything to the conversation.

'Wait, I didn't notice! Is that your – ?'

'Oh, she is a friend,' Karthik said quickly.

Reva came forward but stood at a chaste distance from Karthik. She should just ask Karthik to meet her at a coffee shop the next time, thought Reva, as she nodded and smiled benignly at appropriate intervals to the approving glances his teacher sent her way.

*

On Saturday morning, Reva opened her door to find Jason's panicked expression on the other side. 'The cat! Poons!' Jason exlaimed, his agitation evidently impairing him from forming complete sentences.

Reva raised her eyebrow questioningly as Jason explained, amid pauses to catch his breath, that the cat had jumped from his windowsill down to the edge of the well and, despite his shout of warning (Reva couldn't tell if he was serious), tumbled inside. Reva made a wise seeming 'Ah' sound and followed Jason down the stairs.

Like many older houses in Chennai, Grand Life Apartments had a garden that was shaded from the fiery-breathed morning sun by a tall mango tree that swayed over shorter, flatter plantain ones. In the corner, it had a shed with a partially unhinged door that swung violently when opened, and a neglected well that was usually covered by a metal net pockmarked by fallen leaves from the mango tree.

The net had been left open, and they peeked inside the well to find Poons holding on to a ridge above the murky waters, mewling up at them piteously.

'We'll need something to rescue him with,' Reva said, looking around. She went into the shed and came out with a coil of rope made from coconut coir, which was rough to the touch. She dropped one end of the rope inside the well and steered it close to Poons, who swiped at it suspiciously.

'There, Poons, grab hold of it,' Jason shouted in his best encouraging voice. Poons pawed at the rope a few times before looking up at them with profound disappointment, as if there was no one else to blame, but himself, for expecting better from them.

Jason offered to take over the reins of the rope from Reva and leant forward earnestly over the concrete walls of the well, trying to get the rope as close as possible to Poons. As he lowered his head, his wallet made a bid for escape from his front pocket and tumbled down into the well.

'Bollocks!' Jason exclaimed loudly, his hand windmilling in a vain attempt to catch his falling wallet.

'Oh, no!' Reva said, clamping her hand over her mouth to prevent herself from laughing aloud.

'Meoww,' Poons yelled in consternation as the wallet landed with a loud splash inside the well.

Clutching his right hand to his now-empty pocket, Jason cast a dim look at Reva who was trying her best to sober her laughter.

'Hope you didn't have too much money in there?' She managed to muster some concern in her voice.

Jason said that he had learnt it was best not to carry much money around, given that his wallet seemed to get separated from him quite easily these days. Poons called out to them again, reminding them that there were more important things they should be worrying about.

'We need to drop down a bucket for Poons to jump into, I think,' Reva said, trying to recall the times her mother fished out voyeuristic cats and badminton shuttles from the well behind their house in the village.

'Yes, that's right.' Kamala had made her way to the garden and was holding a red plastic bucket aloft in her functioning right hand. 'I could hear the ruckus you were both making all the way to the terrace,' she said by way of explanation.

Kamala lassoed the rope around the bucket, with the additional showmanship that having an audience entailed, and dropped it inside the well. Poons hesitatingly nudged the bucket and made it sway, as if he were checking if its flight safety certifications were up to scratch.

'Do you have anything a cat would eat? Fish perhaps?' Kamala turned to the two of them, and Jason nodded vigorously and ran back up the stairs.

He came down clutching his thousand-rupee-a-piece Chettinad fish fry preciously in his hands, and Kamala regarded the non-vegetarian piece of fish as she would, perhaps, some highly hazardous nuclear waste, and motioned him to place the fish inside the bucket himself.

After Jason deposited his fried fish inside the bucket, Kamala dropped it slowly into the well again. This time, Poons' ears perked up and he peeked inside the bucket curiously as it made its way next to him. When Poons finally jumped inside, Reva cheered loudly and thought it was only polite to add that the cat had good taste. Jason gestured his hand self-effacingly, looking like he wanted to add that Poons might have preferred his basil-baked fish a tad more.

Poons jumped out of the bucket onto solid ground, his small body vibrating with relief. He splashed water on all of them as a gesture of thanks and scampered away with the half-eaten piece of fish firmly clamped in his mouth.

All three of them trooped up the stairs with the elated air of winning a team sports event. They paused at the balcony on the first floor, replaying the last half hour ('Did you see how expertly Kamala pulled the bucket out of the well with just one hand?', 'Jason really needs to start taking better care of his wallet, doesn't he?')

During a pause in their conversation, Reva looked down from the balcony and noticed that the construction site next to them had now sprouted long scaffoldings that jutted haphazardly into the sky like long blades of grass.

'Do you think we would have any chance of winning this case?' Jason asked, leaning over the railing and looking sideways at the two of them.

'Maybe there is a chance, especially since Sundu Aunty is now representing the apartments.' Reva looked to Kamala for confirmation. She noticed that Kamala was still holding the fish-polluted bucket far away from her and wondered how many washes it would take for the bucket to be accepted back into her household.

'Sundu thinks that it would be a very tough case to win, given that the construction company would have everyone important in their pockets.' Kamala sighed.

'I am meeting a journalist tomorrow by the way,' Reva said, in a casual voice meant to underplay the hope that she had about the meeting. 'He wanted to know more about the harassment at the apartments, especially the link with the famous politician.'

A gentle breeze blew from the trees nearby, and a torn kite that had wrapped itself around a concrete pillar in the construction site freed itself and billowed towards them.

'Well, that's good.' Kamala nodded, but she said it a moment too late for her words to really reassure Reva.

*

Reva had wanted to go to the new Mexican place that had opened in Alwarpet, but she recalled Karthik wanting to try one of the supersized idlis that were now having a moment, so she suggested they meet at a restaurant that served all-day tiffin. Karthik was bringing along his friend, an investigative journalist who had wanted to know more about the situation at the apartments.

'My friend said he can't promise anything, though,' Karthik had warned, but Reva was glad for an opportunity where she felt like she was at least doing something to help.

Reva had arrived early, and she took a seat facing the wall that had a large mural of a tilted cup splashing coffee in artistic waves. The restaurant had exactly two other customers – a girl younger than Reva, who sat with headphones on a chair overlooking a large window, and a man with a salt-and-pepper moustache eating sambar vadai accompanied by satisfied slurping noises.

She watched Mr Moustache beckon the manager and enquire rather thunderingly, 'What is this modern nonsense of giving sugar on the side for filter coffee?'

The manager, a watermelon-shaped man in a formal shirt, bobbed his head in apology. 'Many customers are preferring it this way these days, sir.'

'Which customers, you tell me?' Mr Moustache continued, eyeing Reva who looked away a little too late. 'You tell me! Do you take coffee with or without sugar?'

'With. With sugar,' she responded instantly in the manner of a student woken up mid-doze by a stern professor. The man nodded at her, his bushy moustache twitching its approval. The manager, however, had an expression of profound regret, as if he were rueing the fact that he hadn't gone ahead and taken his job offer at Pizza Hut when he had the chance.

She was quite relieved to see Karthik enter with his friend, Anand, both of them having the cheerful air of two people who had recently shared a joke. From a distance, Anand looked almost a decade older than Karthik, and, as he came closer, she realised that this was due to his prematurely grey hair and buttoned-up shirt with a front pocket that held a clip-on pen.

After placing their orders, Karthik and Anand continued exchanging childhood stories – about the time Karthik had decided to fashion his hair into a quiff so that he could look just like Tintin, about a maths teacher who punished students by making them stand in yoga poses – stories that were not objectively hilarious but caused them to laugh by evoking a shared memory.

'Do you remember the time that we got high on your parents' terrace?' Karthik asked Anand as their food arrived, trailed by the heady aroma of ghee and spices. Reva's rava idli paled in comparison to Anand's glittering butter dosa, and she felt the familiar stab of regret at having ordered something just because she thought it to be the healthier option.

'That must be the only time I have ever seen you high,' Anand observed with a mischievous smile. Karthik gave him a look to show his disagreement, but Anand blithely continued, 'Revathi, I have to tell you that Karthik is one of the nicest guys I know!' and placed his non-eating hand firmly on Karthik's shoulder as if he were a mixer-grinder he was endorsing in a TV advertisement.

Karthik's eyes darted about in embarrassment, and he shot Anand a warning look to stop. 'OK, OK,' laughed Anand in response. 'Anyways, what is the point of having friends if they don't embarrass you now and then?' He smiled good-naturedly at Reva, as if for confirmation.

Reva said she couldn't agree more. She turned to Karthik. 'So, how is your thattu idli?' The idli, true to its name, was as large as the plate and came doused in fiery, full-bodied milagai podi and ghee.

'It's great.' Karthik nodded in-between sips of water. 'Do you remember those table dosas that used to stretch across . . .' Karthik stretched his hand across the table to show the enormity of the dosa under question.

'Yeah, and that Varun – the captain of the school cricket team – used to be able to eat an entire one by himself.' Anand nodded sagely, that act still eliciting his respect more than a decade later.

After a pause in the conversation, Anand tilted his head towards Reva. 'So, Karthik was telling me about the situation at your apartments.'

Reva gave him the highlights – the brick through the window, the forged documents and now the court case – her voice conveying her disbelief at the utter incredulity of it all. Anand humoured her outrage, although she knew that he must have seen far worse, affecting people who didn't even have the cushioning that money gave the residents of Grand Life Apartments. She had read some of his articles online – he had exposed a ring of corruption in the transport department, fought for transgender rights within the police force, rallied against construction projects that encroached on environmentally protected areas. Reva not only did nothing about the social injustices around her, she also actively skipped reading about these topics in the newspaper in her rush to reach the lifestyle supplement.

'I really admire what you do,' she told him. 'I think it's very brave. Really.'

Anand shrugged off her compliment. 'Thank you. Although my mother and wife would use other words to describe what I do – such as crazy.'

'Anyways,' Anand continued, 'I am familiar with this politician's work.'

'Do you think there is an actual threat, you know . . . to Mani's life?' she asked in a hushed tone, as if saying it softly reduced the chances of it coming true.

'I have had several threats issued to my life. And yet, here I still am,' Anand replied. Reva thought that answer was neither here nor there.

'I am sure they wouldn't go that far for a piece of land,' Karthik added, in an attempt to contribute to the conversation.

'I know some contacts in the police who can help if things escalate even further. I will also try to dig around a bit, see if there is some evidence to build a credible story,' Anand mused.

'That will be great. Thank you.'

'Even if I do manage to get a news outlet to publish the story, it may not really help the case,' Anand continued, evidently trying to manage her expectations. Reva nodded to show that she understood.

A waiter in a black T-shirt brought their drinks – coffee for Karthik and rose milk for Reva and Anand.

'There is so much sugar in this coffee,' Karthik exclaimed, looking down at his stainless steel tumbler in surprise. He hastened to add that it was perhaps because he was used to drinking coffee without sugar when not in India. Reva glanced at the moustached man who had effected this change, at least for the day. He was now approaching his scoop of pineapple halwa with the lovingness that she usually associated with the very diabetic, oblivious to her staring. Perhaps, voicing the apartment's story might help it reach the ears of someone who could effect change to the situation, too, she thought, feeling a sense of optimism about this situation for the first time.

14

Jason

Jason rang Kamala's doorbell and was surprised to find Sundu opening the door. 'I can come back later —' but Sundu shushed him and asked him to come inside through quick flicks of her hand, reminding him of the perpetually gesticulating traffic policemen he had seen here on busy roundabouts.

Kamala didn't look up at him when he entered and was completely absorbed in her TV screen, which was zooming into the face of an old woman, in sync with dramatic drumbeats. When the screen switched to a toothpaste commercial, she noticed him with a cluck of surprise. 'Oh, I thought the doorbell was rung by the postman. Hello, Jason, welcome, how are you?' she added rather officiously, although she had seen him just the day before.

Kamala's living room looked exactly the same, except that the calendar that flapped on the wall now showed a new month heralded in by a different, less cherubic god. Jason went closer to inspect a cabinet patched in places by swathes of transparent tape – one shelf was filled with medals and miniature cups that he presumed were won by Lakshmi, and another had little ceramic dolls neatly arranged in descending order of height. The top shelf displayed framed photos of her daughter, each one protected by a layer of clear plastic wrapping.

'That is Lakshmi winning second place in the Rotary Club badminton tournament,' announced Kamala's proud voice from behind.

Jason raised his eyebrows and arranged his face in the way that people do when they decide to appear impressed even when they aren't. He was offered a new chair that still had its packing plastic wrapped around its velvet-and-wood frame, and it squeaked embarrassingly when he sat down.

'Here, I got something for you,' he said, offering Kamala a small, round plastic container. 'I brought some extra slices of the spiced coffee cake I had made for the restaurant. Don't worry, they don't contain eggs. Quite a few customers seem to prefer it this way.'

'Jason is a hot-shot chef back in the UK, and also here, did you know?' Kamala informed Sundu, while Jason demurred politely, feeling a little self-conscious in Sundu's presence. 'Sundu is the one who really likes sweets,' Kamala told Jason, and passed over the cake container to Sundu.

'What is a spiced cake?' Sundu challenged.

'Oh, it just has some ginger, cinnamon and cloves. Gives it some warmth.'

'Sounds like our Deepavali leghiyam, doesn't it?' Sundu quipped to Kamala and they both laughed. 'Leghiyam is like a medicine we make before festivals – to ensure good digestion,' Sundu explained to Jason, and he wondered if he should be offended at the comparison.

'How's the arm?' he asked Kamala instead.

'Perfectly fine. Back to work in a week or so.' Kamala glanced at Sundu defiantly, as if she was expecting her to take issue with this. Sundu simply shook her head and raised her eyebrows in a 'what can you do?' manner at Jason.

'In fact,' Kamala continued, 'the doctor said that it was quite a miracle that I have been able to recover so quickly, except for this elbow, which still needs more time.' All three of them then paused to contemplate the yellowing bandage wrapped across her left elbow. 'All due to God's grace,' she concluded. Jason thought that unlike many people he had heard using the phrase, Kamala actually seemed to mean it.

'Speaking of God's grace, I can't believe those rascals from Olympic Constructions.' Kamala exhaled in the manner of someone who had more choice words to use instead of 'rascals' but preferred showing moral restraint even when expressing outrage. Jason nodded, explaining how Mani was starting to look increasingly forlorn whenever he saw him on the porch. 'Sundu is not going to let them get away with it so easily.' Kamala looked at her friend with considerable pride.

'I am only taking the case because I don't want Kamala to move all the way to some apartment complex in Velachery, what with increasing traffic and petrol costs,' Sundu joked. Even though Sundu avoided any declaration of confidence in winning the case, Jason thought that her representing the case at least held a sliver of hope – he, for one, would not want to be on the other side of an argument with Sundu.

'Oh, where are our manners? Jason, would you like some coffee or cool drinks?' asked Sundu, preparing to get up from the sofa.

'I will make some Mysore bondas. It will take me just two minutes. I had kept the ingredients out as I was planning to make them anyway,' Kamala said, pressing her hand on her knees and getting ready to get up. Both Sundu and Jason loudly insisted that Kamala should not be doing any such thing.

Kamala finally receded back into the sofa after suppressing a sigh directed at Sundu. Seeing the two of them have these wordless conversations that resulted from the comfort of decades of friendship, Jason asked, 'So, how did the two of you become friends?' They both smiled at each other, a little surprised at his interest – then narrated the story, interrupting each other with supplementary facts.

Sundu and Kamala had apparently become friends because of a frog. Over four decades ago, they were both high school students at Saraswathi Vidyalaya – a girls-only school where everyone wore uniforms of a pink half-saree, white dupatta and a dozen strategically placed safety pins ('To hold the dupatta in place around our exposed waist,' Sundu had explained as Kamala sniggered like a schoolgirl at the memory). Sundu was school captain, badminton champion and an all-around shiny person that everyone wanted to see themselves reflected in. Kamala, on the other hand, was very quiet, ranked academically somewhere near the top of the class and went home directly after school without even stopping for one drink at the sugarcane juice stall with the other girls.

Both Kamala and Sundu had taken biology, which was compulsory for students who aspired to become doctors, and the two of them had been paired for the most controversial class in the entire year of the biology group – the dissection. While Kamala revised the procedure from the textbook and rearranged the forceps and scalpels in increasing order of size, Sundu had uncharacteristically become motionless. ('As motionless as the sedated frog pinned to the wooden board,' Kamala quipped.)

Kamala wasn't enjoying the dissection either, considering that she still felt nauseated by the smell of boiling meat that wafted from the neighbour's garden on Sundays. However, her desire to become a doctor was so great that she finished the assignment by herself. She had added Sundu's name to the report as well, partly because she hated conflict and also because she had been a little afraid of Sundu. After the class, when Kamala was scrubbing her hands with mushy pieces of Cinthol soap like a woman possessed, Sundu had stood next to her and spoken her first words to Kamala, 'See you under the banyan tree for lunch,' in a rather high and mighty manner – as if it were Kamala who had been petrified during the class instead of her.

Kamala waved her hand at Sundu and turned to Jason. 'Enough of old tales from us. You tell us, how's the cooking from the *Cook and See* book going?'

'I've just started getting into the dessert section. Not sure if my dishes will receive the passing grade from you, though.' He smiled almost bashfully at Kamala.

'We still haven't given you anything to eat. You will have juice?' pressed Sundu, more firmly this time. She got up without waiting for an answer.

As Sundu went inside the kitchen, Jason looked at Kamala and reached for the topic that he knew was always at the top of Kamala's mind. 'You must be looking forward to seeing Lakshmi very soon?'

'Yes, both Sundu and I will be in your country next month.' Kamala began plumping the blue cushion that Sundu had been leaning on earlier.

'Brilliant! So, it is all set then.' Jason nodded. He hadn't been sure, as Kamala's plan to visit the UK had sounded a little drug-addled the last time she had brought it up. Sundu came out of the kitchen, looking expectantly at them as to what their conversation was about.

'I heard you will be going to the UK soon?' He accepted the stainless steel tumbler of juice from Sundu. He took a small sip. It was sweet, but he couldn't tell what type of juice it was as the steel concealed the colour of the drink.

'It's guava.' Sundu nodded her chin towards his tumbler of juice. 'Yes, we are flying to London. I believe it shouldn't be too cold this time of the year?'

'No, not at all. It's a great time to visit,' Jason enthused. 'Do take some warm clothes, though, as it can get quite chilly in the evening.'

He took another sip of the juice and decided that it was too sweet for his liking. He drank the rest of it in one gulp and firmly refused Sundu's offer for a refill.

'Kamala wears a woollen monkey cap in December here, so we will buy some before we leave,' said Sundu. She placed a plate containing a salty fried snack looped like ringlets next to him. 'Murukku,' explained Sundu as Jason scrutinised the plate.

What he was really examining was the inscription on the stainless steel plate that the murukku came in – it seemed to have been a wedding gift, with the words *Kamal weds Radha, 22-May-1979* inscribed on it.

'Is this your . . . ?' He trailed off, immediately regretting his question when he remembered that Kamala's husband had died a while ago.

'No, no.' She was almost smiling. 'Kamal is a boy's name.' Kamala and Sundu started discussing the couple mentioned on the plate, and it turned out they were doing quite all right – they had downsized to one of those modern apartments on the road encircling the beach, and Sundu had bumped into them at Grand Sweets, where they had been buying fried snacks and sweets in anticipation of the annual arrival of their grandchildren from abroad. ('Nobody cooks anything at home these days,' Kamala had wryly observed.)

He took a bite of the murukku, which crumbled deliciously in his mouth. 'There are a lot of Indian restaurants in the UK, and vegetarian food will not be an issue for you.'

'Yes, I've heard that Indian food is very famous there. By the way, isn't chicken tikka masala considered a British national dish?' Sundu enquired, showing off her trivia knowledge.

'Yes, it's quite popular.'

Jason had been surprised to find that the concept of chicken tikka masala and mango lassi, both very common dishes in Indian restaurants back home, didn't actually exist in Chennai. In fact, when he had asked for mango lassi in a restaurant here, the waiter had appeared flummoxed and brought the chef over, who had enterprisingly asked if mixed fruit lassi would be an acceptable replacement, as if he were a high-strung popstar whose ridiculous demands needed to be met. Later, Aneesh had assured him with suppressed hilarity that mixed fruit lassis were perhaps as commonly found as jackfruit shortbread biscuits.

'Do you want us to bring you something back from the UK?' offered Kamala.

Jason thought about the material things that he missed. Despite his earlier scorn towards sandwiches, the last few days, he had been craving a proper sandwich – not the ones made with square slices of bread and slivers of processed cheese, but nutty sourdough, filled with slices of ham, fresh tomatoes, pickles and a slathering of brie. He explained this as best as he could to them, adding that this wasn't something that could be packed and brought back.

'Have you tried the masala sandwich toast from Iyengar Bakery, though?' was Sundu's response, her raised eyebrows indicating that he would be amazed if he tried it.

Kamala answered on his behalf. 'I don't know why you need to buy that masala toast from outside. In fact, I think I can make that right now in five minutes,' she declared and proceeded to get up, prompting Sundu and Jason to make a fuss over her again.

*

Later that week, after a long shift that ended late, Jason experienced his first Chennai power cut. He was sitting on the sofa, his laptop cushioned on his lap, when his apartment was plunged into sudden darkness. He had just given in to his impulse of looking at Emma's online account, and the power cut had stopped him halfway, like a friend placing a restraining hand on his shoulder.

He got up to check what was going on, taking care not to knock anything over. His eyes soon became accustomed to the darkness of the house, and he was able to make out shapes which resolved into outlines of objects. The sound of loud laughter reached him from the porch beneath. Mani, Reva and Kamala were sitting around an emergency lamp that lit their faces and threw exaggerated shadows on the ground. There was something close-knit about them, soaked in a warm circle of light like friends around a campfire, that compelled Jason to go down and join them.

His presence was welcomed noiselessly, Kamala moving over so that he could form part of their circle. Jason took a seat next to a lounging Poons and scratched his soft neck. Poons' eyes flicked open in immediate alertness, but on seeing Jason, he closed his eyes again to resume his delicate snoozing.

Reva and Mani were listening to a small radio announcing the news headlines in Tamil, occasionally interrupted by merry advertising jingles for Pepsi. Jason nodded good-naturedly, not understanding much except for snatches of a few English words here and there.

He looked around at the buildings and roads, his senses getting adjusted to the surreal aspect of an entire neighbourhood losing access to electricity. It was completely dark, except for the occasional passing vehicle that left a bright streak of light in its wake. The cloud that had fogged his brain the last few weeks finally seemed to shift, and he felt strangely alive, his senses sharpened. Across the wall, they could hear a shout from the neighbouring apartments, which was then followed by an explosion of laughter. Mani leant forward to turn the knob on the radio, feeling some sort of responsibility towards keeping them as entertained as their neighbour. He stopped at a station playing a Tamil song that sounded scratchy with age. Even though Jason didn't know the language, from the affected pleading voice of the man singing the song, he knew that he was singing about love.

Mani seemed to like this song, or at least the memories it seemed to evoke. He hummed along with it softly, sounding like a musically gifted insect.

'They never make songs like these now, do they?' Kamala asked. A question asked by people of a certain age everywhere in the world.

'Now it's all loud noise and dance numbers,' Mani agreed. 'How are you doing, Jason?'

'All good. All good,' Jason heard himself say in an over-emphatic voice. After a moment, he added, gesturing at the emergency lamp, 'I must admit that I have never experienced a complete blackout before.'

'Is that so?' Kamala sounded fascinated at the idea of living a life well into adulthood accompanied by a never-ending supply of electricity.

'Well, you had better get used to these power cuts quickly then.' Mani's tone was apologetic.

Reva was absorbed in her phone, which vibrated with a flurry of texts usually associated with a group chat. She looked up at Kamala and announced in a surprised, cheerful voice, 'Happy birthday, Kamala Aunty!' She held up her phone in explanation. 'I remembered it to be on the same day as a friend's in the US.'

'Thank you, Revathi,' Kamala said quickly, hoping to brush this away into the next topic of conversation.

Jason clapped his hands. '*Happy birthday*! We should celebrate!' Reva and Mani nodded back in agreement.

'Nothing to celebrate,' Kamala hushed him. 'As you get older, your birthday becomes just like any other day. Anyways, today is just my date of birth, my star birthday is not until next week.'

'I think I have some chocolate in my handbag actually.' Reva rummaged around, disregarding Kamala's astrological excuses.

'Hold on, I may have something upstairs. Be back in a bit.' Jason grabbed Mani's orange torch and ventured upstairs, using it to navigate the darkness. Minutes later, he brought down a large bowl of payasam that he had cooked exactly as his *Cook and See* book recommended – by slowly simmering rice, milk, sugar and cardamom into a fragrant pudding. As soon as he came back to the porch, Poons unlounged himself and started circling his feet.

'Be careful, one of my cousins recently broke her hip while tripping over a cat,' warned Kamala.

Mani brought out stainless steel cups of varying sizes from his kitchen, and although it was a little messy serving the payasam out on the porch, every little spill was licked clean by Poons. Mani poured a generous helping of the payasam into Poons' plastic lid and said, 'Have some patience, Mr Poons. You have your own plate.'

'This is really good, Jason.' Reva smiled. Jason thanked her, but both of them knew that the person whose opinion he was really waiting for was Kamala's.

Kamala ate a few spoonfuls quietly before pronouncing, '*Prama-dham.*'

Excellent.

Her response made Jason's heart fill deliciously with pride, and he couldn't help giving Kamala a smile of such high wattage that it could have temporarily made up for the lack of electricity.

Kamala seemed to sense the effect of her words on Jason. 'Thank you, Jason. A payasam should taste exactly like this.' She seemed to be looking at Jason almost affectionately as she said this.

Everyone had second helpings of the payasam and joked about Poons having the largest helping of all.

'Poons must have led a pious past life. He eats mostly vegetarian food,' said Kamala, rather proudly. This made the rest of them laugh, and Kamala, who had made this statement with complete seriousness, wagged her head disapprovingly at them.

'Kamala Aunty is going to come back from the UK and insist on eating only British food,' teased Reva. She then switched to a surprisingly convincing imitation of Jason's accent and said, 'Some buttered crumpets and warm scones with my cup of tea sounds absolutely lovely, my dear,' and mimicked Kamala sipping a cup of tea with her pinky finger extended and nose held high.

Even the mosquitoes that descended on them didn't dampen their good cheer, and they quietened only when Mani brought up the uncovered temple pond as the reason behind the recent excess of mosquitoes.

Kamala lamented on behalf of the gods that she worshipped. 'I can't believe that these greedy real estate developers dragged god's name in vain to do their dirty work.'

Jason could very well believe it – god's name had been dragged in vain for centuries everywhere in the world to do man's own bidding, after all. However, what he didn't want to believe, was that this sense of belonging that he had just recently gained here was going to slip away from his grasp so soon.

'Any luck with your journalist friend?' Jason asked Reva.

After a pause, Reva spoke softly, 'He is working on it, although he hasn't found a news outlet to cover the story yet.'

They fell into a contemplative silence, Mani glancing at his plants in the consoling manner of a parent assuring their children that everything would be all right even when he knew it wouldn't. Poons sat down next to Jason again, placing his tail over Jason's feet.

'You are leaving for UK soon, aren't you?' Jason asked Kamala, trying to force back some positivity into their conversation.

'Yes, I am. I hope I don't disturb Lakshmi's studies too much when I am there.'

'Of course not. If anything, I am sure you will make sure she is well looked after before her exams,' said Mani kindly, looking away from his garden towards Kamala. His sentence was accompanied by the light effect of the roads and houses flickering to life as electricity flowed into them. The bright glare of tube lights and the gurgling noise of television sets coming alive around them made them slowly disperse from their huddle, after wishing Kamala for her birthday once again.

Jason went back to his living room and opened his laptop, the open browser resolving into Emma's face pouting insolently at him. He swiftly deleted his social media accounts. He deleted all the photos on his laptop without lingering to look at any of them again. He knew that he would need some more time to ease the pain in his chest, but being able to do this meant that he was getting there.

*

Jason headed out early for his shift the next day, the air still smoke-coloured from the night before. When he noticed the garden on his way out, he stopped to rub his eyes to make sure that he wasn't imagining what he was seeing. Most of the plants were uprooted and beheaded, and the bougainvilleas that draped the walls now lay unravelled on the ground – it looked as if the entire garden had been destroyed overnight.

He knocked on Mani's door, and Mani nodded at Jason genially and picked up his newspaper from the porch, oblivious to what lay in front of him. When his eyes fell on the garden, he clutched the newspaper close to his chest but, even in his shock, Jason noticed a resigned look pass over his face that showed that he had been waiting for something like this to happen.

Mani walked towards his plants and absently leant against the guava tree, which thankfully seemed to have been spared, although there were bruises on its slender trunk where it had been hacked at half-heartedly. Jason noticed an iron sickle lying next to the tree, the kind used in roadside stalls to splice the hard shells of coconuts and jackfruits with a single, graceful swoop. He wasn't sure what to make of it when he realised that the person who had carried all this out had decided to spare this old tree willingly.

Jason eyed Mani uncertainly. 'Should we inform the police?'

'No use. We all know who is behind this.' Mani sighed, waving his hand at the huge billboard advertising honey-coloured, hive-like accommodation planted across the walls.

They continued surveying the garden morosely for a few minutes, the brightening sky making the plants appear balder. Jason tried to think of something encouraging to say, something along the lines of what his mother might have said in this situation. 'You can get all kinds of seeds online these days. We can fix this up in no time.' The words came out more cheerfully than he had intended them to.

Mani winced, eyeing his rose bush, the fallen flowers still looking pink and fresh against the mud on the ground. Jason realised that he had spoken too soon, that Mani needed time to mourn the plants that were gone before thinking of replacing them with new ones. He said more gently this time that he would stop by later in the evening to help Mani with the garden. However, before leaving for the restaurant, he asked, 'Has this changed your mind? About taking them to court?'

Mani took a moment to consider Jason's question. 'No, I don't think so.'

'Good,' Jason said to Mani. Then 'Good,' more softly to himself.

15

Kamala

Sundu and Kamala reached the airport four hours before the flight was scheduled to take off. Through the glass windows of the waiting area, Kamala could see the novel sight of an aeroplane perched on the ground, its wings extended in anticipation of taking flight. She had flown in a plane just once in her life, to attend a dental conference in Singapore over a decade ago. When she had made that trip, she had expected the country to be as heavenly as it had been described to be – she had heard how people could get fined for as little as dropping a piece of chewing gum on the road, and how taxi drivers dressed in pristine white shirts and spoke perfect English. However, when she actually landed there, she had felt that it was just a slightly cleaner version of India, the humid air tinged with exhaust smoke feeling the same as inhaling a lungful of early morning Chennai air. She also remembered that the residential areas had spilled with bougainvillea and hibiscus plants, reminding her of the garden back at Grand Life Apartments.

Still looking at the plane, Kamala spoke to Sundu, who was sitting next to her, 'I can't believe what those thugs did to our garden. Must be all the evil eye cast on its beautiful flowers, planted with such care by Mani.'

Sundu, who was hunched over her laptop, turned to Kamala with a half-smile. 'Let's blame the evil men this time, instead of the evil eye.' She paused to stretch her back by clasping her hands overhead. 'Anyways, have you registered on the property website as I asked you to?'

Kamala shook her head. She didn't want to admit even to Sundu that she still held out a small bit of hope for some divine intervention to save the apartments, however improbable it seemed.

'Anyways, you can stay with me in the worst case. We can figure it out,' Sundu assured her before answering her ringing cell phone.

Kamala looked around her, trying to distract herself while Sundu spoke with someone at work. On the chairs opposite to them, there was an older couple, perhaps in their late sixties, conferring with each other whether they should really spend twenty-five rupees for a bottle of water in the airport café. This couple had made an effort to dress up for the flight – the woman was wearing a silk saree and diamond earrings that made her ears droop with their weight, and her husband was wearing a half-sleeved formal shirt with matching trousers. Their phone rang, and they became visibly excited as they realised that it was a call from their daughter. Realising that the speaker setting was accidentally on, they shuffled the phone between them, unsuccessfully trying to turn it off. As a result, Kamala, as well as everyone around them, ended up listening to their entire conversation. Their daughter asked them, her voice concerned and affectionate, whether they got to the airport on time and if they had remembered to carry their medicines. Their grandson then came on the phone, and although he spoke in gurgling, barely discernible sentences, the grandparents beamed brightly down the phone and explained in high-pitched sentences that they were going to see him very soon.

Kamala felt a mild pang of envy at the easy relationship that they seemed to have with their grown-up daughter and at the concept of family that seemed to come so easily to others, but somehow continued to elude her. She turned to Sundu, who was engrossed with work on her laptop. Feeling Kamala's gaze, Sundu looked up at her, but Kamala could see that her mind was still on the email that she had left half-typed on her screen.

'Thank you,' Kamala said, as Sundu looked back questioningly at her. She then added, 'For coming with.' Sundu waved her palm, as if her words were a fly to be swatted away, and then went back to peering closely at her laptop through spectacles perched at the edge of her nose.

Once they boarded the flight, Kamala and Sundu reconfirmed their Asian vegetarian meals with the hassled air hostess, clucked sympathetically at the woman flying with two screaming children and distributed a dab of cotton evenly between themselves to stuff in their ears.

Halfway through the flight, Kamala was woken up by the announcement asking them to fasten their seatbelts due to turbulence. The lights had been switched off, and she turned to look at Sundu who was sleeping soundly, oblivious to all this fuss around her. The aircraft quivered and the thought of this small capsule of steel hurtling through the clouds, carrying its cargo of fragile human beings, made Kamala's stomach clench.

She clutched Sundu's arm reflexively. Sundu swatted her hand away, her eyes still closed. 'Goodness, since when did you become such a scared chicken?' she asked groggily before turning away and snuggling further into her blanket.

Kamala spent the rest of the time on the flight awake, her mind restlessly rustling like an open book underneath a fan. She hadn't spoken to Lakshmi in the last few days but had read the news on the BBC website, which spoke of flu going around due to the changing season in the UK. She prayed to her gods for Lakshmi's health, reciting scraps of various prayers that she knew from memory. When the plane rattled again, making her stomach flip, she panicked about something happening to this flight and never being able to see her daughter again. She turned to speak with Sundu, but her friend was fast asleep, snoring, with her mouth slightly open.

After what felt like an eternity, the flight finally landed at Heathrow. The airport reminded her of those new shopping malls in Chennai, with clean white floors and fluorescent tube lights, but there was a foreign iciness in the air that numbed her exposed fingers and face in the short time it took to get to the terminal from the plane. Both she and Sundu had packed woollen clothes in their hand luggage in preparation for just this situation and wore them clumsily on top of their kurtas.

However, within a few minutes, Kamala was asked to remove her woollen layers as she was held back for extra security screening. The airport security guard, a brown-haired man with an unhappy scowl, had addressed her politely but firmly and asked her to remove all her gold jewellery. Kamala removed her chain and ear-rings but struggled with the screws of her nose-ring, which were always difficult to remove without a bit of soap. She explained this to the man who just stared at her and repeated, this time slowly and loudly, as if she were hard of hearing, to remove all her jewellery. She was also asked to remove her sandals, and she flinched as both her sandals and her prayer book were heaped together on the same plastic tray for screening. She touched the book reverently in apology as it arrived on the other side of the screening tunnel. When she was finally let through, she hastily buckled her sandals and stepped out into this foreign country, feeling bruised and dazed.

They got into a taxi that Sundu had booked in advance. A light drizzle had started outside, and they drove down a highway flanked by iron-coloured buildings topped by matching clouds. Their taxi-driver looked Indian and, on further questioning from Sundu, they learnt that he was Bangladeshi. He appeared friendly and was replying to Sundu's questions in that talkative, oversharing manner adopted by some of Kamala's relatives who would later end the conversation by asking Kamala if she could squeeze them in for a free dental appointment.

The driver had lived in Southall for the last twenty-five years, and yes, the lunchbox in-between the two seats had contained his wife's luchis and potato sabzi that he had eaten for lunch (eating out in London was daylight robbery, he warned), and no, his children no longer lived with him as they were both now studying at university (the girl was studying to be a nurse, and the boy an accountant, he proudly declared).

When he asked if they were here to sightsee, Sundu mentioned Lakshmi. 'Wow, Oxford! Your daughter must be very clever!' the driver exclaimed, glancing at Kamala through the rear-view mirror. Kamala thanked him politely and continued looking outside the window. The rain was still pattering softly, the water running tipsily along the glass, blurring the buildings and cars outside into unrecognisable shapes and colours.

'Does it always rain here, like they say?' Sundu asked him, peering at the road ahead through the semi-circle drawn by the windshield wiper.

'Yes, do remember to carry an umbrella with you when you walk around,' he advised. 'Also, be careful with your wallet and belongings while walking in the tourist areas. There are many pickpockets waiting to snatch them in London.'

'Good to know that we can feel right at home here,' joked Sundu as they arrived, and the driver laughed loudly, especially after noting her generous tip.

Kamala was lost in her own thoughts, though, and was far from feeling right at home, but she nodded and smiled at Sundu and the driver.

*

Kamala had been surprised to note the musty blue carpets of their hotel room and the unidentifiable stains in the hallway, considering that the cost of a night's stay was nearly the same as the monthly wage of a nurse at her hospital. 'Everything is very costly here, like Bipin said,' Sundu declared, naming the taxi-driver as if they were the closest of friends.

The food on the flight had not been enough for either of them, so they decided to venture outside to find a place to eat. It was six in the evening in London, and the air now felt distinctly chillier than it had in the afternoon. Their hotel seemed to be close to a busy train station around which a large crowd of people milled, walking purposefully in all directions. Kamala had never seen so many foreigners in one place before, and she watched them enthralled – there were young travellers carrying backpacks as large as gunny sacks of rice, office-goers wearing long coats that swept the floor, and men begging in corners and yet wearing laced-up shoes.

In front of the station, a man in a black suit approached Kamala with a flamboyant smile that she could identify as fake even from a distance. He thrust a brochure in her hand, offering tickets for an original, exclusive tour of London on a double-decker bus with apparently very limited availability. While she was an expert at dealing with this sort of hustle in Chennai, where everyone from the fruit-seller to the auto-driver heckled at you for business, she was tongue-tied in front of this well-dressed man until Sundu elbowed her away from him.

'Victoria station is the Chennai Central station of London,' explained Sundu in her best worldly-wise manner. 'Maybe we should walk outside on one of those quieter roads and find a res-taurant? This place looks like it only has fast-food joints, which may not have vegetarian food,' she added, thumbing at the neon-lit signs around them.

'We should have packed a small pressure cooker in our luggage like Aruna recommended. Then, we could have just made some pongal in the hotel room and not roamed around the roads with empty stomachs like this,' mumbled Kamala as they left the station to walk along a quieter tree-lined road a few minutes away.

Sundu ignored her comment. Instead, she pointed to one of those iconic red London phone booths by the side of the road. 'Look, this unused booth has been dirtied just the way it would have been done back home,' she said with more glee than Kamala thought was necessary. Kamala chuckled in response, although she had noted that the roads were pothole-free and tree-lined, and not a single street-lamp flickered.

They decided to stop at the first restaurant that they saw, called Olive, after Sundu explained that Italian food was usually vegetarian friendly. Kamala wondered if the restaurant was under construction, as the walls had bricks showing through, and the room was lit by naked bulbs suspended from the ceiling by exposed black wires. She pored over the menu, which was typed on an unlaminated piece of paper, which she thought made no practical sense. Although the menu was typed in English, there was nothing much that she recognised apart from the word pizza.

'I know pasta, but what is antipasti? Is it the opposite of pasta?' she asked Sundu who was frowning over the menu with her spectacles perched so far down her nose that it looked like it was about to fall off.

Sundu started to hazard a guess but then shrugged. 'I don't know. Maybe we can ask the waitress?'

'Don't bother. Let's just order a pizza. God knows when I last had one, though – it must have been when Lakshmi used to order home delivery from Pizza Hut years ago. Even then, I had to eat some curd rice later to settle my stomach.'

They placed their order with their waitress, whose attitude was as sunny as her glossy, blonde hair. She enthused to everything they said with: 'Excellent choice!', 'Oh, I am vegetarian, too,' and 'Did you know our pizzas are freshly baked in our stone oven?' By the time they finished placing their order, they both felt that they had been extremely clever to have come in here and ordered their pizzas topped with roasted vegetables and cheese.

The pizzas arrived after a long wait, looking slender and dressed in melting cheese. Even Kamala, who would have usually said, 'I can just add cheese on bread at home and make this,' had to admit that it was quite tasty.

'So, should we buy tickets to Oxford tomorrow at the station, on the way back?' Sundu asked once they had finished eating and refused the enthusiastic offer for desserts that apparently were the recipes of the owner's Italian grandmother. ('Is she here? Can we meet?' Sundu had enquired earnestly, and stunned silence had ensued.)

'No, let's stay in London for one or two more days.' Kamala quickly averted her eyes from Sundu who stared at her, making a show of wanting more explanation without having to ask for it. Seeing none forthcoming, she just sighed. 'I will extend the reservation for a couple more days. The hotel doesn't seem to be full anyways.'

*

The next day, Sundu claimed that it had been her lifelong desire to take a photo next to the Prime Meridian, although Kamala couldn't recall her mentioning the Meridian or having even a vague interest in geography until then.

'Isn't Buckingham Palace more famous? Why didn't you want a picture there?' asked Kamala as she paused for rest while climbing the steep hill in Greenwich, on which the Royal Observatory was located. Sundu had convinced Kamala to buy sports shoes for this trip, and Kamala, who had never worn anything other than sandals all her life, was not used to the restrictive, hefty feeling of having her entire foot enclosed. As she wiggled her toes inside her trainers, she thought that the sight of her in such shoes was certain to make Lakshmi smile in that wry, half-dimpled manner that she did whenever her mother tried out anything 'modern'.

'We can go see the palace, too.' Sundu, who had climbed up the hill with surprising sprightliness, was now taking pictures of Kamala holding on to the side rail and catching her breath.

Once they reached the top of the hill, Kamala sat next to Sundu on a mound of green grass and complained that her new shoes were biting her feet.

'Look at the view ahead,' Sundu cajoled, adopting the voice of a parent speaking to a disgruntled child.

Kamala could see the tips of what looked like tall buildings across the horizon, but most of the view was covered by foggy, grey clouds. 'I am going back to wearing my sandals tomorrow onwards,' Kamala announced in a defiant voice, without commenting on the view.

'It takes a bit of time to get used to new shoes, doesn't it?' was all Sundu said. 'If you are wearing sandals, make sure you wear them with socks so that your feet don't get cold.'

As they talked, the air around them lightened, and rays of sunshine flooded the hill, revealing the view of a sparkling river that encircled the sharp outlines of buildings and spires that formed the city of London. Everyone around them seemed to let out a collective sigh on seeing the sunshine and putter about with renewed energy. Sundu took out her camera from her handbag and turned to Kamala, who was staring at the view vacantly.

'What's wrong? Why the long face?' asked Sundu, taking a woollen cap out of her handbag and placing it on her head at a lopsided angle. Kamala wanted to straighten the cap for her but left it untouched out of childish sulkiness.

Sundu continued, 'You tell me, who doesn't have issues with their children? Just last week, my son called me, and I was so happy – it was my birthday, and although it was late in the evening, I thought he had finally remembered. Did he call to wish me? No. He called because he had lost his passport, degree certificate and all important documents on a train and needed legal help in getting new ones.'

'These young people are all just so busy with their lives, Sundu. What can you do?' Kamala looked commiseratingly at her friend. She leant over and straightened Sundu's cap.

They both then continued looking at the view while alternating between drinking hot water from a flask and eating banana chips, both of which they had in their handbags.

'We haven't taken any pictures with the view! Go stand in front,' instructed Sundu, nudging Kamala to get up. Kamala posed in front of the view shyly, adjusting her saree and holding her handbag close to her, conscious of people glancing at her as they walked past to an ice cream van parked nearby.

As Sundu snapped multiple pictures of her, Kamala noticed two young men seated behind Sundu kiss each other briefly on the mouth before going back to eating their vanilla ice cream cones, as if it were the most normal thing in the world. The sight unnerved her, and she wondered for a second if she had actually imagined it. If she went to Oxford, would she have to witness the unimaginable – Lakshmi kissing another girl?

She came back and sat next to Sundu, forgetting to ask Sundu to go and pose for a photo. 'I don't want to go to Oxford. We should just head back home. This was all a very bad idea.'

'What got into you all of a sudden?' Sundu asked Kamala and then followed her gaze to the two men sitting next to them.

'I see,' she said, non-committedly, peering more closely at the camera and at the pictures that she had just clicked.

'I am not as modern as you are. I am just not fine with all of this.'

'You need to be, Kamala. Pretend, if you have to.' Sundu took a gulp of hot water from the flask with the swiftness of someone drinking a much stronger beverage. She then continued in a softer tone, 'Remember how you were feeling at the hospital about Lakshmi and how you left things with her? This is your chance to make things right with her again. It's OK if you don't agree with her on everything. Sometimes, you need to pretend to approve of your children's choices in life so that you don't lose them altogether.'

Kamala didn't reply. She knew that Sundu was projecting her own feelings about her son's choice of a life partner but had to admit that there was some truth in her lecture. She turned slightly and continued looking at the gay couple who were now taking out some biscuits and strawberries from a wicker basket and laying them out on a chequered napkin. She watched them closely, as if they were a magic trick that she could figure out if she looked carefully enough. The two men seemed to notice her interest and waved pleasantly at her before she could quickly avert her gaze. She turned away from them, feeling ashamed, wondering if they had read her mind and knew exactly what she was thinking.

*

It was Kamala and Sundu's third day in London when they got lost. The receptionist at their hotel, an old man with a heavy accent, had enthusiastically given them directions to a place that had the 'best curry in town' when they enquired about Indian restaurants nearby. They had been walking for over half an hour now, and Kamala thought that they were either lost or there was something lost in translation about the meaning of the word nearby.

'Let's just go back the way we came from,' said Sundu, poring over a piece of paper on which she had scrawled some directions with a pen. As they walked back, evening descended quickly, and all the residential streets started looking indistinguishable in the shadows of the tall lamps lined at perfectly equal intervals along the streets.

'Let's ask someone where this restaurant is,' Kamala suggested, although there was nobody else on the road.

As they turned a corner, they came across a group of young men huddled together by the side of the road. 'I'll go ask them,' said Kamala in an unusual show of bravery. Sundu sniffed the air in the manner of someone awaiting a sneeze and turned to Kamala to say something, but Kamala had already started walking purposefully towards the group of young men by then.

There were about five of them, all dressed similarly in slouchy jeans and sweatshirts, and looked to be in their early twenties. They shuffled slightly as Kamala approached them. One of them, the tallest, with freckled skin and a large mop of blonde hair falling over his face, eyed Kamala's salwar kameez and grey hair in a manner that he perhaps imagined to be astute. He then looked at the shortest one, who was fidgeting with the zip of his sweatshirt, and asked, 'That your mum?'

The boy he was addressing rolled his eyes. 'Piss off, dude. How many times do I have to tell you that I am Egyptian, not Indian?'

Kamala could smell something sweet and pungent in the air around them, not quite unlike the smell that filled her kitchen when she brewed her tulsi tea for too long. She wondered if they hadn't taken a shower and sprayed on some strange cologne like some of her patients did during the brief Chennai winter period of December. Just as she was about to show the printout of the hotel address to one of them, a police car stopped ahead. Two police officers dressed in blue uniforms walked towards them, looking rather tired and weary. Their eyes widened slightly after spotting Kamala in the midst of these young men.

Sundu came to her side and told one of the police officers that they were only looking for directions. It turned out that they were just another corner away from the restaurant, and they sighed in relief and left after thanking them.

'Those young boys were so strange,' said Kamala in a stage whisper as they walked away from them. 'Why do you think the police wanted to speak with them?'

'They were strange, indeed. Who knows what they were up to?' replied Sundu, but it looked to Kamala like she was smiling.

The restaurant, Curry Leaf, had just opened for the evening. The smell of rose incense perfumed the dining area, and napkins folded into starchy swans floated on a sea of red tablecloth. An old Hindi film song, popular when Kamala had been in college, played softly in the background. A man dressed in a black vest welcomed them inside and seated them on a table by a window that overlooked the road. The restaurant was completely empty except for a middle-aged local couple, who were seated in the opposite corner. Seeing Kamala and Sundu, they nodded at each other, secretly pleased that they must have come to a very authentic place if the likes of Kamala and Sundu had chosen to eat there.

A man who looked like the owner of the restaurant walked up to their table to welcome them with a greasy grin – he was short and pot-bellied and wore more rings than there were fingers on his hands. He reminded Kamala of one of her patients, a pawnbroker from Usman Road, who had insisted that his molar cavity needed to be filled with nothing less than twenty-four-carat gold.

'Travelling from India, or from around here?' he asked, giving them each a laminated menu with a flourish.

'Yes, we are coming all the way from Chennai. Previously known as Madras,' Sundu added in explanation, confused by the British-accented English from the Indian-looking owner.

'Yes, I know Madras, of course. The land of idli and dosas! Although, unfortunately, neither of them are on the menu here.' He laughed unnecessarily.

A young man, perhaps in his mid-twenties, hovered near their table with a large jug of water. 'This is my nephew, Krishna. He will be looking after you today.' The owner patted him on the back before turning away to greet the other two diners.

'Hello, I heard you say that you are from Madras. I was there five years ago – very beautiful temples,' Krishna said in a genuinely enthusiastic tone that made Kamala warm to him.

'Oh really, what were you doing there?' Sundu asked him.

'I was there for an internship project during college. I used to live in a side alley behind Loyola College,' he explained.

'Oh, that's a very central area. How long did you stay there?' Sundu asked him as Kamala started looking at the menu. Kamala would have liked to question him further on what he was doing in London now, but she felt a little bashful, so she let Sundu do the talking.

'Only two months. I really liked the food in Madras, but I have to admit, I didn't like dealing with the auto-drivers there.' The last statement was said in a somewhat low, conspiratorial tone, as if he knew Sundu well enough to confide in her. There was something effeminate about the way he spoke, which made Kamala look closer at him. He was wearing a black vest that was cut more fashionably than the rest of the staff's, and he kept tucking his long, curly hair behind his ear, from where a solitary gold earring glinted.

'Those auto-drivers can be quite the rascals,' Sundu said, nodding approvingly at his statement. 'I can't make head or tail of this menu, by the way. What in God's name is a motor paneer?'

'Oh, that!' Krishna laughed delightedly as if Sundu had said something very charming. 'That is just a typing mistake. It is supposed to be mattar paneer – paneer with peas. But if you were to ask me, I would recommend the black dal and paneer tikka masala, if you are vegetarians. Let me also get some extra poppadoms for you while you wait. On the house, no need to pay.' He smiled brightly at the two women.

'What a nice young man!' exclaimed Sundu once he left.

Kamala started tentatively, 'You know, I have read something about men who wear earrings in their left ear. Do you think he is — ?'

'Do I think he is what?' Sundu was looking at her curiously.

Kamala lowered her eyes and continued looking at the menu. Her mind was constantly thinking about Lakshmi, and she wondered if she was projecting her thoughts on everything she saw – the way a newly pregnant woman suddenly notices all the babies on the road or how a newly single person realises that the world is populated with happy couples.

'What do you think?' Sundu was asking. 'Maybe we can get some peas pulao as well? I was really looking forward to some idlis or dosas after all the nonsense we have eaten these last two days. The internet said there is a Saravana Bhavan half an hour away by train. Maybe we should have gone there instead.'

Kamala, however, was busy observing Krishna, who was now talking with the other couple. It looked as if he was saying something funny to them, too, making them laugh loudly.

'Let's go to Oxford tomorrow,' Kamala said finally. 'It is Saturday, and we wouldn't be disturbing any of Lakshmi's classes.'

'Very good. I wasn't sure what sort of auspicious hour you were waiting for,' said Sundu, and continued, 'Should we get the cucumber raita as well?'

'Yes, let's get it with the pulao,' Kamala replied, straightening the unnecessary knife and fork kept on their table. 'You know, I am still not sure what I would say when I meet Lakshmi.'

Sundu looked up at her and closed the menu. 'You could always start the conversation by saying how you almost got arrested for smoking weed here,' she said, her eyes twinkling with amusement. It took a moment for Kamala to connect the implication of the word weed with their recent encounter with the police car. Her eyes went wide, and her face took on a horrified expression, 'Really? Drugs? Dear God!'

'Yes, really.' Sundu grinned as Kamala continued to look at her with utter disbelief.

'Everything all right here? Any more questions about the menu?' Krishna came to their table with an earnest expression.

'Yes, everything is more than all right here,' Sundu assured him, looking over at her friend for confirmation. Kamala nodded back. Her eyes were still widened with surprise, but the corner of her mouth was fighting unsuccessfully against the arrival of a smile.

16

Revathi

Reva and Karthik were sitting by the Marina beach, listening to the sound of waves breaking gently against the shore. It was still early for a Sunday morning, and the beach didn't have many people, except for those trying to make a living from it. Young boys drenched in seawater dredged their canoes laden with nets of silvery fish. A woman swept the sand briskly with a broom before setting up her stall that would soon start serving battered green chillies wrapped in newspaper. Overhead, crows and pigeons squawked and flew in circles.

'I am sorry to hear about the garden at Grand Life Apartments. It was so beautiful,' Karthik said sincerely as he turned to look at Reva. The morning sun glinted off his metal-framed spectacles.

'I don't think I have seen Mani Uncle actually smile since then.' Reva glanced at Karthik before turning to look at the ocean ahead. 'Really nice of your friend to agree to write the article about all this, though.'

'I'm sure he is not doing it just to be nice.' Karthik shrugged. 'I admire him for what he does – bringing about social change here, you know. Making a difference.'

Reva tried to adjust her hair, which flew wildly in the breeze. She wanted to say that there was nothing stopping Karthik from coming back to India and making a difference, if that's what he wanted to do. However, she didn't, because she knew that it was easier to admire someone else who made difficult decisions rather than make those decisions yourself.

'Look, *kili josiyam*. A parrot fortune-teller!' Reva translated as a man walked close to them, carrying a cage inside which a bird flapped its wings pointlessly.

'I know what *kili josiyam* is! I have lived here for twenty years of my life, remember?' Karthik placed his bare feet gingerly in the sand in an attempt to avoid the pieces of broken glass bottles that they had seen earlier.

'Who knows? I thought you could potentially mistake him to be taking his pet parrot for a morning walk,' teased Reva.

Karthik smiled at her joke, but his brows had a tiny furrow, as if he were smiling at someone he recognised but couldn't recall their name. Reva and Karthik had met around half a dozen times, mostly for coffee and dinner, and once to watch the latest *Star Wars* movie. She knew that he didn't entirely like being teased, which only made Reva try harder.

The man with the parrot stopped in front of them, parking his cage in the sand. His face was coarse and wrinkled from being out in the sun too long, and he wore a faded white veshti that he had folded high above his knees, displaying the chequered shorts that he wore underneath.

'Josiyam, sir? Arularasi can tell you your future.' He gestured to the parrot that was desperately trying to peck at something in the sand through the bars of its cage. He rapped the cage with his hand, after which the parrot stopped pecking and looked down glumly at the sand.

Reva looked at Karthik, willing him to refuse politely, as the man obviously ignored her presence. As Karthik hesitated, the fortune-teller quickly placed a stack of cards on a piece of cloth and opened the tiny door of the parrot's cage. The wing-clipped parrot waddled out, picked one of the cards with its beak, and brought it back to him.

'Ah-aha,' the fortune-teller sang in exaggerated wonder while looking at the card. 'She has picked Mahalakshmi – which means that you are going to be blessed with a lot of wealth and prosperity,' he announced and then quickly glanced at both of them to check if he had said the right thing.

Noticing Reva and Karthik looking rather unimpressed, the fortune-teller cleared his throat and made modifications to his pre-diction to add some specificity. 'It is an extremely lucky time for you with the goddess of wealth by your side, sir. If you buy a lottery ticket in the next two days, a hundred-and-fifty per cent chance that the jackpot will be yours.'

'Thank you. That was –' Karthik started but was interrupted by the fortune-teller rapping the side of the cage for the parrot to come out again and pick another card. 'This one will be for you, madam. What is your good name?' he asked as the parrot came out and tilted its head towards her in a very human-like manner.

'No, that's enough,' Reva said, raising her palm towards the parrot.

'Are you sure, madam? I can tell your fortune for half-price.' He was now looking at Karthik as if expecting him to overrule her. Karthik merely opened his wallet and paid him without bargaining for the amount. The fortune-teller quickly pocketed the money as Reva mouthed to Karthik that it was too much.

The fortune-teller threw in an additional bonus prediction. 'You will live a very long life, sir! May the divine grace of the Goddess always be with you!' and gave Reva a look that implied that any such divine grace was unlikely to be bestowed upon her. The parrot eyed the transaction and walked resignedly back into its cage with-out any bidding.

'I need in on this supposed windfall of yours,' Reva said as they both watched his retreating figure approach another couple in the distance. Karthik gave her a rare, loud chuckle that made her feel quite pleased with herself at having prised it out of him.

'So, what do you think about the future? About us, I mean,' Karthik asked. He asked this seriously and Reva knew that anyone else might have adopted a more deliberately casual tone.

Reva took a deep breath of the air that was wet and salty, with a hint of kerosene. 'Maybe we should call the parrot again and ask,' she joked nervously.

'So, what do *you* think?' she rallied the question back.

'I think we should take the next step,' he said, in the matter-of-fact voice of someone who had worked out a decision by following a series of flowcharts. 'I like you, and I like spending time with you.' He paused. 'I also think you are a good person.'

'I think you are a good person, too,' she replied, rather inadequately. She thought of how subdued she felt, compared to the women she saw in films, where at this point, the girl would be making a flapping movement with her hand near her face, trying not to cry with happiness at the sight of an open velvet box.

Reva swatted a fly away as an excuse to break eye contact with him and looked ahead at the soapy blue horizon. 'I think I need more time,' she said, finally.

'Of course. I understand that.' Karthik sounded like he really did. However, both of them knew that he was flying back to the US in a few days, and she was going to be away visiting her mother and grandmother. If she decided not to marry him, this was probably the last time that she would see him. She felt sad at that thought and then wondered what feeling sad at that thought meant.

They sat quietly for a while. The smell of burning oil wafted from the bajji stall, and they watched an old woman decorate the cart with garlands of large green chillies.

'Tried the bajjis here?' Karthik asked.

'No, my mother never allowed me to. She was always listing the illnesses that would befall me if I did.' Reva was feeling quite talkative now that they were back to normal, safe topics of conversation.

'Mine, too. I have never had one either.'

They stared at the stall, watching the woman dip the chillies in orange batter and expertly slide them into the boiling oil. The sharp smell that came from the battered chillies getting crisped in oil was mouth-watering, but neither of them ventured to buy one, not daring to defy the disapproving voices of their mothers in their heads.

Later that evening, Reva's mother emerged as a green bubble on her phone.

'How was meeting with Kodak? Sorry, Karthik.'

Reva felt a twinge of annoyance at having to report back on everything to her mother. *It was OK,* she texted back and left her phone untouched, although it foamed with multiple new green bubbles.

She went to bed, feeling slightly better at having left her mother worried overnight.

*

The bus depot was soupy with people trying to go back home from the city over the weekend. Reva was able to get on the bus as soon as it arrived and found a seat next to the window, where the blue resin was slashed in the middle to reveal its yellow foamy interior. The bus smelled of diesel smoke and cigarettes and the still, humid morning air made Reva break into a sweat. Through the glassless windows of the bus, she noticed a billboard advertisement for Olympic Constructions that showed a happy family with alarmingly bright teeth super-imposed in front of a tall apartment complex. She checked her phone and confirmed with Anand, the journalist, that she would call him back from

the village. The last time she had spoken to him, he had been trying to restrain his excitement while adding cryptically, that 'this
could all be part of something bigger'. He had then tempered
both their optimism by adding that he still hadn't found a news
outlet to take on the story.

As she opened the book that she had brought with her in the
bus, a girl in a black purdah came and sat next to her with a huge,
audible sigh that she listened to with mild foreboding. She knew
that noises such as loud sighs or questions about the bus schedule
usually indicated a fellow passenger who wanted to chat, so she
avoided making eye contact and pretended to be glued to her collec-
tion of short stories by Stephen King.

'I was hoping to get to the bus before it got too crowded. It is the
Theemithi festival in Tiruttani this week, isn't it?' her neighbour asked
chirpily through the black veil of her purdah. Her entire body and face
were covered by silky fabric and Reva could only see her eyes, which
looked startlingly pretty, outlined in inky black kajal. It was difficult to
guess her age, but with the smooth skin around her eyes, put together
with her too-cheerful voice that was just trying itself out in the world,
Reva guessed that she must be somewhere in her early twenties.

Reva nodded although she hadn't remembered about the festival
at all. The Theemithi festival was a yearly occurrence at the Amman
temple in Tiruttani. 'Theemithi' in Tamil translated to 'walking on
fire', and that's exactly what the devotees of the temple did, as an
expression of their devotion. While only a few people walked over
the pit of burning charcoal, hundreds of people gathered in throngs
to watch the spectacle. This explained why the bus was more
crowded than usual, Reva thought, as more people crammed onto
the bus, with elbows of children and corners of suitcases getting
pushed and shoved to fit tightly around one another. She regretted
not renting a car, as she usually did, but was glad that she had at
least got onto the bus early enough to get a seat.

'Are you going to Tiruttani for the festival, too?' the girl asked.

Reva shook her head. 'No, I am getting off at a few stops before that, at Arugoor.'

While Tiruttani was a big town with air-conditioned hotels and restaurants that supported the thousands of devotees that flocked to its famous temple, Arugoor was a smaller village that didn't have the infrastructure that came from having a popular place of worship. Reva's grandfather had been a teacher at the only school in Arugoor, where an average of five students passed the high school board exams every year. Her father had thankfully turned out to be one of them and ended up moving to the city afterwards.

The girl took a magazine out of her handbag and started fanning herself with it. She was wearing her black purdah over what looked like a purple polyester saree that fell in pleats around her feet. Reva thought that she must be feeling very hot, then chastised herself for being judgemental – a foreigner wearing shorts and a tank top in such weather would think her own salwar kameez to be ridiculously stuffy.

As the bus started on its way with a belch of black smoke, her phone pinged with a text. *Have a good trip, Revathi*, it read, with no exclamation points or yellow smiling faces at the end. Reva observed that Karthik somehow managed to convey the unwavering steadiness of his voice through his texts as well.

'My name is Aaliyah,' the girl announced, turning towards Reva again. From the way her eyes crinkled at the corners, Reva guessed that she was smiling at her. With absolutely no encouragement from Reva, Aaliyah decided to tell her all about herself. Aaliyah was going back to her husband's house after spending a week with her parents in Chennai – she had come down to help her sister shop for jewellery and sarees for her wedding. She then spoke about her own wedding, and how the first time that she had seen her husband was only on the day that she had got married.

Reva looked at her in surprise, not for the way she had got married, but at the candour in which she was narrating these details about her life. Arranged marriage was pretty much the only way people got married in the village, with 'love marriages' usually ending with failed drowning attempts in the temple pond.

'— Thankfully, when I sneaked a look at him on the day of our wedding, he looked fine!' Aaliyah said with a suppressed giggle at the end. She added that her husband worked as an electrician, wanted only one wife and even knew how to make an omelette. All her friends repeatedly told her that she was very lucky indeed. She ended this statement by thanking Allah and raising her hands to the sky, revealing a sudden flash of gold bangles beneath her black sleeves.

The bus took a ten-minute break at the terminal at Tiruvallur, where hawkers flocked to the windows of the bus, trying to sell their wares. A flower-seller, carrying a bamboo saucer of jasmines, eyed Reva and Aaliyah dismissively before entreating a young man ahead of them to buy some flowers for his wife. Reva noticed a man selling nongu, the sweet fruit of the palm with the colour and transparency of ice, and called out to him. She bought some for her mother, thinking nostalgically about those afternoons when her mother would peel the thin brown skin off them patiently for Reva so that she could suck on their sweet juice while she studied for her exams. Even now, she knew that her mother would peel them all for her anyway. She could hear her saying, 'I get more than enough here – you must be the one finding it difficult to get these fruits in the city.'

Reva watched a white Ambassador car stop next to the bus, and at the sight of the car, a group of people cheered and rushed towards it. A man stepped out of its humming air conditioning in the black robes and white collar of a priest. His shoes gleamed black like freshly laid tar and seemed magically untouched by the layer of dust that covered every surface of the bus terminal. He held up his palm and gave that oily smile that sometimes passed for benevolence, and the throng of people – mostly farmers and their barefoot children – extended their hands out towards him in an attempt to get a piece of divine grace through his touch. Another man dressed in white walked around with a cloth bag, collecting money from these people who already looked like they had so little. Recognising her impotence to do anything about this situation and feeling guilty for not giving back enough despite having so much more, Reva turned her gaze back to her book until the bus started again.

Halfway through the journey, the bus started moving fast, and Reva could finally feel the tug of a strong breeze that pleasantly ruffled her hair, which was now gritty with sand. The crowd inside the bus had trickled down and there were now people sitting languidly on the floor of the bus, next to fruit baskets and cages of chickens. Reva closed her book and watched stretches of green fields give way to pockets of small towns before giving away to green fields again, all stitched together by black threads of electric lines that ran alongside the road.

Aaliyah, who had been dozing on and off, stirred herself awake and looked out of the window past Reva's shoulders. '*Akka*, are you married?' she then asked, in her sweet sing-song voice, with no preamble leading to this question.

'No.' Reva waited for the censorious stare that usually followed this answer.

'Not yet,' Aaliyah corrected her. 'You are lucky, *akka*. You have freedom.'

Reva didn't know how to respond to that.

Aaliyah's phone beeped and she looked down at it while saying, 'I am pregnant. Five months now.'

'Oh! Congratulations,' exclaimed Reva. The purdah had made it pretty hard to tell.

'If it's a girl,' Aaliyah looked at Reva with eyes that had the very adult expression of unspent worry, 'I want her to grow up and have what you have – freedom to do what she wants.' After another pause, she added, 'My husband also agrees with me.'

Reva smiled and replied that she was very glad to hear that. She didn't know what else to say, so she placed her hand on Aaliyah's elbow reassuringly – a hopeful reassurance for her daughter and for many other girls who would hopefully have a choice – and then looked out of the window as the bus blew its loud horn and continued its way after kicking up a cloud of turmeric-coloured dust.

Reva got off at her stop, thinking how the surroundings of the bus stop always looked familiar but had significant changes every time she visited. Murugan Cool Bar, next to the bus stand, which usually had orange and brown cola in its display case, was now called Ritz Kiosk and sold colourful packs of sanitary napkins and notebooks. The school opposite the stop was covered with scaffolding to support the building of an extension. As Reva straightened her suitcase, a motor-rickshaw driver who had been drowsing inside his vehicle perked up, and she signalled to him.

Within a few minutes, she had left the dust and smoke of the main road and was surrounded by emerald green rice and sugarcane fields on all sides. The gravelly road was bumpy as always, endlessly waiting for a layer of tar to even it out. A bullock cart ambled alongside her rickshaw, and she waved at the kids in the cart, who were sitting cross-legged on brown sacks of rice. They eyed her curiously and waved back half-heartedly at her. A shiny black car passed by, and when someone inside the car aimed an expensive camera at the cart, the kids got up and started dancing and waving exuberantly at them. Reva chuckled wryly to herself.

17

Jason

'Emergency lamps? You will need them for power cuts?' Salim asked, placing a large burlap sack on Jason's doorstep. Jason peered inside to find plastic lamps in primary colours jostling with unkempt coconuts.

'How much?' He picked one up, turned it on and off. Its light appeared feeble when viewed under the brightness of the noon sun.

'These are eight hundred rupees outside. For you, special price, only six hundred.'

'I will give you five hundred, and I will take the red.' Jason took it out of the sack.

Salim raised his eyebrows and looked back at him with a stern expression, but there was a hint of a smile tugging at the corner of his lips. 'OK, OK, but extra fifty rupees for the battery.'

As he handed over the money, Salim continued praising Jason in a way that he now knew to mean that he hadn't bargained hard enough. 'You have got the cheapest price you can get for this lamp. This is an even better price than the one I gave to Jet Raja from the opposite apartment.'

'Raja means king, right?' Jason commented. 'Here, have some onion bajjis that I made this afternoon.' He extended a handful wrapped in newspaper – the way he had seen them sold on roadside stalls here.

'Thank you, sir. By the way, Jet Raja is not his real name, did you know? There are three people called Raja in that apartment complex, and Jet Raja is the one that used to work for Jet Airways. He is now an old, retired man and, with nothing better to do, has started his own investment company so that he can pocket other people's money.'

'Let's see if his investment company takes off.' Jason raised his eyebrows at Salim who looked back expressionlessly at him. 'That was a joke,' Jason started to explain, 'because—'

'Take off and Jet Airways? I get it, I get it. It just isn't good comedy.'

'Or maybe you are just afraid that pearls will fall off if you smile,' was Jason's rejoinder. He had learnt this phrase while watching a Tamil movie with subtitles.

Salim examined one of the bajjis before finishing it swiftly. 'Very good, sir!' he exclaimed, the tone of surprise in his voice indicating that his praise was sincere this time. He wrapped the remaining bajjis more securely in the newspaper with a firm twist before placing them in his sack. 'You are learning. Both with cooking and everything else. These bajjis are superb.' Jason found himself blushing at the unexpected compliment. Salim waved goodbye and walked down the stairs, dragging the sack behind him.

Jason was working through the snacks section of *Cook and See* and, as a result, the acrid smell of burnt oil hung permanently in his kitchen. He plated some bajjis, brewed a cup of Three Roses tea and placed them both next to his laptop. As his hands hovered over his keyboard, he realised with relief that he no longer needed to fight that uncontrollable urge to type Emma's name into the search bar and click through her pictures, his heart beating maddeningly fast whenever he came across something new.

As he peered towards his laptop, he was taken aback when he heard the jubilant ringing of his video messenger, something that had remained dormant on his laptop for as long as he could remember.

'Hello there, Jason love, it's your mum,' his mother announced after he had spent the last few minutes staring at her round chin bobbing up and down as she adjusted her webcam.

'Mum! I didn't know you were on Skype.' He found himself inexplicably smoothing his hair down, although it was only his mother squinting back at him on his computer screen.

'You remember that girl next door? Tiny slip of a thing? She's been helping me sort out this computer business and other bits and bobs.' She looked rather pleased, both with herself and her ability to see Jason on video.

'That's rather nice of her,' Jason found himself saying encouragingly, in the same way that his mother used to when, as a boy, he told her that his friend had shared a bag of sweets with him.

'Your father is at it again – shouting at the telly while watching football,' she genially explained his father's absence.

'Well, of course he is,' he genially empathised in return.

'How's everything, Jason love?' she then asked, her voice sounding a little older than he remembered. His mother explicitly avoided mentioning Emma ever since the breakup, but in the loaded way that she said 'everything', he could see the asterisk and footnote explaining that 'everything' expanded to 'everything after Emma'.

'It's all right, all good.' He shrugged in a manner that indicated that even if everything wasn't all good, she was not really going to hear about it.

'How's everything, really?' she repeated, somehow managing to move the webcam again. Jason could now see the corner of his parents' kitchen where their family cat snoozed away next to a kettle and a packet of Doritos, all of them coloured the same shade of orange.

'How's Daisy?' he asked, changing the topic of discussion to their cat.

'Doing grand. So would you be if all you had to do was eat and sleep all day.'

'That's true.' Jason wiped his sweaty forehead with the sleeve of his T-shirt. The sofa was in a far corner of the living room and did not get enough breeze from the ceiling fan that swirled as fast as it could but still drowned in the Chennai afternoon heat.

'It is starting to get quite nippy here. You need to send some of that Indian sunshine our way,' his mother instructed.

'It gets really hot here. In fact, there are only three seasons in Chennai – hot, hotter, hottest.' He was repeating something that he had heard from several people here, who usually laughed loudly when they said this statement, as if the weather here was any laughing matter.

'Sounds absolutely lovely,' his mother enthused.

Jason smiled thinly in response. He thought that the sun his mother imagined was probably closer in benevolence to the cartoon suns drawn by the children at the school she taught. The sun here, on the other hand, emanated a heat that seeped in through his skull and threatened to knock him out unconscious if he dared to roam outside for too long.

'How is all the cooking going?'

'I've been trying more dishes from that recipe book, you know, the one I've talked about,' Jason told her, almost shyly.

'That's nice. I hope you learnt how to make a proper chicken korma. Your father and I order that every time we get takeaway curry from Spice of India down the road now.' His mother paused, perhaps contemplating the extravagance of this statement, and added, 'Everything is under a tenner there.'

'South Indian food is actually quite a bit different to that,' Jason started explaining. However, he was distracted by the sight of his mother's eyeballs and inexpertly applied mascara peering closely at him through his screen.

'Don't move. There is something behind you,' she whispered rather theatrically.

Jason turned around to look. A mustard-coloured lizard was inching across the wall towards the ceiling, where it usually cooled off on hot afternoons. A few weeks ago, he had Googled remedies to get rid of the lizard and strewn the recommended and rather peculiar repellants of coffee and eggshells around the house, which just made the house messier. He ended up cleaning the house and embracing the fact that he had a housemate by naming the lizard Lizzie.

'That's just Lizzie, the lizard,' he said, enjoying the look of surprised consternation that came across his mother's usually unflappably genial face.

'So, when are you coming back from your holiday then?' she asked, in clear disapproval of his seeming existence in the wild. She kept insisting on referring to his move as a holiday, even though he had been here for four months now and had a job that probably gave him a better standard of living than all of his previous jobs had in London.

'I thought I could make a trip back for Christmas, maybe?'

'And what about after that?'

'Well,' he started, but was saved from planning out his life by the Tamil Nadu Electricity Board, his mother's questioning face suddenly frozen on screen. He took that as a sign and closed his laptop and walked downstairs, where he knew Mani would be sitting by himself at this time of day.

Mani's shaded porch somehow seemed cooler than his living room, and he sat down on the chair next to Mani, both of them taking care not to be caught staring at the dishevelled garden in front of them.

'I've got something with me.' Jason opened his palm to show small sachets of seeds that had optimistic pictures of their future selves drawn in front. 'I thought we could have a small vegetable patch – tomatoes, spinach, some bottle gourd maybe?'

Jason could see worry dart through Mani's face as he wondered what the point of it all was, if the apartment was no longer going to be theirs. However, after a momentary pause, he pointed to the corner of the garden. 'They would grow well in that shaded spot near the guava tree.'

Jason nodded, thinking that the court case would be just around the time when the spinach plants were likely to have their first harvest in about six weeks.

'No time like the present. Let's sow them.' Mani got up from his chair and folded up his veshti, sounding incrementally more cheerful than he had earlier. Jason followed him, the bare, crusted soil feeling almost as solid as the cement floor of the porch.

Mani brought out a pair of small shovels and a bucket of recycled soap water and gave specific instructions to Jason on the location of each plant. Watching Mani's contained smile as he folded a tomato seed gently into the dampened soil, Jason realised that he had never seen Mani outside his natural habitat of this garden and porch. 'Have you lived at Grand Life Apartments all your life?'

'No.' Mani smiled knowingly at Jason, as if he understood why he could have been mistaken to have. 'When I was very young, I actually tried to stay away from home as much as possible.' He told Jason stories of his travels around the country – about snowy mountains stalked by shadows of leopards, about bridges made out of the living roots of trees and of people who were all much the same although they spoke a multitude of languages. He ended his stories of travels by resting his eyes on the guava tree. 'I came back when my mother was taken ill and decided to stay.'

He then nodded encouragingly at Jason, perhaps realising that he had been talking for a while. 'You are doing the right thing by travelling when you're young.'

Jason didn't mention that his reasons for coming here were quite different from that of the regular traveller's, but admitted, 'Coming here has been really good for me.'

Mani patted down the soil reassuringly. 'These plants should start showing themselves in a few days.' Jason had no reason to feel optimistic about the outcome of the court case, or these plants, but added, 'We should also grow some herbs like basil and mint.' His eyes fell on the stalks of the rose bush next to him – although there was nothing left of it except one scrawny stem, it was stubbornly sending hope into the world with its tiny new leaves of bright, unblemished green.

18

Kamala

Kamala couldn't stop staring outside the window. It was a clear day, and the scenery on the way to Oxford looked uncomprehendingly foreign to her – she had never seen a sun that cast such soft buttery light, or a sky that looked so dewy blue or grass that came in so many different shades of green. She took out Sundu's camera and took many pictures of the landscape, mainly because she didn't know how else to respond to something so beautiful.

Most of the people inside the train, however, were oblivious to the beauty passing by and were looking down at their phones, expressionless. Some others were closing their eyes to catch a little nap, while one young girl, who looked to be Lakshmi's age, was expertly applying make-up with a brush while looking critically at a mirror propped on her handbag. Throughout the last few days, Kamala had closely observed girls who were Lakshmi's age – some dressed strangely in all-black costumes, some looked pretty as Barbie dolls but walked in a lopsided way – wondering which one of them fit the way Lakshmi behaved here. Did Lakshmi, whom she never thought to have worn make-up, also paint her already black eyelashes to be even blacker?

'Here, try some.' Sundu interrupted her thoughts with a shiny brown pastry studded with raisins. 'It is a cinnamon bun,' she explained, although Kamala had been standing right next to her when she had bought it at the station.

'It might have eggs in it, don't you think?' Kamala forensically examined the glazing on the pastry.

'You may be right. Oh well.' Sundu shrugged and finished off the pastry in swift bites before inspecting the paper bag from the bakery for something more to eat.

Sundu's childishly impudent behaviour reminded Kamala of Sundu's son when he was younger, but she waited until Sundu had finished eating and crumpled the paper bag into a ball before asking, 'I heard you speaking with your son this morning. How is he doing?' She avoided mentioning the daughter-in-law because all of Sundu's evidence seemed to paint her as a devious schemer who had stepped right out of a dramatic scene from her television soaps and into Sundu's son's life. Just over a month ago, she had heard that the daughter-in-law had suddenly acted all nice and spoken words of honey to Sundu, only to sting her like a bee and ask her for a large sum of money.

'He said he is coming home for Deepavali at least, so that's nice. I am going to keep my eyes peeled for any new schemes from that cunning fox, though.'

'I'm glad that they are coming to Chennai to be with you for the festival,' Kamala said, struggling to adopt the right positive tone for her response. She didn't know how she herself would deal with someone like Sundu's daughter-in-law but knew that there was no person better equipped to handle this than her friend.

'Wait, let me show you something.' Sundu attached earphones to her phone, mimicking everyone else on the train. She gave Kamala one of the earbuds, which she wore gingerly – she had never had reason to use earphones before, although she was familiar with them since Lakshmi's ears had sprouted them when she turned fifteen.

Sundu was playing a grainy video of her son standing on some sort of stage on her phone. Kamala thought that he was dressed rather smartly and unnecessarily warmly, in a leather jacket and jeans. 'You would not believe it is the same boy who would remove all his clothes when it was too hot and run around the house naked, would you?' Sundu exclaimed, and they laughed, knowing that these were the kind of jokes that now elicited extremely irritated stares from their grown-up children.

It seemed to be a comedy show, and Sundu's son was trying to tell a joke about astrologers by simply stating facts about how astrology worked in a silly voice. Kamala didn't find it to be in the least bit funny but made an effort to smile for Sundu's sake. However, the next topic he moved to was about body parts, and it took Kamala a while to figure out that he was talking about the awkwardness of sex education in his high school. His hand gestures, and the words he used, made Kamala shift uncomfortably in her seat. She turned around to look at Sundu, who was watching the video with a fascinated expression on her face.

Kamala didn't say anything but quietly removed her single earphone in disapproval and held it in her palm, not wanting to disturb her friend. Sundu noticed it and laughed, 'I knew you wouldn't like hearing that.'

Kamala could not bring herself to say anything positive to what she just heard. 'Comedy these days is quite different from our time, isn't it?' was the best she could come up with.

'Kamala, let me be honest with you. I don't like this nonsense either.' Sundu sighed as she disentangled her earphone from her greying hair. She craned her neck to check where the train had stopped, and muttered, 'Half-way there,' before continuing, 'However, I watch this because at least now I know more about what he is thinking, and more about what is going on in his life. He calls me once every hundred days, and you know what he talks to me about?' Sundu shook her head in an expression of disbelief. 'The weather and the traffic. As if I am some useless old lady who cannot read that on the internet herself.'

'That's true. They all have sides to them that they don't tell us about. Don't I know that?' Kamala replied with a slight bitterness that made her wonder, for the hundredth time that week, if the conversation ahead with Lakshmi was perhaps beyond her.

*

Lakshmi's apartment block was a tall, thin building with peeling blue paint. Unlike its neighbouring houses, it didn't show any signs of domesticity, such as a newly painted mailbox or a blooming rose bush. Instead, it had an overgrown front garden lined with dented garbage bins and a bicycle that stood forlornly without its wheels.

Kamala pressed the doorbell to Flat F, which was indicated by a careless scrawl on a thin scrap of paper. They weren't sure how doorbells worked here and suspensefully waited for something to happen. After futilely pressing the doorbell for the fifth time in five minutes, Kamala looked over at Sundu, who shrugged as if to say she was as clueless as Kamala.

'We should have called Lakshmi this morning to let her know,' Sundu added, more pointedly than Kamala would have liked.

After twenty minutes of standing around, both Kamala and Sundu sat on the pavement next to a few withered potted plants. The road was extremely quiet for four in the afternoon, and they saw no one apart from a young woman with a pushchair who eyed them curiously before opening a door much farther down the road. Kamala wondered how safe this road was for Lakshmi to walk alone, especially at night.

An hour and a half later, Kamala noticed Lakshmi's slight frame at a distance, carrying a large cloth bag. Both Kamala and Lakshmi stood up immediately in attention, willing Lakshmi to set eyes on them.

Lakshmi was typing something on her phone while walking and didn't look up at them until she was only a few metres away. When she finally did, she looked completely and utterly shocked, her mouth dropped open in an expression of total surprise that Kamala had never seen on Lakshmi's grown-up face before.

'*Amma!*' she exclaimed in disbelief. Instead of dropping her bag of groceries to the floor in shock, she seemed to hold on to it tighter, as if she was making sure that its weight, and what she was seeing, was real.

'How are you, *kanna*?' asked Kamala, her face blooming with such happiness at the sight of her daughter that she temporarily forgot her nervousness.

'I am good, Ma. Just really surprised to see you both here. How long have you both been waiting on the road for me? What if I had gone out for the day? You could have just called me, you know?' She sounded more than a little overwhelmed.

Sundu exchanged a familiar glance with Lakshmi. 'I told your mother to call. You know how she is, never listens to any good advice.'

Lakshmi dug out her keys from deep within the recesses of her cloth bag and jangled it into the keyhole, struggling to open the door. Once ajar, she looked back at them as if to reconfirm that Kamala and Sundu had really appeared, in person, on her doorstep. She warned them that they needed to climb three flights of stairs to reach her flat before nimbly climbing ahead. Both Kamala and Sundu struggled with the stairs, pausing often to catch their breath, leaning against the peeling sour milk coloured wallpaper that lined the stairway.

When they finally reached the cramped landing of Lakshmi's flat, Kamala knelt down awkwardly to remove her shoes.

'Are you really wearing sports shoes?' asked Lakshmi, in a voice that had still not lost its tone of surprise.

'Sundu made me buy them. I am actually finding it very comfortable now,' Kamala replied. 'Have you been eating properly? You look like you have lost even more weight than the last time I saw you!'

'You always say that, Ma.' Lakshmi shrugged, ushering them into her flat.

Kamala was surprised to see that it was even smaller than it had looked in pictures – the living room so tiny that you could do away with a remote and change TV channels directly from the sofa, and the kitchen consisting of just a stove-top and a small cupboard.

Kamala and Sundu sat down on the sofa, while Lakshmi sat hunched on a small, foldable chair. Kamala had rehearsed topics of conversation on the train ride and immediately brought up the court case that threatened Grand Life Apartments, eliciting an alarmed gasp from her daughter. They discussed this topic with the concentration of stilt-walkers at the temple festival, careful not to take a misstep towards anything else – they talked about Sundu's experience with these types of cases, Kamala's strong belief that misusing god's name would backfire as per the universally renowned concept of karma, Lakshmi's concern about where Kamala would live if the case didn't go well.

After they had exhausted those topics, Sundu made an excuse about going for a walk and left Kamala and Lakshmi alone together. They talked about Lakshmi's academics and Kamala's new patients, although a bit more awkwardly without Sundu's opinionated presence.

Lakshmi suddenly got up, exclaiming, 'I didn't ask if you wanted anything. Shall I make you some coffee? I don't have filter coffee, though, only instant.'

'OK.' Kamala smiled. After a minute, she moved to stand next to her daughter and watched her pour hot water into a yellow ceramic mug and mix in spoonfuls of metallic smelling coffee.

'How much sugar should I add?' Lakshmi asked, holding up a glass jar with perfectly shaped sugar cubes of the kind that Kamala had never seen before.

'Add however much you are adding to yours.'

'I have it black,' she said and, looking at her mother's confused expression, added, 'I don't add sugar to my coffee.' Her daughter's eyes then flitted over the wine and whisky bottles arranged neatly on a shelf next to the kettle before returning back somewhat defiantly to meet her mother's.

'So, how did you both like London? Did you find it too cold?' Kamala knew that this was probably the closest Lakshmi would come to asking her why she was here.

'It was all very nice. Sundu took me walking around everywhere – my knees aren't what they used to be, though, you know.'

'I am really glad that you have made a complete recovery after your accident, Ma.' Lakshmi touched Kamala's elbow.

'So, while I was at the hospital, I was thinking –' She was interrupted by a young girl who came out of a door next to the kitchen stove. The girl was around Lakshmi's age, blonde-haired and wearing nothing other than a long, white T-shirt. She stopped short and looked at Kamala with an expression of shocked surprise. She then turned to Lakshmi and exclaimed, 'Oh Lux! You didn't tell me your mum was visiting!'

'I didn't know she was, either. She decided to surprise me.' Lakshmi's English accent as she spoke to this girl sounded so different that Kamala had to guess at what she was saying.

'Oh, great! I need to rush to a class now, but very nice meeting you. I will see you around,' the girl chirped in Kamala's direction and disappeared as suddenly as she had appeared.

'She seems nice.' Kamala looked down at her coffee mug, then glanced up with a start, a bewildered look coming across her face. She spoke in flustered half sentences, 'Is she your . . . Wait. You didn't mention –'

'She is my housemate. Rent is too expensive otherwise,' Lakshmi said quickly.

'Oh, all right, I see.' Kamala exhaled, sipping her coffee. Her head was thrumming with the migraine that had settled permanently into a corner of her brain ever since Lakshmi had made her confession to her, and never really gone away. She knew that she had a sad expression on her face and her daughter was watching her closely, missing nothing.

She turned to Lakshmi and spoke in a deliberately bright voice, 'Wait, I forgot to give you the badam halwa that I bought for you from Krishna Sweets.' She got up, then turned towards Lakshmi. 'You still eat sweets, right – you were mentioning something about not taking sugar?'

'That was only for coffee, Ma,' Lakshmi replied, her voice sounding a little too even. They went back to meaningless small talk, even more awkwardly this time, and when Sundu returned, had a dinner of frozen pizza reheated in the oven. Kamala thought that this pizza, unlike the one she had in London, tasted like salted cardboard, but she told Lakshmi that it tasted good.

Lakshmi had given Kamala and Sundu her bed, explaining she would sleep on the sofa, which expanded out to become a bed. Kamala couldn't sleep, however, and observed the unfamiliar room around her in the dim light that came from the streetlamps outside.

The room was small, but neatly kept with a study table next to the bed and a compact bookshelf on top. Kamala leant across the table for her spectacles and prayer book so that she could pray to calm her mind. Her hands felt Lakshmi's familiar leather wallet, which had been a New Year's gift from Kamala's hospital and had her name embroidered on it. Kamala opened the wallet, and beneath Lakshmi's IDs and credit card, she saw a rectangular card that she had given to Lakshmi around her eighteenth birthday.

'It is a protective chakra that I got from the temple. You should carry it in your wallet. It will protect you wherever you go,' she had said with absolute belief when she had given it to her.

'All right,' Lakshmi had replied, giving her that look of mild irritation mixed with indifference – the look she gave every time Kamala involved her in anything religious.

Kamala hadn't expected Lakshmi to carry that card for this long in her wallet, and she traced the outline it had wedged inside the leather pocket thoughtfully. She finally fell asleep, still holding the wallet in her hands.

The next morning, Kamala woke up early and wandered into the kitchen to find Lakshmi drinking a cup of coffee, facing a window that overlooked a roof. As she looked out of the window, her chin was gently and thoughtfully tapping the rim of her cup – a habitual childhood gesture that had remained well into adulthood. Something about that familiar gesture that Kamala had seen every day for years tugged at her heart, forcefully reminding her that she loved her daughter more than anything else in the world. Sensing her presence, Lakshmi turned around and smiled tentatively at Kamala, but at that moment, two slices of bread popped up from the toaster, distracting them.

'Wait, let me make a hot breakfast for you – maybe I can make some bread upma with the bread you have already toasted,' Kamala offered.

'No, Ma, don't bother. I am running late for my classes anyway,' Lakshmi replied, walking around briskly, multitasking between eating her toast and packing her bag with books.

'Here, you didn't have any of the badam halwa I bought for you.' Kamala picked up the sweet box that was left unopened on the kitchen table and offered it to Lakshmi.

'It is too early in the morning, Ma. I will eat it later, maybe.' Seeing her mother's slightly crestfallen expression, she gave a forced smile. 'Maybe just a little. I am trying to watch my weight, you know?'

'I don't know why you are always trying to go on diets,' Kamala said, tearing open the plastic wrapper of the box. After a moment, she added, 'You are perfect the way you are.'

Lakshmi looked at her, startled at the full import of this statement. 'I can finish early and then show you around campus? Maybe we can go to the Indian grocery store and get some things to cook dinner after?'

'That sounds nice.'

She watched Lakshmi put away her dishes – it was barely perceptible, but there was something lighter in the way she carried herself as she walked around the kitchen. Kamala's migraine was throbbing less as well, although it had not entirely gone away. However, she now understood that, given enough time, it would.

19

Revathi

Their house in the village was over twenty years old and freshly painted pale brown, the colour of the chocolate wafer that you could buy for two rupees apiece from the shop around the corner. The door was always left open during the day, and you could see right through the house and view the garden as a bright rectangle of yellow and green. The garden was expansive and had mango and coconut trees interspersed with flower bushes, which used to be lovingly tended to by her grandmother every day. Now, with nobody to keep them in check, the plants had fallen in favour with wilder company and clambered against the fences and paths in unkempt abandon.

Her mother appeared from the side of the house, walking eagerly and wiping her hands on her saree. She was not used to hugging, but Reva held her in a tight embrace anyway. Her mother smelled familiarly of talcum powder and coconut oil, and Reva suddenly felt nostalgic for her, although her mother was right there with her.

'How long has it been since you last visited!' her mother exclaimed, her diamond nose-ring catching the noon sun as she appraised Reva's appearance. Reva noticed guiltily that there were new wisps of grey in her mother's hair every time she visited, as if her hair were carefully watching and marking the time intervals between Reva's visits back home.

Later in the evening, Reva sat on the cool, concrete floor, avoiding the resin sofa that would feel sticky with her sweat. Her mother sat next to her, shredding coconut with a metal scraper while her eyes were fixated on the evening soap playing on the television. Reva felt herself relax in the house where she was intensely familiar with everything – the cobweb behind the goddess Saraswati photo that you couldn't reach without a ladder, the switchboard where the switch for the fan had faded a murky yellow from overuse, the plastic bucket in the corner of the verandah that caught rainwater that dripped through the thunderbolt-shaped crack in the ceiling.

'How is *Paatti* doing these days?' Reva eyed her grandmother's room where she had found her curled up in sleep, covered by one of her mother's old cotton sarees.

Her mother turned to Reva and spoke over the high volume of the television, 'The new medicines seem to be working a little better, Revathi. Although she is far from doing well – just last week, she threw her food on the floor thinking that someone was trying to poison her.' A look of sadness fluttered across her mother's face before it settled down to an expression that was more hopeful. 'Maybe the new medicines will help her get better soon, and she will actually know who you are at your wedding.' Reva knew the line of questioning that would soon follow and made an excuse about going into the kitchen to get Fanta from the fridge.

'So, am I allowed to ask what is happening with Karthik?' her mother asked as Reva stood up.

'No, you may not,' Reva replied in a deliberately defensive voice.

'Revathi, listen to me,' her mother said, with a sigh that usually implied the start of an advice-giving monologue. 'Karthik is from a good family, and they don't mind that we are not as well-to-do as they are. I am sure they have hundreds of alliances lining up at their doors, but for some reason, the boy seems to like you. So, I hope you make a good decision quickly.'

Reva didn't respond to her mother but walked into the kitchen instead.

'You never told me, what do you want me to cook for dinner?' her mother shouted across the corridor. Reva pretended that she couldn't hear.

Reva had trouble sleeping that night. It was too hot, and she missed the zealous air conditioning in her apartment that acted like a blast chiller, routinely frosting the bottle of water she kept next to her bed. The windows here were open, but it was pointless, as the air outside was still and thick with no sign of a breeze. Through the windows, she could see fireflies hovering outside, signalling to each other with flashes of yellow light.

She recalled mentioning these fireflies to Karthik when they had been exchanging childhood stories while sipping fancy coffees in a café on Khader Nawaz Road. 'I have never seen a firefly,' Karthik had said seriously, but not wistfully, as if never seeing a firefly in his life would not really bother him. He had then added, 'Did you know that fireflies are the most efficient sources of light in the world – hundred per cent of the energy in the chemical reaction is transmitted as light?' Reva knew other trivia about fireflies that could be considered more fun – for instance, the fact that some fireflies tend to snack on each other when they feel peckish – but she had simply nodded back with feigned interest. Shortly after, though, she remembered that he had borrowed two sachets of sugar from the nearby table and placed them next to her cup, although he took his coffee without sugar.

Her recollections of Karthik started becoming more distorted the longer she stayed awake. She tossed and turned in her bed, trying to come up with rational arguments that would help her decide on where she stood with him. However, the longer she watched the ceiling fan draw empty circles in the air, the more incomprehensible her thoughts became. She finally started sleeping fitfully only after the darkness in her room started giving way to the soft light of daybreak.

Reva's mother had let her sleep in, and she woke up close to noon to find the house searingly hot and empty. She walked to the garden, where the air smelled of sun-scorched earth and manure. Despite the lack of breeze, Reva knew that it would be cooler to sit under the dense canopy of trees rather than indoors under an over-whelmed fan. She sat underneath the shade of her favourite mango tree and called back Anand, who picked up her call immediately.

'Revathi, hello, one minute—' She could hear a song with high percussive notes playing in the background. The volume of the movie song decreased as he walked away someplace quieter. '—So, about the article,' he said, pausing to exhale down the line.

'Do you need any other information? Mani Uncle said he shared everything about the apartments, including copies of his ownership documents, with you.'

'So, the forged documents for Grand Life Apartments is just a very small part of what I discovered about the politician . . .' He paused again.

'That's good because it makes the story better, doesn't it?' Reva asked hopefully.

'Revathi, the thing is,' Anand started in an apologetic voice that made Reva's hope flicker, 'I just learnt that I am going to be a father.'

'Congratulations!'

'Thank you. But this also means that I can't be taking these kinds of risks anymore. From what I have learnt, these guys can be quite dangerous. I would ask Mr Mani to be careful when dealing with them.'

Reva told him that she understood and thanked him for his help, although she didn't quite manage to hide the disappointment in her voice as she said it.

She had just ended the call when she was startled by the sound of her grandmother's voice next to her.

'Revathi, do you remember the story behind this hibiscus bush?' Her grandmother had managed to wheel her chair outdoors, and Reva could tell that she was having one of her rare moments of lucidity. She was pointing at the overgrown bush next to her, which was covered in large white flowers the size of Reva's palm.

'Ah, yes.' Reva nodded, smiling at her *paatti*. When Reva had been around seven or eight, she had poured a perfectly good bottle of Brill ink into the soil to see if the white flowers would turn blue. She could no longer tell if she had the actual memory of the incident or if it was a memory created after repeatedly listening to her father's recording of this conversation on a cassette tape. It never ceased to amaze her how, even now, she could switch on the black tape recorder, watch the reel of the cassette turn, and listen to her father's voice come out of it and ask her teasingly about this bottle of blue ink.

'Do you remember how *appa* used to keep recording everything on tape? Especially when I sang, although my voice was horrible?' she asked her grandmother.

Instead of replying to her, her grandmother closed her eyes and started humming an unrecognisable song while tapping unrhythmically against the handles of the wheelchair with swollen knuckles that looked like knobs of ginger. Reva sighed, spread the patch of prickly heat powder at the back of her grandmother's neck more evenly, and wheeled her back inside, thinking that whatever happened with the apartments, she would always have the memories associated with it.

She walked to the kitchen, where her mother was toasting a garnish of curry leaves and mustard seeds in oil, the smell making her stomach rumble involuntarily. Her mother was making lemon rice for lunch – something that Reva knew was considered too modern for her mother's tastes but was being made exclusively for her daughter's benefit. There were also baby brinjals roasted in oil, avial made with yoghurt and vegetables and a coconut thogayal to go with everything. Reva winced looking at the amount of work that must have gone into this and glanced guiltily at the remnants of her mother's cooking – piles of peeled vegetable skins, blender jars of various sizes waiting in the sink and husks of coconuts lying next to a sickle.

She dipped a spoon into the lemon rice. 'So tasty.' It took her a moment to realise that her mother had added too much salt. If there had been anything in her life that she could have taken for granted, it was the fact that her mother could make a flawless South Indian meal with her eyes closed.

'Is the lemon rice all right?' her mother asked, ripping coriander leaves from its stem.

'Just as I remember it,' lied Reva, a lump forming in her throat. She went over to her mother and hugged her across her shoulders as her mother multitasked across three stoves.

'Do you want beetroot or carrot halwa for evening tiffin?' her mother asked, pleased at this rare display of affection from Reva.

'Neither. They contain too much sugar and are not good for either of us.'

'You need a little bit of sugar and butter every day as part of a healthy diet,' her mother declared authoritatively.

'By the way, it is looking very likely that the construction company will win the case in court.' Reva sighed, temporarily reverting to her childhood habit of confiding all her worries to her mother.

'Mani should have sold it to them when he had a chance,' her mother said matter-of-factly, making her remember why she had outgrown this habit. 'Anyways, you may be living in the US very soon with Karthik, wouldn't you?' her mother added, glancing at Reva before stirring the baby brinjals that had acquired a glossy sheen. 'It is true that it will take a few months to get the wedding organised, especially since good caterers get booked out in advance. In the meantime, it will be good for you to live in a flat surrounded by normal families, wouldn't it? – '

Reva dropped her hands from around her mother's shoulders.

' – Velli *Athai* has invited herself for dinner today, by the way. She heard that you were in town and wanted to see you,' her mother added in a casual tone that fooled neither of them. Velli was her father's sister, and as siblings, they couldn't have been more different from one another. She was circling their ancestral home more closely now that her grandmother was ill. The last time that Reva had visited, Velli had stood very close to her and touched the chain on her neck. 'Is this real gold? Looks a lot like something that used to belong to your grandmother,' she had said with a smile that was all teeth. The memory of her aunt's fingers on her neck made Reva shiver slightly in the balmy kitchen.

'Why couldn't you just tell her not to come?' asked Reva indignantly. 'Why do you always have to be such a pushover?' She regretted her words as soon as she said them. Her mother just shrugged tiredly. 'What can you do, Revathi? She is your father's sister. You tell me, how can I ask her not to come to her own childhood home?'

Over dinner that evening, Reva tried her best to not engage in conversation with Velli. They were all seated on the floor, eating from round stainless steel plates with separate circular compartments for rice, brinjals and pickles. Velli's thin frame was bent over her plate, and she ate by rolling rice and sambar into a round ball before popping it into her mouth. In her green saree that day, she reminded Reva of a grasshopper with its spindly legs and arms, picking its way through its food. Reva wondered idly about countries where she had heard that they fried and ate grasshoppers as a snack.

Reva's grandmother was placed on a chair at the side of the room next to the television and was eating a bowl of curd rice that had been put through the blender so that she could swallow it easily. She seemed oblivious to the three of them and was watching the flickering screen on mute, occasionally murmuring instructions at the characters on screen.

Velli was complaining about the rising costs of everything – of onions at the vegetable market, of archanai tickets at the temple, of the salwar-kameez set that her daughter had just bought. She then looked up at Reva and asked, more to make a point than to know the actual answer, 'You and Gita are almost the same age, aren't you?'

Reva heard the taunt in the inflection of the word 'age' but decided to ignore it. Although Reva had always disliked her aunt, she was fond of her daughter, Gita. She was sweet, eager to please and had been married off at twenty-one and now had two children who were almost as tall as Reva. Sometimes, when she met Gita at weddings and watched her admonish her children, Reva couldn't help thinking that Gita herself hadn't had the chance to grow up from being a child. They spoke to each other formally and politely when they met now, both of them over-assuring each other that everything was going as well as it could in their respective lives.

Reva didn't respond to her aunt's question, knowing the subtext of what she was getting at.

'Actually, Reva is a year older than Gita,' her mother chipped in unhelpfully.

'That's right.' Her aunt turned to her mother and Reva could have sworn that she could see her eyes glint. 'If my brother was around, things would have been different, obviously. He would have made sure that his daughter got married at an appropriate age.' Reva bristled as she watched her mother's face crumple.

'There's a certain age beyond which it will be difficult to find a husband, you know, leave alone bearing children,' she added, now looking at Reva, while continuing to knead the ball of rice in her hand.

'That's enough advice, Velli *Athai*,' Reva said evenly, before turning her gaze back to her mother who was quietly looking down at her plate.

'That's the issue, isn't it? You have been spoiled by your mother, who has let you do exactly as you please. You have now become so stubborn that you wouldn't be able to adjust to the role of a good wife,' she admonished.

'Like you have adjusted, *Athai*?' Reva asked. She paused before continuing, her voice low but taut as a tightrope, 'Like you have adjusted to pretend that your husband doesn't have a second wife in the neighbouring village?'

There was a stunned silence as her aunt looked at her, her hand stopped midway to her mouth. Reva felt a moment of gratification looking at her shock, but then immediately felt crass for stooping down to her level.

At that point, Reva's grandmother started fidgeting with her bowl and spoon and started hitting them together. Humming the same tune that she was singing earlier, she looked down at Reva, her face as bewildered as a young girl's. 'Do you know what this song is? We used to sing this at night to make you sleep.' Reva got up and kissed her grandmother's cheek. She murmured softly that she didn't remember the song and pulled up a chair next to her grandmother and finished her dinner.

An hour later, her mother came into Reva's room without knocking, although she had closed the door. Reva continued reading her book in bed and didn't acknowledge her mother's presence as she sat on the corner of her bed and watched Reva with a put-upon expression. After a minute, Reva closed her book and looked at her mother, waiting for her to say something.

'That scorpion has left,' her mother finally said, in an unusual open display of dislike towards Velli. 'She was obviously trying to taunt you, but you needn't have brought up the mistress. She was unstoppable in her laments after you left.'

'I really don't care much about what she thinks,' Reva shrugged. She placed her bus ticket as a bookmark carefully inside her book and closed it. 'Ma, tell me honestly, you don't think it's your fault that I am not married, do you? It shouldn't be any parent's responsibility. What matters is that I am happy, or at least happier than I would be if I was in a relationship that I didn't want to be in.'

'Of course, I am doing all this so that you can be happy. Who is going to look after you after I am gone? You wouldn't really understand all this until you have a child of your own.' Her mother smiled despairingly.

Reva wondered if she should make her mother despair more by declaring that she didn't know whether she wanted children at all but decided to make a concerted effort to be kind. 'Well, we just have to disagree on that then,' she said, smiling with her lips straight, and went back to her book.

'I'll get going. Shouldn't forget to sour the milk like I did the other day. We had to go without curd for an entire day. And your grandmother doesn't like to eat anything other than curd rice these days,' her mother spoke rapidly, getting up from the bed.

However, she didn't leave until she had closed all the windows and sprayed eucalyptus-scented repellent in Reva's room so that the mosquitoes didn't keep her daughter up at night.

*

Reva's mother sat hunched at the edge of Reva's bed and observed her daughter sullenly as she zipped up her bag. 'You are going to leave despite the bus strike? You don't have any more holidays to take, is it?'

'I have told you about the situation at work, Ma. I can't be away for too long.' The taxi honked loudly outside, announcing its arrival.

Reva dragged her bag to the living room, where her grandmother sat dozing after taking her morning medications. Reva touched her *paatti*'s feet as she said goodbye. Although her grandmother was in a peaceful mood, she didn't recognise Reva and looked down at her curiously like a child watching shoes being fitted for the first time.

'Don't forget to say your prayers before you leave,' warned her mother as Reva carried her bags further to the front porch. Reva obediently went back inside to the prayer room and applied the smallest dab of vermilion on her forehead as proof.

Outside, she hugged her mother, who awkwardly patted her back. She got into the taxi, which was an old white Ambassador car, and hand-cranked her window down.

Her mother bent down and spoke across the car window, 'Don't wait too long to make a decision, Revathi. Let me know the good news soon, and I will come to the city for official discussions.' Reva looked up and squinted, the sun in full bloom behind her mother's hopeful face. She smiled thinly and waved her goodbyes, deciding it was just easier to nod at everything at this point.

'– remember not to roam around too much in the sun and darken your skin,' her mother ended, and walked ahead to dispel more advice to the driver. 'Drive carefully, Babu. Don't take any short-cuts away from the main road and make sure you turn the AC on in the car.'

She furtively gave him a tip that Reva considered to be embarrassingly low. The driver pocketed the money and nodded his head vigorously anyway. As the car started, Reva waved a final goodbye to her mother and cranked her window up. She didn't need to look back to know that her mother would be waving at the car until it was nothing but a tiny speck on the horizon.

The entire drive back felt different when viewed through the clean, tinted windows of her taxi. She realised that she needn't be alert and keep her eye on her luggage, but could get lost in thought as she watched bright green fields and mud houses flip by from inside the cushioned perch of her car. She imagined herself in similar car drives, if she were to move to California with Karthik – perhaps through one of those ocean-lined highways that swerved next to impossibly tall redwood trees. She wondered if this future version of herself would be nervously excited for the new life that she had chosen or be regretful of transplanting her entire life to be with someone she didn't entirely know. She finally felt like she was getting closer to finding her answer to this question.

Once she reached her apartment, she opened her laptop and checked her emails. The tech start-up that she had interviewed with had offered her a more senior title with a large team but with no increase in pay. Her eyes then skipped over to an email from Karthik. He had sent an email containing a link to an article in the *New York Times* debating the benefits of drinking coffee – a follow-up of something that they had discussed the last time they had met. She knew that the subtext of the email was really a reminder that he needed answering to.

*

When Reva went into work the next day, she was surprised to find the interiors of the office repainted a red so bright and vivid that it almost hurt her eyes. Previously, when her company was called Informatics & Co., it had been painted various shades of grey with blue lighting, making her sometimes wonder if, to an external observer, they all looked like fish swimming pointlessly inside a tank. Now, with the company being renamed Zip Technologies, it seemed to have gone through an image overhaul, and the interiors of the office were being replaced by the same exuberant colour that was part of their new logo.

'The office looks great, doesn't it?' enthused a young intern as she walked to her desk.

Reva thought that this shade of red didn't look great on anything with the exception of perhaps Kanjeevaram silk sarees but nodded agreeably in return.

She could have hardly been at her desk for fifteen minutes, when Subbu stopped by. 'Hello, Revathi. How was your holiday? Everyone fine and well back home?' he asked in a surprisingly attentive tone. 'I saved one of our new monogrammed cups for you.'

He handed her a coffee mug with a cartoon letter Z with over-zealous eyes that looked a little bit like Subbu's. Reva thought of lambs that got fattened up before getting converted into dinner and accepted the mug cautiously.

'Have a few minutes for a quick discussion?' he asked solicitously, instead of the usual curt head-nod he gave to anyone he wanted to talk with.

They went inside a meeting room where the chairs had been replaced by red beanbags. Reva slipped into one and watched Subbu with mild amusement as he gingerly lowered himself down, the beanbag squeaking a little in protest.

'The reason I wanted to talk to you is that I want you to be the lead for the B56 project again.'

'Isn't that the project that Vijay is leading? You transferred the project from me to him, remember?' She raised an eyebrow, not altogether displeased with where this conversation was going.

'You will be the right fit for it,' his flattering manner falsely implying that he had always thought Reva the right person to lead this project.

'Does Vijay know about this?'

'Oh, don't you worry about him. He has transitioned.' Subbu flapped his arms as if Vijay had transitioned into thin air and evaporated from the office building. It was only later that she learnt that Vijay had upgraded to a larger company, where he would have a bigger playground for his political exploits.

'Well, I am assuming you are giving me the promotion?' she pressed.

'Promotion?' Subbu peered at Reva as if it were a new word that he had never heard before. He then reclined, somehow managing to find a comfortable position in the beanbag as well, and placed his hands underneath his head. 'We will have to revisit that after the delivery of the project, obviously,' he said, giving her his slipperiest smile.

*

Later, over lunch, Ranji repeated everything Reva said, but replaced Reva's informative tone with one of absolute disbelief. It was first, 'You are planning to leave your job for a start-up?' which was then followed by, 'You don't want to marry Karthik?'

'About the job, it is really a no-brainer. I simply cannot work in an office that looks like a tomato ketchup explosion,' she joked weakly before adding, 'I have been wanting a change anyways, and working for a smaller company feels exciting. I am going to try negotiating my pay with the start-up, though.'

'I get that. Although start-ups are very risky, with an average life span of less than two years,' Ranji warned. Her face then took upon an injured expression. 'But what about Karthik? I thought it was going well?'

'Well,' she started, reserving her energy for a more apologetic explanation that would be later forthcoming with her mother.

'I really don't know him well enough to commit to spending my entire lifetime with him.' She felt incredibly guilty even as she said this, knowing that she was behaving from a place of complete selfishness, something that she was not sure she had the right to.

Ranji looked uncomprehendingly at her and then stared down, as if she were mentally trying to formulate an argument, and the missing words were scrambled inside her open lunchbox.

'Even love marriages are not perfect, you know that?' Ranji looked up triumphantly. 'One of my friends who had a love marriage is now getting a divorce.' She shook her head in disapproval at all the unhappiness that seemed to accompany these so-called modern values.

'I am not denying that,' Reva replied, shrugging. She found herself backing away from providing further explanations, knowing that her decision would probably be voted as unreasonable by an overwhelming majority of Chennai's population.

Looking at Reva's closed-off face, Ranji sighed. 'By the way, my manager has agreed to consider letting me work part-time after the baby, on a trial basis. Let's see how that goes.'

'That's great news, Ranji!' Reva exclaimed, taking a spoonful of the vegetable biryani that had become cold over the course of their conversation.

They ate silently for a few minutes, each of them inhabiting their own, different worlds. Ranji finally murmured, 'We need to have a send-off party for you.'

'That would be great.' Reva smiled back.

It was quite late by the time Reva sat down in front of her laptop to compose her reply to Karthik. Throughout the day, she had mentally rehearsed the sentences that she wanted to write, and she typed them, glad that the subject line still said *Re: Hello*. She then drafted and redrafted her words several times. Over eight sentences, she told him that he was a great person, but she was just not sure about making the decision to marry him in such a short period of time. She hit Send, feeling a wave of relief sweep over her. She knew that the wave of panic would visit later, when she would worry about the loneliness ahead and wonder if she would ever meet someone she really wanted to marry. But at least for now, she was giving herself the chance to find out.

20

Jason

The best part of Jason's new scooter – a crimson Honda with blindingly bright headlamps – was its helmet, which gave him the superpower of invisibility. When he wore it, people no longer knew that he was a foreigner and, hence, no longer stared at him. In fact, he could now openly stare at the fruit-seller who split a jackfruit open with a single hack of his sickle, at the family of three on a moped waiting patiently for the traffic signal to change and at the children who dodged vehicles as they played cricket in the middle of the road.

Jason was driving his scooter through the residential alleys behind his apartment, whiling away a spare afternoon. Although he had taken an auto-rickshaw on these roads often, viewing them from his low perch on his scooter gave him a different perspective. It made him wonder about the history of the crumbling old houses overgrown with plants and about the hundreds of people who lived their individual, busy lives from within boxy apartment complexes. He had just driven past the temple with a giant banyan tree, when a stray dog started following him, wagging its tail. Jason then heard an English accent behind him, exclaiming, 'Looks like you have a stalker here!'

He turned in surprise to find the same girl who had joined Aneesh and him for a drink a while ago. She waved and gave him the broadest of smiles, as if he were a close friend she was reuniting with after several years. She was wearing a bright pink salwar kameez, and her hair had bleached even blonder under the sun.

'Well, hello there,' said Jason, stopping his scooter and switching the ignition off. The dog also stopped to stare at the two of them, wagging its tail furiously. Sensing that there was no attention forthcoming from either of them, it slinked away to examine the nearest dustbin.

Jason smiled back at the woman while trying to recollect her name. She seemed to realise that and offered good-naturedly, 'Jason, right? I am Sarah. We met briefly at The Tamarind, remember?'

'Yes, of course! Are you still staying at The Tamarind?'

'What? Are you insane? That place is bloody expensive – I only stayed there because my friend had already paid for it. I've been travelling in the South, well, Kerala mainly, and am back in Chennai for a few days before my flight back to London.' She hesitated, then asked, 'How about you? Been here all along?'

'Yes, right here. Making heart-shaped mango tarts in The Tamarind Room, as always.' Sarah tilted her head back and laughed, as if he had said something exceedingly funny.

'Well, I have some time to kill before meeting a friend, so, I was planning on waiting at a café nearby. Want to join me for a coffee?' she asked, tucking a stray hair behind her ear.

Jason followed Sarah to a rambling bungalow that had been converted into a café. It was tastefully decorated with a posh Indian sensibility, with henna designs drawn on its ochre walls and bougainvillaea plants spilling their purple flowers onto the iron-wrought tables outside.

They sat on a glossy wooden table overlooking a bamboo garden and ordered ice creams and French fries. Sarah talked about her travels around India, gesticulating with her hands as she talked, widening her eyes in places for effect.

Even without knowing her well, Jason could tell that she would be the type of person who would forge easy-going friendships with fellow travellers wherever she went and wouldn't spend much time by herself, despite travelling alone. For him, however, this was a social novelty – she was the first British person that he had met in weeks, and he realised that he had missed listening to the straight-jacketed vowels of the British accent as he listened to her ramble on about her adventures here.

'You wouldn't believe who I met on my train journey back from Pondicherry.' Sarah leant forward conspiratorially.

'Who?' asked Jason, gamely leaning forward as well.

'None other than God himself.' She nodded her head slowly in a mock-serious way.

'No!'

'Yes, he apparently wears an orange robe, sports a long white beard and has a soft spot for filter coffee with lots of sugar.'

Jason laughed. A waiter dressed completely in black placed a bowl of ice cream between them ceremoniously. The mango ice cream came as firm, plump scoops, yet unaware of what the world outside the freezer had in store for it.

Sarah prodded the ice cream thoughtfully with a spoon before asking him, 'Do you ever think of giving back?'

'Giving back what?' asked Jason, a little surprised, thinking of the auto-driver's question about the Kohinoor diamond for a startled moment.

'You know, to be a more mindful tourist – volunteer to teach or help out here.' She raised an eyebrow at him knowingly.

'No, I haven't really given it much thought,' he replied truthfully. He could, however, imagine Sarah's social media picture – dressed in a colourful kurta, she would be surrounded by a huddle of Indian children, their smiles brighter than usual because they were posing for a photo with her.

'So, you are really in India to cook at this posh restaurant then?' she asked, licking the ice cream first, before swallowing the spoonful.

'Well, I am really here because I found myself unexpectedly single in London and wanted a change of scene.' This was the first time he had admitted this to someone, and he felt a little free for saying it, like a handkerchief prising away from a tight clothespin.

'Oh!' She placed her spoon on the table and gave him her complete attention. He didn't go further into the story of his breakup, but his confession made Sarah open up about her own life in return. She had also broken up with a boyfriend before her travels here, but it had been a relationship that had lasted for only six months, so it hardly counted. However, what bothered her more was that she had never been in a relationship that had lasted for longer than a few months despite being thirty years old.

'—I know this is probably quite clichéd, but travelling around India has also made me have second thoughts about my career, you know.' She was currently on a sabbatical from her job at an ad agency and didn't want to go back to it. She wanted to do something meaningful and was wondering if it was too late to start training to become a teacher.

'You are so lucky that your profession matches what you are passionate about.' Sarah picked up one of the French fries that came clustered in small buckets.

Jason shrugged. He didn't know why people always assumed that all chefs were passionate about cooking, but in his case, at least, it was true. He bit into a French fry and winced when he realised that it didn't have a single flicker of heat.

'Yes, they're pretty tame,' Sarah said, but picked up another one anyway. 'The best food is always found in these hole-in-the-wall kinds of places. Have you been to Ratna Café by the way? They have something called ghee roast dosas on the menu – they're simply the best things that I've ever tasted.'

'No, I haven't.' He had passed by the café she mentioned, though, and knew that it was a bustling hotel with sturdy wooden tables and not exactly one of those stalls next to auto-stands where people spilled on the pavement, eating biryani by the handful. He didn't correct her, however.

Sarah typed something furiously on her phone and then dropped it on the table with a sigh. 'This friend I was supposed to meet has now cancelled. Should we go get one of those ghee dosas instead? The café is right around the corner from here.'

'Sure, let's do it.' Jason shrugged casually as if he were a more spontaneous person than he really was.

By the time they reached Ratna Café, it was filling up with people for the evening. Their waiter, a brisk young man, seated them both at a large table for four and got them bottled water. Sarah ordered for both of them, and the dosas arrived on stainless steel plates, glistening with ghee. She ate a small bite of the dosa with her hand and nodded her head with her eyes closed, relishing its taste in a rather exaggerated manner. She then looked at him with widened eyes as he took a bite. Jason raised his eyebrows and nodded back to show that he was equally impressed.

He imagined how it would have turned out if Emma had come here with him on a holiday or for their honeymoon. She would have tired him out on shopping trips for the perfect saree souvenir or dragged him up and down those boutique shops selling golden tapestries of elephants and peacocks. He was fairly certain that she would have turned her nose up at the greasiness of the dosas and asked him whether he had remembered to carry those pills for digestive problems. He knew, however, that he would have indulged her shopping and researched for Emma-friendly places to eat uncomplainingly, as long as it made her happy. As if realising how lucky he was to no longer be encumbered by the likes of Emma, he ate the dosa with additional gusto.

'So, when are you flying back?' he asked Sarah, filling her empty glass with water.

She thanked him more profusely than was necessary. 'My flight is on Friday, with several hours of layover in Dubai. When are you planning to get back to London?'

'Not made any concrete plans yet.' The more he had thought about it, the more he felt that he was finally beginning to feel like his normal self and was in no hurry to leave.

'Well, you know, I wish I could stay for longer, too, but real life awaits at the other end.' She smiled back at him, her eyes crinkling at the corners. Jason knew that he would probably never see her again, but he also knew that it was a good thing that he noticed that one of her eyes was greenish blue and the other bluish green.

*

It was another ordinary day in Chennai where the afternoon sun spilled generously onto the floor of the kitchen. Jason stood in a corner, inspecting the little red ants that marched in a neat, single file. They turned a perfect ninety degrees at the corner of the wall before entering the kitchen cupboard and attacking a plastic jar of sugar. He took the jar out and saw that it teemed with ants swaying about in the white grains like overweight holidayers on a sandy beach. He had never seen this many ants in one place before, and he spooned out a heap of sugar and placed it on the kitchen counter just to watch the ants mill about in confusion. This completely childish amusement, somehow, brought upon a sense of optimism that he hadn't felt in months.

He flexed the spine of his cookbook, careful not to dislodge its cover. As he worked through the recipes in the book, he had started accumulating unfamiliar ingredients in his kitchen – flours in different shades of yellow, vegetables that grew in strange shapes and ground spices that seemed to escape out of their neatly labelled jars and hover around the kitchen in a permanent fug of spice.

He opened the book to the recipe that he was planning to make that day – a cluster bean jaggery koottu. By now, Jason had understood that there were many variations of koottu, but in essence, they were flavourful vegetable stews that were almost always eaten with rice. This particular one was a sweet and sour stew made from cluster beans – a type of green bean that came in a leaner and bendier frame than the one that he was used to back home. The recipe called for *a lump the size of a big lime* of jaggery, and he rustled inside his cupboard for the chunk he had bought from Diamond General Stores. He was relieved to find that the ants had not gotten to it yet, although it was wrapped half-heartedly in a piece of newspaper. He sliced the jaggery with his knife and enjoyed the sensation of cutting it – it felt satisfyingly smooth, like scribbling on skin with a ballpoint pen.

He dissolved a piece of tamarind in hot water and left it to soak. He needed to wait till it imparted enough sourness to the water, so that even a few drops on his tongue would make his nose pucker up involuntarily.

He toasted the finely sliced beans with turmeric and salt, added water and sambar powder – the rust-coloured mixture that carried the heft of chilli and lightness of roasted coriander seeds – and let the beans simmer in it for a few minutes. He added the tamarind water and jaggery to the fragrant mixture and watched the jaggery flakes melt and fold their sweetness into the sourness of tamarind. He then added the mixture of rice flour and water that gave the stew its thick consistency. The last step for garnishing was something that he was very familiar with by now – the blistering of mustard and dal in oil that was then added to the main dish with a sharp sizzle.

He looked outside his window as he left the dish to stand on the stove. It was a searingly hot day, and the clouds melted shapelessly into the sky like soft-serve ice cream. The mango tree stood still, laden with fruit. He savoured this moment of quiet stillness in his kitchen, which felt bittersweet with the knowledge that the presence of this very house could be transient.

He scooped some rice onto a plate and submerged it in the piping hot koottu. After a couple of spoonfuls, he set aside his spoon and gingerly mixed the rice and koottu with the tips of his fingers. He brought it to his mouth in an awkward motion, liquid dripping on his chin and shirt. He tried again, with more rice and less koottu, and felt the warmth of the spices go down his throat and linger in his hands after. He then licked his fingers clean.

*

One week before the case was due to be argued in court, Jason and Kamala were seated on the low parapet wall on the terrace of the apartments, wagering on crows.

'My bet is on that plump fellow in the middle,' said Jason, scrutinising the row of crows perched on the electric wire that ran by the side of the terrace.

Kamala craned her neck and adjusted her spectacles before stating her pick. 'The tiny one on the right, sitting a little distance away from the rest.' She had barely finished her sentence when the small bird took flight, forming the silhouette of an open book against the reddening sky.

'So, who is winning?' asked Reva, climbing onto the terrace with a black camera slung around her neck. Jason had noticed that Reva had recently started walking around with her camera, taking pictures around the apartments – of Poons surveying the world from his perch on a blistered yellow windowsill, of mango leaves and neem flowers scattered on dark concrete – pictures that evoked a sense of nostalgia in Jason, even as he stood right next to the fallen leaves.

'Kamala Aunty is the expert. She doesn't believe in sharing her secrets, though,' Jason pointed out, almost petulantly.

'Well, I've had years of practise,' Kamala admitted. 'Sundu is even better than me. We used to play this secretly, though, because any kind of betting was frowned upon by our families.'

She turned away from the crows to look at Reva. 'You need to come pick up the chocolates I brought for you from the UK, Revathi. Lakshmi chose them, so I think you will like them.'

'I will drop by later today, Aunty. Thank you.' Reva joined Kamala and Jason on the parapet wall, all three of them now making a crow-like row.

'Look, look, Jason's one has just flapped its wings,' Kamala exclaimed with an unrestrained excitement that made her younger neighbours exchange an amused smile.

'Aren't crows supposed to be respected as our ancestors and all that?' Reva asked Kamala, appearing confused just for Kamala-teasing purposes.

'That's correct.' Kamala nodded seriously, while Jason pointed to one of them and observed, 'I must admit that one rubbernecking at the passersby below does bear a startling resemblance to my grand-uncle.'

The droning of machinery from the construction site next door increased in volume, and they had to shout over the noise to make themselves heard. Although a film of cement covered every surface of the apartment, and the thought of the court case weighed heavily in all of their minds, none of them brought it up. Instead, they sat with the air of people who knew that they were at the cusp of something good coming to an end – like the last day of summer holidays or the day of college graduation – and wanted to make the most of what was left.

In-between their bets, Kamala asked Jason about his cooking, and Reva pretended to be interested in his answers while focusing her camera on things at a distance.

'You can now go back and open a South Indian restaurant in London,' Kamala mused. 'We couldn't find one good place there, let me tell you.'

'I'm sure you could find one, if you had searched properly, Aunty,' said Reva, who took it upon herself to mellow down Kamala's often hyperbolic statements. 'Is that something you would want to do, though?' Reva looked at Jason with interest, as if this would finally help her make sense of why he was spending so much of his time on these recipes.

'Not really.' Jason shrugged. He still considered himself to be far from an expert on South Indian cooking. His purpose of recreating the recipes from the *Cook and See* book had been to know more about this place, in the same way learning to swim helps you wade out a bit more into the sea.

A loud squawk from a new arrival caused a small frenzy among the crows, and they all flew away, perhaps hearing about the availability of a loftier electricity line with panoramic city views. Reva turned to take a picture of Kamala and Jason as they groaned dramatically at the sight of the fleeing birds.

21

The Four Residents

On the morning of the court trial, Mani found himself cleaning his apartment with unnecessary fastidiousness. He swept his porch with the broom made from the spines of coconut leaves and polished all the surfaces of the apartment – the writing desk, the mahogany swing, the kitchen countertop – until they acquired a perspiring sheen. He only stopped when an already snagged piece of tile on the kitchen walls, the chequered blue-and-white kind that was a relatively recent addition, came off in his hand as a result of his vigorous scrubbing. He was still clasping the broken piece of tile in his palms when the doorbell rang.

On the other side of the door, there were three stocky men in lungis and banians, and for a moment, Mani wondered if he had asked for pesticide to be sprayed in the garden that day and forgotten all about it. It was only when the shortest of the men smirked, accompanied by the twitch of a well-maintained moustache, did Mani recognise him to be the same person who had threatened him at the gates of the apartments. He took a sharp intake of breath, his heart drumming rapidly inside his chest.

'*Vanakkam*, sir, can we come in?' the tall, well-built man with a gold chain around his neck asked with exaggerated politeness, but walked inside anyway without waiting for Mani's response.

'This is not a good time, actually. Why don't we do this another time?' Mani asked, worried about whatever 'this' was.

Meanwhile, the three men had already entered the house and were making themselves comfortable – the tall man sat on Mani's cane chair, the man with the moustache reclined on the sofa with his legs outstretched, while the young, plump one sat on the swing, pushing his feet against the floor to make it sway.

'How about some cold drinks for the boys? Some juice, Coca-Cola?' the tall man, who appeared to be the leader, asked Mani before casting a quick look around the apartment to ensure he didn't have company.

'I can get something from the fridge,' said Mani and walked towards the kitchen, wondering if he would have a moment by himself inside to call for help. However, the young man got up from the swing and followed him into the kitchen, his eyes watching Mani's every move.

'I have some lemon juice chilling in the fridge, or I can make some spiced buttermilk,' offered Mani, going with the pretence that these were guests with whom he was discussing beverage options.

'Lemon juice is fine,' the man said while leaning against the kitchen countertop, his white banian stretched taut against his round belly. 'Make sure you add some sugar and ice,' he added.

Mani took out the jug of lemon juice from the fridge and poured it into three tumblers. He spooned sugar from a porcelain container, his shaking hands spilling white granules on his newly polished counter.

'Why are you all here?' Mani entreated the young man supervising his actions. The man looked around twenty-five and carried himself with the genial air of someone who used to work behind the counter of his father's biryani shop, but had recently switched career streams to join the people-threatening business to optimise his earning potential.

The young man shrugged and pointed at an open container and asked, 'Are those roasted cashews?' with interest. Mani nodded, poured some into a bowl, and placed it next to the glasses of juice on a tray.

'If you don't mix the sugar in the juice, it will stay in the bottom,' the young man further instructed.

Mani reached for the spoons next to the sink, and his fingers grazed the plastic handle of the small vegetable-cutting knife kept next to the spoons, and hesitated. He thought that it was very likely that the men were carrying weapons behind the folds of their lungis, and even if they weren't, he could be knocked cold by just a mild thump from this young man. Better sense prevailed, though, and he picked up only the spoons.

In the living room, the other two men had switched on the television, and were watching a movie song from the nineties where the hero and heroine hopped with kangaroos and cuddled koala bears in Australia.

Mani sat quietly on a chair, listening to the three men exchange heated critical reviews of hero Kamal Haassan's latest offering. Finally, he addressed all three men, his voice wavering more than he would have liked. 'I actually have somewhere to be soon.' The song switched to another one where a young girl danced buoyantly against the backdrop of bright green sugarcane fields.

The tall man replied with his eyes still on the television, 'It is better for all of us if you don't go anywhere.' Understanding finally dawned on Mani – they were here to ensure that he never left the apartment. As the defendant, if he didn't turn up at the court, it was likely that a default judgement would be made against him.

The young man, who was now back on the swing, was humming along rather melodiously to the song, when a knock on the door put pause to his singing. The tall man tilted his head towards Mani to open the door and for the young man to follow.

Reva and Jason stood outside. They had come to pick up Mani so that they could all go to the court together. Reva was the one closest to the door, and her eyes widened as she saw the men inside.

'Mani Uncle, isn't it time for us to . . . ?' Reva started, tilting her head to look further inside. Jason waved hello to the man standing behind Mani, who waved back rather pleasantly.

'They are here to do some repairs on the air conditioner,' Mani told her a little too quickly. So far, the men had been peaceful, but he didn't want to see their patience tested, or worse, get Reva and Jason into any kind of trouble. Reva tried to keep the door open with her palm, but Mani asked her to leave without meeting her eyes, and slammed the door shut.

*

Reva gestured to Jason to follow her, and they climbed up to the balcony on the first floor.

'It's a bit strange that Mani needed work done in the house the morning of the case,' Jason observed.

'Well, it is even stranger since Mani does not own an air conditioner,' Reva whispered, although they were well out of earshot from the men in Mani's apartment. 'I think these men were sent from the construction company to make sure he doesn't turn up at court.' Looking seriously at Jason, she added, 'Or worse.'

Jason stared back at her, his eyes turning round as a cartoon's. 'What do you think we should do?'

Reva contemplated their options. From their perch on the balcony, she could see the plump man who had followed Mani to the door standing under the guava tree. He was talking into a phone balanced in the crook of his neck while rotating his right hand in the manner of someone practising his spin on an imaginary cricket ball. She wondered if distracting him was even an option since she had noticed at least two more men inside. She knew that Jason, who yelped on spotting a scurrying cockroach, and herself, whose only foray into self-defence was limited to signing up and then cancelling karate lessons, were a laughable match against these men.

She checked the time on her watch – there was less than an hour before Mani was due to appear in court.

'If they are threatening Mani, surely, we should call the police?' Jason suggested.

'And report some suspicious drinking of lemon juice?' Reva responded wryly. She sighed. 'Although that's probably the only idea I can think of, too.'

She scrolled through her phone, a little too frantically, and stopped at the journalist's name.

'Let me check with someone who may be able to help,' she told Jason and paced on the balcony with the phone held against her ear as the phone kept ringing at the other end. She was about to give up, when Anand picked up the call. She explained the situation to him in hasty sentences, her voice overlapping with the booming voice of a television newscaster in the background.

Anand asked her to stay put, promising to see what he could do. 'Don't try to handle the situation yourself,' he warned her before ending the call.

Jason looked at Reva expectantly. 'He will get back soon. Where is Kamala Aunty, by the way?' Reva asked, looking around.

Jason told her that Kamala had left earlier with Sundu in order to pick up some blessings from the temple on the way to the court. Reva nodded distractedly, gently rubbing the phone as if it were a magic lamp that she was willing to conjure up a solution.

They heard a shout downstairs, making the young man who had been ambling outside, rush into Mani's house. Both Reva and Jason exchanged worried glances and tiptoed downstairs, trying to see if they could eavesdrop on whatever was happening downstairs.

They were halfway down the stairs, when Reva's phone rang. She picked up Anand's call on its first ring. 'So, my friend in the police said that he would ask one of his officers doing the rounds around your area to stop by.' Reva thanked him profusely, with a promise to keep him updated.

Within ten minutes, a policeman in neatly pressed khaki clothes made his appearance, and his presence was welcomed insolently by the men, like high-school students who thought they were now too cool to get busted by their teachers for skipping lessons. But they all came out onto the porch nevertheless and made a big show of being Mani's personal security posse. 'We are not here looking for any trouble. We are here just to look after Mr Mani, aren't we?' The tall man looked at Mani for confirmation.

Mani looked too stupefied by his comment to respond.

Reva, who had come downstairs, thanked the officer, and spoke to Mani, 'We are already running late. We need to get going right now,' and pointed at her watch, which indicated that there were just fifteen minutes left for the court proceedings to start.

The policeman said tiredly to the men, 'You don't need to worry about his safety. I will drop Mr Mani where he needs to go. And, Pazhani,' he called out to the young man who looked a little more worried about the entire situation than the other two. 'If I were you, I would think carefully about whom I am roaming the roads with.' He then gestured for Mani, Reva and Jason to follow him to the police jeep parked outside.

*

Kamala and Sundu had reached the court well ahead of time – Sundu armed with her bulging black briefcase of notes, and Kamala with her blessed basket of coconut halves and jasmines.

Sundu asked her to take a seat in the courtroom while she went and did whatever lawyers were supposed to do before they presented their case. The room in which their case was argued was small but had large windows that overlooked a garden edged by neem trees that grew neatly in a row. Kamala looked around the fast-filling room, wondering what was taking Mani, Reva and Jason so long to get there.

Around five minutes after the case was scheduled to start, the judge entered the room, and everyone stood up in respect, Kamala being one of the last ones to do so. She noticed that the judge, a tall bespectacled man around her age, had dyed his hair completely black but left his moustache whi te, making her wonder if it was careless-ness or simply lack of time to finish what he had started, and which one of these two would be a preferable characteristic in the person who was going to decide where she lived for the foreseeable future. He ignored his audience and sat down behind his large table with a sigh, checking his watch impatiently even before they had begun.

Sundu entered immediately after, exchanging a joke with the opposition lawyer while adjusting her black lawyer cape. Kamala found it reassuring that the opposition lawyer, a short man with an elaborate comb-over, was eyeing Sundu warily despite her overly friendly demeanour. Sundu approached Kamala with a smile painted on her face, and hissed into her ear, 'Where has Mani dis-appeared? We can't start without him. I can stall the judge only for so long.'

'It's not like him to be late.' Kamala looked around the room anxiously. 'He should be here any moment,' she added, although she had no idea if he would.

She texted Reva asking where they were, knowing that Reva, like Lakshmi, never let her phone slip too far away from her finger-tips. As she waited for a response, Kamala fidgeted with the bangles on her wrists and cast frequent glances towards the entrance door, willing Mani to make an appearance.

Sundu entreated the judge for more time, but he had now assumed the impatient air of a man who had eaten lightly for breakfast and was looking forward to the prospect of an early lunch. The judge's rapidly disappearing patience was not helped by the opposition lawyer announcing the time every two minutes either. The judge had already got up from his chair, when Mani, Reva and Jason rushed into the room, looking all aflutter like sparrows who had narrowly escaped the swiping claws of a cat. Sundu exclaimed loudly in relief and the judge sat back in his chair rather ruefully, perhaps contemplating the delicacies in his tiffin box that were now out of his reach for some more time.

The other three residents of Grand Life Apartments sat down in chairs nearer to the entrance and Kamala raised her thumb at Reva in the modern gesture of good luck that she exchanged with Lakshmi before her exams.

Within a few minutes into the hearing, Kamala lost track of what was happening in the courtroom. Both Sundu and the opposition lawyer spoke directly to the judge, using terms and words that were hard to follow even when she tried to pay close attention. The opposition lawyer paced around as he spoke, making startlingly quick movements as he walked back and forth, while Sundu, in contrast, seemed to stand completely still while talking, using a deferential voice that she had never heard her use outside this courtroom.

Both the lawyers kept giving the judge papers – some of them single sheets, some of them wrapped in colourful folders sealed with white bows – and the judge kept rolling his glass paperweights on top of them in the casual manner of a child playing with marbles without keeping score.

This went on until the lunch break, when Sundu came to where Kamala was sitting, and sat down next to her. 'Enjoying the show?' she asked with tired amusement.

'I can't make head or tail of what's happening here,' Kamala replied. Sundu had outlined her defence strategy to all of them earlier – she was going to prove that the construction company's documents were fake by bringing in expert testimonies.

'What experts?' Kamala had asked doubtfully. Sundu had assured them that this was pretty standard procedure, and that she had a long list of people who specialised in this sort of thing, and that they shouldn't worry themselves with these particulars.

'It will all boil down to how closely the judge wants to look at the evidence,' she had said knowingly and paused, as they had fallen silent. 'It depends on whether the judge accepts offerings under the table?' she had said and laughed uncomfortably. Kamala had not laughed along with her. In fact, she had felt the exact opposite of laughing.

'It's going as well as it can,' Sundu now replied, asking Kamala to follow her to a rickety bench underneath one of the neem trees outside. Kamala opened the tiffin box in which she had packed curd rice seasoned with ginger and chillies, with a tart lemon pickle wedged in the middle.

'I forgot to bring the containers of appalams and potato roast that I had packed to go with this,' lamented Kamala as they washed their hands discreetly with water from a bottle.

'This is the best lunch I've had here recently,' Sundu assured her. They shared the box between them and took turns sharing observations, and providing reassurances, just as they used to while eating lunch under the banyan tree in their high school several decades before.

*

Jason could not believe the day he was having. He had helped to rescue Mani from a bunch of thugs (OK, 'help' might be a bit of an exaggeration), travelled in a police jeep that came complete with blinking lights on top and set foot in the arched walkways of a High Court – and it was still only one in the afternoon. His striped shirt, which he had got pressed for the occasion, was soaked in the perspiration brought about by all the distress and excitement of the day.

He rolled up the sleeves of his shirt and reached out for the packet of tamarind rice that Reva had bought for him and Mani from the court canteen. They were seated on the steps outside the courtroom, with people milling busily around them, several stopping to cast openly curious glances in his direction.

Mani ignored his lunch in favour of narrating the story behind the statue in front of the court building – the figure was Manu Needhi Cholan, the king who killed his own son to provide justice to a cow whose calf had been trampled by the wheels of his son's chariot.

Although Jason was in no mood for a history lesson, he put on an interested air, understanding that Mani needed to distract himself by telling this story. Reva, who had been hmm-ing along, observed, 'Wait, didn't some god then bring back both the calf and son to life?' in a suspicious voice to show how far-fetched she thought the entire moral of the story was.

After lunch, the judge appeared sleepier but less peeved than he had been during the morning session. All the residents of Grand Life Apartments had reconvened to sit together, and Jason looked sideways to see if the others were faring better in following the case. Kamala seemed to concentrate hard on whatever Sundu was saying earnestly, in the same way Jason imagined her to listened to prayers at the temple. Reva was also looking at Sundu, but with a distracted expression that showed that her mind was elsewhere. He heard the woman sitting adjacent to Reva reprimand her for sitting with her legs crossed, which apparently showed disrespect to the judge. Reva rolled her eyes in the woman's direction, but Jason quickly uncrossed his legs, assuming this was another cultural thing he wasn't aware of.

Finally, after entire reams of paper had been handed to the judge, the arguments drew to a close. Sundu had a relieved air about her, but in the quick manner she packed up her papers, Jason wondered if it wasn't because of the success of this case specifically as much as the more pedestrian relief of seeing the end of another workday.

It turned out to be a combination of both. 'We ended up having a good enough case – we presented some compelling electronic evidence that my private investigator dug up.' Sundu then paused to look at Reva. 'And also the proof of similar harassment by the construction company sent by your friend.'

'What do you think the verdict will be?' Kamala pressed.

'Be patient, Kamala. The judge will be back, and we should know soon.' Sundu said this while fiddling with the clicker of the pen in her hand impatiently.

'Fingers and toes crossed!' Jason said, holding up his scissored fingers. Mani awkwardly imitated his gesture and moved his hand, as if he were waving a flag of hope, making all of them break into the kind of brittle laughter usually used to cover up anxiety.

After what felt like a very long time, the judge entered the court again, and they all rose in unison, Mani stumbling a little as he did so. The judge cleared his throat and looked down at the sheet of paper in his hand, pausing significantly for the moment it took for the courtroom to fall completely silent.

All the residents stiffened with nervous anticipation as he then started reading out the verdict that determined the future of Grand Life Apartments.

22

Mani

Three months later, the sound of hammers and drills, combined with the discomfort of the afternoon heat, woke Mani from his afternoon nap. He felt a momentary sense of panic as he watched a mechanical crane dangle a heap of bricks from its claws. It took him a moment to completely awaken and remember that the court had ruled in his favour and that the crane was hunched over the neighbouring construction site. He turned to reorient himself by staring at the dust-furred ceiling fan that had stopped mid-rotation following a power cut, and felt his panic slowly ebb away in waves of relief.

He came outside to his porch and found Reva and Jason seated on the steps, having a modern conversation that involved talking while typing things on phones.

'There are only three constants in life – death, tax and power cuts,' he quipped as he sat down on his chair. They both smiled back at him tolerantly, making him wonder if he was repeating something he had said during the last power cut.

He looked over at his garden, which was beginning to slowly regain its nourished air. The newly planted shrubs – ixoras, hibiscus and samanthi – had flowered in the arresting yellows and reds of the morning and evening sun, and Jason's vegetable patch underneath the guava tree had evolved into a herb garden that lent a fresh, cleansing fragrance to the air.

'Well, hello there, Mr Poons!' he exclaimed as the cat walked past the porch in a swirl of orange and white. Hearing his voice, Poons paused mid-stride to look at him, his ears twitching enquiringly. Mani held his open palm to the cat, who sniffed at it half-heartedly, as if he knew that this was a decoy for his affection but was playing along for Mani's sake. Poons then folded himself to sit upright next to Mani, the white tuft of his head within patting distance of his hand.

Mani scratched Poons' neck with one hand while gesturing to the large bag seated between Reva and Jason with the other. 'I thought your flight wasn't until much later, Revathi?'

'I am meeting a few friends for dinner before.' Reva glanced up from her phone, her eyes having a shine to them, both from the indigo glow of her phone as well as the prospect of her upcoming travels.

Mani thought that Reva had a lighter air around her ever since she had started her new job (although he couldn't keep track of the names of companies these days – this one, he believed, was called Instant Mix, but was surprised to learn it had nothing to do with making ready-to-eat breakfast items but instead sold software). She seemed to have made some new friends as well, who dropped by, always respectfully wishing him a good day and pausing to admire the garden before they went out on their young people adventures that he imagined involved spending way too much money just to keep themselves entertained.

Jason was helping Reva adjust the straps of the backpack he had lent her, and Mani mused, 'You should also travel up the country to see the Himalayas someday, Jason. Very beautiful, although I hear it has become quite commercialised these days.'

Jason shrugged, saying that he would like to travel around South India first, but his voice was languid, as if he was in no particular hurry to do this. When Mani had first rented an apartment to Jason, he had imagined him to be a fleeting occupant of Grand Life Apartments, someone who would hastily retreat after dipping his toe into life here. (It hadn't helped that Jason's first question to him had been whether it was all right to drink the water straight from the tap, asked nervously with an empty glass in hand.) Mani surmised that Jason was indeed bound to haul his adventures here over his shoulder and leave, but perhaps not as soon as he had thought.

Kamala joined them from upstairs, fanning herself with her prayer book covered in its jacket made of newspaper. 'I don't understand what's wrong with carrying bags with wheels, really,' she said, eyeing Reva's bag with sincere confusion. She added, 'Lakshmi has one of these bags as well – I keep telling her it cannot be good for her back to carry this around.'

'Everything well with Lakshmi?' Mani enquired. He was glad to notice that Kamala was back to inserting her daughter's name in conversations like superfluous punctuation marks ever since she'd returned from the UK.

'Yes, she is coming to visit in a month after her exams are over.' Kamala folded her hands around her prayer book gratefully as if it were personally responsible for summoning her daughter here.

Reva followed Mani's line of sight to the newly flowered white hibiscus. 'When I come back from the village next time, I will bring back a stem from ours. It has red flowers as large as my palm.' Reva held up her hand.

'The juice of the hibiscus is good for the heart.' Kamala directed this educational comment towards Jason. 'Only if it is red hibiscus, though,' she warned with urgency, as if Jason were preparing to get up and follow her health orders immediately.

There was a clanging of the metal door at the front of the apartments – Mani had thought it prudent to implement safety measures for the apartment and had added a padded lock on the front door and sharp glass pieces on top of the surrounding walls. He had to admit that his heart still tripped whenever he saw a group of strangers loping around an apartment, or when he heard a particularly loud noise, like the sound of a tyre bursting from the heat.

Mani got up to let Salim inside, who had shot up in height, as well as responsibility at the store. He was followed by his new assistant, and Salim, in typical manager style, was carrying a small part of the load and giving detailed instructions to Iqbal on where to place the rest.

'Let me get some lemon juice for you both,' Mani said, walking into the house. Poons got up from his perch as if to follow him, but then jumped onto the shaded balcony above, and was soon lost to sight.

Mani came back with two tumblers of chilled juice. Salim held up his and asked Jason, 'So, Jason sir, what would you call this in your restaurant?'

'Hmm, maybe a fizzy lemon tonic?' said Jason, in the game voice of someone who knew they were being teased.

'No, the name must show how exotic the drink is. Something like—' Reva pursed her lips in the exaggerated imitation of someone thinking deeply and supplied, '—Sweet nectar of the Indian gods.'

Kamala, who didn't entirely understand the game, but wanted to play, added, 'Mani's Special,' which Mani voted as the best name of the lot.

Iqbal spoke to Jason in the shy manner of someone who had been preparing what to say for a while, 'I've heard all about you from Salim.'

'Have you now?' Jason asked a bit warily.

'I heard you sell South Indian food to the people of Chennai for thousands of rupees. You are an expert at selling halwa to Tirunelveli itself, isn't it?'

'Halwa to what?' Jason turned to Mani questioningly.

Mani thought for a moment to find the closest translation. 'It is a Tamil phrase similar in meaning to "selling ice to Eskimos".'

'That sounds about right.' Jason nodded, looking pleased, as if this was the best compliment that he could receive.

Salim gestured to Iqbal that it was time for them to leave for their next delivery, looking down importantly at the new Titan watch that hung loosely around his wrist.

'You should get the strap tightened so that you don't lose that,' Kamala said sagely as they waved the boys goodbye.

Electricity suddenly flowed back to the neighbourhood, the construction site next door coming alive with the furious sounds of machinery. As one, they turned to watch the tall crane tilt and deposit a heap of bricks in a cloud of red dust. This visible reminder of what Grand Life Apartments had just escaped made all of them recollect the court trial again, the details of it getting watered down with each retelling, but always ending with the collective exclamation of gratitude for the way things had turned out.

One by one, each person was pulled away from the porch by the tug of life unfolding elsewhere. Reva left as her taxi arrived, Jason for his evening shift at the restaurant and Kamala to buy fresh coriander to make Sundu's favourite chutney for dinner.

Mani continued sitting on his candy-striped chair as the sun lowered across the horizon, leaving shadows of his house in shapes that he could recall with his eyes closed. He watched a group of dragonflies hover over the hibiscus plants in the garden, the smell of rain bubbling up pleasantly in the air around him. It was only when the mosquitoes came nipping at his elbows that he got up, patted the pillar holding up the porch reassuringly, as one would the shoulder of a good friend, and went inside.

Acknowledgements

This book is dedicated to my parents, to whom I owe everything. Thank you for your unwavering love and unconditional belief. Thank you for finding creative ways to get my hands on second-hand books as a child, which opened up worlds of possibilities.

Thank you to my agent, Diana Beaumont, for believing in my writing and making this book possible. I feel very lucky to have you by my side. Thank you to Melissa Cox for editing this book with so much heart and much-appreciated humour – it wouldn't be what it is without you. Thank you to editor Hannah Black for championing this book and helping to send it out into the world. Thank you to Erika Koljonen for the thoughtful editorial support and for taking very good care of the words in this book. I am also grateful to everyone else at Coronet and Hodder, who have each played a part in this book's journey.

I want to thank Sampath for his excellent advice, and Elane and Sarah for organising their writing events. Thanks also to the agents who eventually passed on my manuscript but took the time to give kind, constructive feedback that improved my storytelling and kept me going.

Thank you to my friends who read early drafts and reassured me that I had something worthwhile in my hands. Thanks also to the friends and family who have cheered me on from the sidelines for the many years it takes to write and publish a book. I am so glad to have you all in my life.

Thank you to N for caring deeply. For being there for every draft, every sentence, and every crisis of confidence. For clearing away the worldly clutter to ensure that I have the space to write. Thank you, also, for all the mor kozhambu.

I also want to thank you, dear reader, for choosing to spend time with this book. It means so much to me that you did.